# DEAD DROP IN LILY ROCK

## ALSO BY BONNIE HARDY

For a full list please go to

bonniehardywrites.com/Books

**Welcome to Lily Rock Holiday Mystery Novellas**

'Tis the Season *

All Aboard for Murder *

Wrap it Up! *

**Lily Rock Mystery**

Getaway Death *

Influenced to Death *

Deadly Admission *

A Thymely Death *

Deadbeat Dad *

A Very Tidy Death *

Sit. Stay. Play Dead. *

**An Avery Denning Lily Rock Mystery**

Dead Drop in Lily Rock *

**Redondo and Rose Palm Desert Midlife Mystery**

A Doula to Die For *

Between the Sheets *

Sight Unseen *

Class Dismissed *

Harvey House Detective Mystery

An Unsuitable Job *

* Available for listening on Audible

# DEAD DROP IN LILY ROCK

---

AN AVERY DENNING LILY ROCK MYSTERY
BOOK 1

BONNIE HARDY

ON THE OTHER HAND BOOKS

By Bonnie Hardy



This is a work of fiction. Names, characters, places, and incidents either are the product of the author's imagination or are used fictitiously, and any resemblance of fictional characters to actual persons living or dead, business establishments, events, or locales is entirely coincidental.

AI has not been used in any aspect of this story.



**Ebook ISBN:** 978-1-954995-50-5

**Paperback ISBN:** 978-1-954995-51-2

**Hardcover ISBN: 978-1-954995-52-9**

Cover Design by Ebook Launch

Editing by Proof Positive

"I wouldn't be a songwriter if it wasn't for books that I loved as a kid."

Taylor Swift

# PROLOGUE

Stella Rawlins held her to-do list at arm's length. "My eyes aren't what they used to be," she muttered. Fortunately the sun peeked over the mountains just in time to illuminate her scrawl. She squinted, sighed, and sorted her priorities. Her first chore was her favorite: the early visit to her little library. After that, a few finishing touches before her weekend boarder turned up, fresh off the Pacific Crest Trail.

Over the past year, Stella had developed a keen eye for her little library customers. She replaced popular titles, like Harry Potter books, daily. They were hard to come by, so she snatched a used copy whenever she could find one.

Stella also kept her eye out for any early reader books about unicorns. But her personal favorite was one about mermaids. She felt especially proud of having recently purchased several new copies of *Julián Is a Mermaid* by Jessica Love.

As she bent to pick up her book basket, a chuckle escaped her lips. The faces of her small group of other little library enthusiasts had been priceless when she'd told them *Julián* was a personal favorite.

"That's not a classic," someone had insisted.

Stella knew she was stepping on toes. After all, the Switchback Syndicate's motto was to make older classics available to new readers. She admitted to her critics that her book didn't fit, but that didn't stop her from making it readily available in her own little free library.

Prepared to step outdoors, Stella tucked her to-do list in the basket, next to her recently acquired copy of *All American Boys* by Jason Reynolds and Brendan Kiely. That book, like *Julián*, flew off her little library shelves. Popular with young adults, *All American Boys* was rarely returned. *A nice touch*, she thought. *To offer* All American Boys *on the Fourth of July*. It would give the next reader the chance to see there was more than one way to be all-American.

A stack of bookmarks, held by a rubber band, lay in her basket. Stella had designed them herself. On the front was a photo of Mayor Maguire, the town's famous labradoodle politician. Underneath was a list of addresses, inviting people to visit the other little libraries in town.

She stepped out the front door and onto the gravel path, her basket swinging lightly from one hand. Just ahead, the familiar outline of her library came into view.

The sunrise cast a soft golden glow across the yard. The little library, stationed at the top of a post, was painted bright blue. Still pleasing to Stella's eye, it made her smile.

Setting her basket by her feet, Stella rubbed at a smudge on the glass with her elbow. She wanted everything to look just right, especially since it was a holiday. With fingers outstretched, she turned the wooden toggle and opened the glass door.

A quick scan of the shelves revealed a few missing

books. Two Redondo and Rose mysteries had been removed. She lifted *All American Boys* from her basket and slid it into place beside a copy of *Julián Is a Mermaid.* She smiled faintly at the pairing.

Then her breath caught.

*Are You My Mother?* by P.D. Eastman was back. She groaned and shook her head.

Someone in Lily Rock persisted in dropping that same book in her little library nearly every day. Stella suspected who it was, which only made her more uneasy.

There was a time when just seeing the cover made her feel hollow. Reminding her of the baby she'd carried to full-term and then given up for adoption. She'd made peace with her past...

Until that book kept appearing.

Staring at it now, her hand hovered just above the spine. She left it inside and closed the door.

Stella took a moment to ground herself, admiring the little brass sign that read, Take One, Leave One. She heard a rustle from behind the hedge. *Is someone watching me?*

"Who's there?" she called out.

A blinding flash.

Heat.

Smoke.

The distinct sulfur smell of a firecracker igniting just inches from her face.

Stella reeled backward, arms flailing. Her heel struck the uneven edge of the roadway. And then...nothing.

The book basket spilled on the ground.

A red bloom from a mandevilla floated through the sky, drifting past Stella's face to the dirt below.

# CHAPTER ONE

Avery Denning wiped her hot face with the sleeve of her shirt, wondering how soon she could ask her landlady for a bath. Her oversized backpack, held together with duct tape, hung off her shoulder.

*I feel like I'm carrying a ten-pound elephant*, she thought as the pack slid off her arm into the dust. She inhaled deeply, remembering herself just a month ago, her hair shiny, her shorts and tee clean, her perfect smile for that selfie she took at the upscale tea shop in the South Bay.

That girl was no longer visible.

It had taken a fire in Palos Verdes to burn her house to the ground and to catapult her onto the Pacific Crest Trail. Now she was one of the unhoused and unwashed hikers, looking for a place to lay her head for the Fourth of July weekend.

"If my friends could see me now," she muttered. With a swift kick to her backpack, she looked up. The house, set back behind a thick hedge, looked like the photo Stella had sent.

"I invite one hiker at a time to stay in my room," Stella

wrote. "That way I can focus on them without being distracted."

Before Avery could type her reply, Stella sent another email.

"I hope you like homemade baked goods. I have a standing order at the local bakery, Thyme Out."

Avery did her best to assure Stella that she'd be a good lodger. It wasn't as if she planned on staying that long. Once she got a good night's sleep and a warm bath, she'd be back on the trail.

"What's that?" Avery blinked and then squinted at a bright blue house suspended on a pole. Her breath caught. She kicked her backpack to the side of the road and stepped closer.

The sharp irritating buzz of a fly swooped past her ear. She flinched. Swatted. "Go away," she whispered, not sure if she meant the fly or the rising dread curling in her stomach.

Her shoulders stiffened, followed by a deeper sense of dread. Her glance drifted to the dirt underneath the little library. A woman's body lay supine, her legs sticking out like stumps. Her shirt was twisted at the waist. Avery's eyes traveled to a pair of worn jeans, then socks, finally a sturdy pair of walking shoes, as if she'd prepared for a long morning walk. Then she looked back up to her head, where a red, white, and blue bandanna had slipped to one side.

A thin plume of smoke drifted upward from behind the bright blue box. She could see a glass door off the hinges, books inside. *What a mess. Sabotaged by some local kids...*

"Are you okay?" Avery called, crossing her fingers. *Please say yes. Please say yes. Please say yes.*

With breath held, she waited.

No response.

No movement. No reply. Only what appeared to be a lifeless corpse.

*Look at her eyes*, Avery thought. Wide open, staring up at the blue sky.

She tentatively leaned closer. Black soot covered burns on the woman's arms. Smudges ran up her neck, leaving residue on her cheeks.

Avery's legs began to tremble. She didn't want to admit it, not even to herself. But she suspected the identity of the lifeless woman from a photograph she'd sent.

Taking a deep breath, Avery kneeled to examine her more closely. Holding her fingers over the woman's wrist, she waited for a pulse. *She's a goner*, Avery thought, and a shudder ran down her spine.

On her feet, she took a step backward. *Should I just leave Stella here?* Avery knew that was wrong, but she felt frightened.

Her eyes glanced toward her backpack. She couldn't imagine picking it up one more time, leaving Stella to be discovered by someone else. She knew she was supposed to be responsible and call 911. But she wasn't sure that was the best decision because being responsible rarely paid off. At least for her.

Her cell phone showed two bars of connection. Despite her misgivings, she made the call.

"Lily Rock Constabulary," came a young man's voice. Avery blinked. A voice she'd never forget from her teens, when they'd last seen each other.

Her heart clenched and tears came to her eyes. "I have an accident to report on Honeysuckle Lane. There's a woman lying in the dirt, and I can't find a pulse."

"On it," the voice said. "Can I have your name?"

Avery clicked her phone off. She didn't want to start that thing people do. The "hey, don't I know you?" conversation.

The peal of a siren filled the air. If she hurried, she might be able to disappear, now that she'd reported the body.

She exhaled a deep sigh and changed her mind. Dragging the pack across the road, she sat down to wait. Her only thought was, *Good deeds never go unpunished.*

# CHAPTER TWO

"You the one who called this in?" Janis Jets glared at Avery, her hands on her hips. Dressed in her cop uniform of navy blazer and tan slacks, she looked ever the professional.

Avery felt herself bristle. "I can neither confirm nor deny," she said stoutly, clamping her lips closed.

"Easy there, Elf Two. This isn't a gift-wrapping operation. There's a dead woman to consider."

"You're never gonna let that go, are you?" Avery scowled.

"Not until you give me a better nickname to work with." The cop's eyes traveled from Avery's askew ponytail, to her stained shirt and baggy shorts, down to the thick layer of dust on her boots. "How old are you now? In your twenties?"

"Twenty-three," she muttered.

Janis continued to assess. "Elf Two wouldn't have been caught dead in that outfit." The cop's raised eyebrows had a sting of judgment.

"You don't know me," Avery snapped.

"Never mind. I assume that's your backpack." Jets pointed.

"I planned on getting it repaired in Lily Rock before hitting the trail after the holiday."

"Backpack Betty it is." Jets smiled. "Are you sure you're not smuggling something illegal in there?"

Avery felt her hand twitch. *If only I could smack that smug smile off her face.* But before she could manage a retort, Jets turned away. She hitched up her pants and glanced toward the little library.

"So what's going on exactly? You come into town and there's another dead body. This is number three, if I'm not mistaken." Jets's eyebrows rose over her sunglasses.

Before Avery could explain, an old Ford rumbled up and stopped on the side of the road. A woman stepped out.

"I called an hour ago," barked Jets.

"Fifteen minutes," the woman mumbled, eyes focused on Avery. She had a bemused expression for Jets and then a bright smile for Avery.

"This is Olivia Greer." Jets kept talking. "She didn't live in Lily Rock when you were here." She took out her iPad and nodded toward Avery. "This is Avery Denning, better known as Elf Two. She's a real magnet for murder, not unlike you.

"First it was Betty King, then Baubles the Clown, and now..." Janis waved three fingers in front of Avery's face. "Three dead people. Count 'em."

Avery dropped her gaze in embarrassment. The truth was she felt like she did have a problem. The first dead body could be considered an unfortunate circumstance. The second one a coincidence. But the third... *I really am bad luck.*

She interrupted Jets. "I planned on spending one night at Stella's to get cleaned up and repair my hiking gear. Like I said, the backpack..." She pointed to the strap hanging by a string. "I made a reservation with Stella weeks ago. So when I showed up, there she was. I assume it's Stella. I only saw a photo. We communicated with email."

"You must be in shock," came Olivia's soft voice.

Avery's shoulders slumped, tears filling her eyes. Her bottom lip trembled. One short sentence from Olivia and she was a puddle of emotions.

Olivia stepped closer to place a hand on her shoulder.

"She's a constabulary consultant," Jets explained. "You can do your confessing to her."

Avery wanted to throw her arms around Olivia and burst into tears, but she pulled away, admonishing herself. *You don't even know this woman. Stop being so needy.*

Olivia eyed her face carefully. "I moved to Lily Rock soon after you left," she said. "But I heard about the nutcracker and the clown."

Avery liked that she didn't say "dead bodies." Just the memory made her shudder.

"Enough getting to know you," snapped Jets. "What about my dead woman? You were the one to call it in."

She turned and nodded toward the paramedics who leaned over Stella.

"Is sh-she...really dead?" Avery stuttered. "I couldn't feel a pulse, but I wasn't sure."

"Looks like it." Jets closed her iPad. "Let me check with them."

It only took a moment before she returned with a report. "The doc told me Stella must have expired when her head hit that rock with the bloodstain. Probably before you arrived, right?" She stared closely at Avery. Her directness made Avery squirm with discomfort. She had nothing to hide from the cop, but she felt as if she did, the way Jets looked at her.

"Dead on arrival," Avery muttered.

"What time was that exactly?" Jets opened her iPad.

Avery sighed and said under her breath, "I have no idea."

"Right, you wanna play that kind of game. Go ahead then, make my day. Confess. Then I can arrest you and get lunch. It's July 4. There's crowd control and the mayor to corral. He gets really fidgety with the fireworks."

"You mean Tater Tot gets fidgety," Olivia corrected her. "Mayor Maguire is used to the commotion."

"I know the mayor, or I did, when he was a puppy." Avery felt her spirits lift. "He's still here? That's so cool. What about Sparkles? The pony. Is she by any chance..."

Jets frowned. "Sparkles is mine. I board her at Paws and Pines. She's eating me out of house and home. No one can ride her, not even children. Just an overgrown pet without a purpose."

The crabby circus pony brought back fond memories for Avery. Just the thought of seeing her and the mayor brought a smile to her lips. She felt her heart open, a bit of energy return.

"I think Avery needs to take some time, gather herself after finding Stella. No more questions for now," Olivia said in a firm voice. "Why don't you come home with me? I have plenty of room, a bed, and a hot shower."

Then she turned to Officer Jets. "Since you'll probably need to cordon off Stella's house and property for a complete investigation right away. This is a good idea, right?"

The "thank you" died on Avery's lips. The word "investigation" made her wince. "Do you think Stella was murdered?"

"With your record for finding dead people, I'd bet on it," mumbled Jets.

Avery felt her eyes fill again. *I must be tired*, she thought. *Big wuss.*

When Jets gave her a hard stare, she turned away. "Don't get all weepy on me," Jets said. "I was just kidding. Olivia has a point. We'll do this right. If you stay with her while Mike's away, you won't go far. I can get your statement after the Fourth."

"Mike..." Avery turned to Olivia. "Is that Michael Bellemare? I knew him."

Jets answered in place of Olivia. "They're a couple. Like peas in a pod, Mike and her." Janis gestured toward Olivia with her thumb. "She's kind of a..." Janis hesitated. "A catalyst. I guess that's the nice way to put it. I usually refer to her as a pain in the A." She shrugged. "But not to her face."

Olivia chuckled. "Enough about me. Is that your backpack?" She gestured toward it.

"Yes," Avery answered quietly. "Such as it is."

"You okay coming to my place?"

"I really appreciate your offer. If you don't mind." She'd been mailed a key to Stella's, but the thought of staying in the house of her dead landlady... It didn't feel right.

Olivia took the backpack with one hand and Avery's elbow with the other. "My car is right over here."

As soon as she got into the car and the door slammed shut, Avery felt her body slump. Her feet were sore and her legs ached from days of nonstop hiking. A sharp pain in her right shoulder began to throb. She already regretted not taking the advice to pack lighter.

Olivia started the car. "Where did you stay the last time you were here?" she asked as she pulled away from the side of the road.

"I was at the music academy the first year because Elf One and I didn't go home for Christmas. We stayed in the dorm. When we came back the second year at Christmas, Sage said we could use the rooms again."

"Elf One?"

"A guy named Logan. He was nice." Avery sighed. She'd lost touch with him after the last holiday stay. But the memories lingered. *Speaking of memories...*

"Does Meadow still bake those to-die-for cinnamon rolls? I've never had anything like them before or since."

"She does." Olivia nodded. "Sage has taken over a lot of the holiday planning. But her mom is the cinnamon roll queen."

Olivia drove around the curve. Avery grasped the edge of the seat.

"Oh, sorry. I'll slow down. So you know, Lily Rock locals take these roads really fast. Kind of unnerving." Olivia tapped the brake to reduce the speed.

Avery released her grip. "So you and Michael..." She was dying to know how they'd gotten together.

"It's been five years now. He built this house for us." Olivia pulled down a gravel road and pointed to an all glass and redwood structure ahead. Two stories, it spread over the land with the flare of a cabin, finished in an ultramodern city style.

Avery gasped. "Spectacular," she sighed, and then lifted her eyes to the mountain range beyond. She gulped. "This is..."

"A Bellemare architectural wonder," Olivia finished. "Our house has already received two awards and lots of write-ups. He's really quite something, my man."

"Is he here?" Avery felt her heart quicken. She had fond memories of Michael. How he'd guided her and Logan and even took care of them. He'd seemed emotionally detached over the holidays but very kind. "Is he still sad?"

Olivia looked surprised. "Not so much," she said. "He's not here at the moment. Finishing a design commission in Chicago. I hope you'll stay long enough to say hello when he comes back."

"Do you think he'll remember me?"

"I'm sure he will." Olivia smiled.

Avery wasn't so sure. Why would a famous architect have any memory of a high school girl, abandoned over the holidays by her parents, who was called Elf Two.

"Leave your backpack by the door. I'll show you around first. I bet you're exhausted." Olivia's quiet voice of authority filled Avery with a sense of relief. Usually she rejected people telling her what to do, but Olivia she didn't mind.

They made their way across a footbridge toward the front patio of the house. A clear stream trickled over rocks beneath, stirring the water with soft calm.

Olivia pointed toward the mountain range. "Say hello to Lily Rock."

Avery stared into the distance. Glimmering in the sun, the alabaster white rock looked like an omen for good. "She watches over the town," Avery commented.

Olivia nodded. "You feel it too." Her bright eyes stared directly into Avery's. "That means a lot. I'm so happy that you're able to stay."

# CHAPTER THREE

The word "stay" echoed in Avery's mind. She stood under the warm stream of shower water, feeling Olivia's words like a blessing. Stuck in Lily Rock for longer than she'd planned, she was happy it was with her. Especially now that Janis Jets was investigating a murder.

Holding her hair to the side, she rinsed her back. Then she considered her next problem. *I have nothing clean to wear.* She'd packed a minimal change of clothes to take on the Pacific Crest Trail—nothing she'd be caught dead in under usual circumstances. "Caught dead," she mumbled. Not exactly the best phrase, considering...

She turned off the water. Stepping onto the fluffy white mat, she reached for a towel and dried her hair. The shampoo—mint and eucalyptus—reminded her of an apothecary in Hollywood where they overcharged to make everyone smell like the great outdoors.

"I left you a change of clothes," Olivia called from the hall. "We're about the same size. I also took the liberty of tossing the items you wore and the rest of your clothing in your backpack into the washer. I hope that's okay."

Avery's throat caught. Had Olivia read her mind, or was she perhaps the kindest person she'd ever met? "Thank you," she called. "I'll be out in a minute."

"Meet me on the front patio," Olivia shouted back. "Up the stairs, through the great room." Even though they'd just met, Avery was quite certain they would get along. She wasn't used to being so comfortable with other women, let alone one a bit older. But Olivia was different.

The worn jeans fit her perfectly. The tee with a photo of Mayor Maguire on the front made her smile. The irrepressible puppy had turned into quite a celebrity since she'd last seen him.

Her fresh clothes smelled heavenly and clean. She sniffed with appreciation.

A comb and a toothbrush, still wrapped in cellophane, and a small tube of toothpaste lay in a drawer. She ran the comb through her wet hair. *I can't remember ever going this long without an appointment at my salon.*

Bracing her hands on the marble counter, she rotated her shoulders and groaned at the pops and crackles. All the hiking and carrying... She sighed and rotated a few more times.

Feet bare, her toenails looked ragged. Both big toes were blistered, the tips black and blue. *I need a pedicure,* she concluded. Then she felt a stab of guilt. *I can't walk around Olivia's house with these nails.* She looked in the drawer again and found a pair of nail clippers, using them before leaving the bathroom.

*What's wrong with me? All I can think about is how I look, when I just found Stella's dead body.* Avery made her way from the bathroom into the bedroom.

She opened the door and peeked out to the rest of the house, remembering Olivia's instructions. Bare feet padded against the wood plank flooring as she made her way down the hall and up the stairs.

At the landing, her eyes stopped on the enormous stone fireplace. It dominated the great room, open to two sides. An L-shaped sofa filled the center of the room, its back to the staircase. She caught a glimpse of a kitchen on the other side of the fireplace. The vaulted ceilings made the room feel enormous, especially with all the light pouring in from windows and glass walls in every direction.

Avery was used to luxury, raised by wealthy parents who were Hollywood actors. So this wasn't her first house built in the style of the rich and famous. Friends of her parents had vacation homes just like this in Aspen. They were more A-list and could afford more of the luxuries than her family. But this Bellemare design in Lily Rock, it felt special. Not staged, nothing extra—casual and elegant. A home.

Avery approached the massive stone mantel filled with photographs. There was one of Michael and Olivia. He had his arm around her and stared into her eyes with a mischievous smile. Olivia looked up at him, her mouth slightly open, her eyes half closed, obviously laughing.

*He was pretty funny*, Avery remembered. But mostly he looked so at ease in her presence.

"I'm out here," Olivia called.

Avery moved past an oversized dining room table, stopping to take in the view. There was a wall of glass, with a floor-to-ceiling door, that separated the kitchen dining area from the patio. She saw Olivia outside, with her legs curled up underneath her body, staring toward the bridge that connected the parking area to the main house.

Avery's neck tingled. Olivia had placed an empty barrel chair close by. Only then did she experience a niggle of fear.

*Is this a setup?* she wondered. *After the shower and the fresh clothes, will she interrogate me now?*

*Don't forget, no matter how nice she seems, Olivia works for the constabulary*, Avery cautioned herself. *Until they find out the details of Stella's death, I would be a convenient scapegoat for murder. Better be careful. Stay alert. Even well-meaning people can come to the wrong conclusion.*

With slow deliberate steps, she walked through the opening onto the patio. "Hello," she said cautiously.

"Have a seat." Olivia gestured, then stretched out her legs to stand. "I suspect you're hungry, so I'll get us a snack. I've got the best cookies." She kept talking in her low calm voice. "Janis's boyfriend is the town baker. He brings out a July 4 bake that hikers stand in line for. Sierra Snowcaps, he calls them."

The thought of food, especially a cookie, made Avery grin. "I've heard of them. Hikers can't stop talking about Thyme Out on the Fourth, how a guy named Cookie Kravitz bakes for the hikers. So he's Janis's boyfriend? I remember him from the music academy."

"Yes, that's where I first met him too. Let me get a plate," Olivia said.

Once she headed to the kitchen, Avery leaned back in her chair. She heard the sound of water trickling past. *What an amazing vibe*, she thought. *Right on a front patio.* She welcomed the quiet which slowed her racing thoughts.

"I'll bring herbal tea. Lavender okay?" came Olivia's voice.

Avery's eyes flew open to find Olivia standing over her. "Come on inside," she invited. "It's getting breezy out here."

Avery took a moment to run her hand through her still-wet hair. She wiggled her toes, stood, and followed Olivia inside.

A large blue ceramic platter filled with oversized frosted cookies sat in the middle of the quartz-topped island. They made her mouth water. The thick kind, ladened with creamy frosting. Nothing fancy, unless you counted the American flag on a toothpick stuck in the top.

*That's why they're named Sierra Snowcaps,* Avery thought. It was as if someone had climbed a great height and stuck the flag there to mark their accomplishment.

The sight of the frosting made her want to raise a finger and dip it in for a lick.

She'd never liked overly decorated cakes and cookies, the kind her mother got at the Beverly Hills bakery. They never tasted as good as they looked.

She'd always wanted a grandma who taught her to bake. Ones just like those Sierra Snowcaps. She sat down and reached toward the platter as Olivia passed her a napkin. Avery's hand stopped midair. "Do you mind if I go first?"

The corner of Olivia's mouth twitched. "Not at all. I have plenty in the freezer if these run out. Cookie makes me a special batch and I store them just for people who drop in."

*The hostess with the mostest,* Avery thought, licking her fingers. *I could never be her. I don't even like people that much. I bet Michael loves this kind of treatment.* "When will your hubby be back?" she asked, brushing the crumbs off her lap.

"Oh, we're not married." Olivia poured tea into a mug from an enormous pot. "Not planning on children, so we didn't see the need. Are you? In a relationship?"

*Why does everyone ask me that?* Avery fumed to herself. "Not me. I stay out of entanglements. I made some friends on the trail, but nobody I'd live with. Too messy. Inconvenient."

Olivia's gaze softened. *She's digging into my soul,* Avery thought. She abruptly changed the subject.

"I've never met anyone who needed a bridge to get to their front door," Avery commented, reaching for another cookie.

"Michael's idea." Olivia sat down. "At first I thought it was his way of making me feel like a princess in a castle. You know, with a moat." She nodded to the front of the house. "But now that I've lived here awhile, I realize it's his way of protecting me, not like I'm a princess, but someone who needs a lot of space to think my own thoughts."

"Sounds complicated." Avery reached for her third cookie.

"I am rather," Olivia admitted. "I used to think I was low maintenance, but now..." She laughed. "Not so much.

"For instance, you must be wondering if I'm going to interview you about finding Stella Rawlins. That I may be softening you up with the hot shower and a batch of cookies." Her eyebrow lifted.

Avery burst out laughing.

Olivia's eyes sparkled.

"Do you read minds?" Avery asked, her voice slightly annoyed.

"Sometimes," Olivia said. "But not really. I feel energy patterns, so I just say what I assume. You have to confirm or deny. Are you, by the way, confirming?"

*How can I be mad?* Avery realized. *She's so transparent. Not like I have to lie or make up a story. She doesn't even seem that judgy.*

"I'm an open book." Avery waved a cookie in the air. "The shower. The clean clothes that fit. And man, these Sierra Snowcaps. They're to die for." One bite into the soft goodness and Avery's face froze. The remainder of the cookie dropped from her grasp, landing on the floor. *To die for… Really, Avery?*

Olivia rose from her seat. "Don't worry. Mayor Maguire will include crumb cleanup with his next meal. Have some tea." She handed her the mug.

Avery wrapped trembling fingers around the warmth, tears returning to her eyes. "I've been trying to put the sight of Stella's body out of my mind, but it's so not working."

Olivia rested a hand on her shoulder. Warmth radiated down Avery's arm. "This may sound odd, but I've been in your position," Olivia explained in a low voice. "The first time I visited Lily Rock I found my friend Marla dead in the woods behind her house. It's a terrible thing to experience. There's no hurry. You can sit quietly. Talk to me now or another time, but not until you're ready."

Avery took a sip of tea. She glanced through the glass wall toward Lily Rock. A light breeze from the open doorway brushed against her cheeks.

"Is this, you know, off the record?"

"I don't keep a record," Olivia said. "That's up to Janis. I just give people a chance to speak. Everything you say is between us two."

# CHAPTER FOUR

"I wanted to revisit Lily Rock and stay for the Fourth of July weekend," Avery explained to Olivia. "So I contacted Stella in advance. She rented one room to hikers and posted on the Pacific Crest Trail website. Her place was popular. She took the first dozen applicants, reviewed them, and picked me. That's when we started exchanging emails.

"Nothing complex. Just a little about her life in Lily Rock and mine in Los Angeles. I told her my house had recently burned down. She told me that she'd lived here for decades. That she found solace in the quiet and the woods and eventually in the community.

"Mostly she talked about her little free library. How she loved all kinds of books and that she really liked sharing them with others. There was a group of people who were her friends. They called themselves the Switchback Syndicate."

"The what?" Olivia looked surprised. "I thought I knew all the small groups up here. Lots of AA and book clubs. But the Switchback Syndicate? Sounds like a pack of retired spies."

"I suppose." Avery sipped her tea, feeling her nerves settle. *It's so comforting to talk to Olivia*, she realized. *And to think about Stella, how open she was, writing to me before I left*.

"The Syndicate thought of themselves as liberators," Avery said. "At least that's what Stella said. They took switchback, a hiking term, as their name and their motto. You know, a zigzag road where you get to your destination, but it's not the shortest path."

*I should know*, Avery thought. *In that I've never done anything the easy way*.

"Stella explained in an email that switchback also referred to how the Syndicate wanted to turn back to the old ways. Encourage people to read classics without interference from librarians and critics."

"I'm familiar with the term." Olivia nodded. "Not the shortest but more accessible route, right?"

"Right. There are several well-known switchbacks on the PCT," Avery said. "So obviously I was interested in Stella's clandestine group. She was so cute, with her daring choice of books. I like that too."

"It's the syndicate part that concerns me." Olivia put her mug down. "What was that about?"

"So there were six people, including Stella, who all had LFLs. They stocked their libraries with personal choices. Stella said they didn't always agree which books were best, but the conversations at their meetings were interesting.

"They wanted to switch back to the old days," Avery continued, "when libraries weren't so controversial. One of their members was a classic sci-fi guy. One woman a romance author. Not spicy but clean behind-closed-doors kind of stuff. Two moms were very picky about books for children."

Olivia's jaw set. "Just so you know, we don't ban books in Lily Rock. Our librarian, Meadow McCloud, wouldn't stand for that. No politics on her watch. She'd tell you as much."

"I know her," Avery said at once. "I stayed at her place that one Christmas and she ran our gift-wrapping station. Nosy old bird, watching us from behind her office window." She sniffed. "Logan and I wore elf costumes and wrapped gifts. That's how I got the name Elf Two."

Olivia's phone lit up. Meadow McCloud's name flashed on the screen.

"Looks like ol' Meadow's ears are burning," Avery muttered.

Olivia picked up the phone. "I haven't heard that expression for a long time, ears burning. She usually calls me this time of the morning, so we can catch up on family news. Hold on for a minute while I see what she wants."

"Hey, Meadow," Olivia said into the phone.

Avery watched her settle in for a chat, a smile on her face. Olivia listened and then finally spoke. "Star loves to ride, that's for sure. I wish Sparkles would be more amenable. Uh-huh. I do have her here. News travels. Wait a minute." She handed her cell to Avery. "Meadow wants to have a word."

Avery held the phone to her ear. "Hello," she said tentatively.

"Avery, dear, so good to hear your voice. I'm very sorry about Stella. She was a good friend of mine and will be missed." Meadow's voice, pitched in sympathy, reminded Avery that she wasn't really that bad.

Meadow sounded just the same. That combination of soft-heartedness and no-nonsense. Mixed with a rock-solid certainty. It was the certainty that Avery didn't want to cross, not when she was younger and certainly not now.

"Thanks, Ms. McCloud," she said. "It was kinda difficult, finding her like that. But I'm getting better."

"Olivia is an excellent listener," Meadow admitted. "But I want you two to stop what you're doing. I could use some help. The July 4 crowd is already lining up for the parade, and Mayor Maguire requires assistance. Hurry, dear. No time to dillydally."

"Okay, I'll tell her," Avery mumbled. She handed the cell back to Olivia. "We're being summoned."

"So it seems." Olivia stood. "Let's leave the rest of the cookies for later. We'll be in charge of the mayor, keeping him in sight as the tourists gather. His tendency to mooch treats from strangers might get the better of him."

She stared at Avery's bare feet. "I have some shoes that might fit. Your toes look very sore. Maybe we can soak them in Epsom salts later, when we get back. Come on, then."

Avery pulled on the worn pair of slip-on sneakers. Hurrying outdoors, she met Olivia in her car. Her toes weren't cramped, but the shoes clunked along because they weren't a good fit.

Olivia sped down the hill. When she came to a screeching halt behind a row of traffic, her brakes squealed. "Why don't you get out while I park," she suggested. "You'll find Meadow at the Fort, where the parade will start. She'll be in the mayor's convertible. I'll catch up in a minute."

Avery stepped out into the street and slammed the car door shut. She made her way between two truck bumpers to the boardwalk. The loose-fitting canvas shoes felt like wearing boxes on both feet.

She stopped under an old oak tree to rest her sore feet and to have a look at the town. Not much had changed in

Lily Rock. The redwoods in the park looked bigger and more vibrant. The library still stood side by side against the constabulary just like before.

The Fort, a two-story mercantile building with Old West charm, looked as if it had been recently painted. Maybe a few of the shops had changed hands. She didn't remember the beef jerky one, where Old Toy Trains used to be.

People lined the boardwalk, waiting for the parade to begin. Many had dogs on leashes. Lily Rock was known as a canine-friendly community. LA people often drove up the hill for a day trip to experience small town Americana this time of year. The parade for one. The quirky dog mayor for another, who was known as free-range because he walked and slept and ate wherever he chose.

Plus the eccentric but excellent food choices, from trucks to upscale restaurants, made Lily Rock a popular destination.

The street in front of the Fort was blocked off for the parade to assemble. At the front was a yellow convertible, with a red, white, and blue sign labeled Mayor Maguire. No one sat in the car.

Avery felt a shove to her knee. She looked down. The bright black eyes and furry face looked up, his tail wagging with excitement. "Bork," he said.

"Hey, buddy." She reached down to scratch behind his ears. "I think they're looking for you. We'd better find Meadow. You're the main attraction, you know."

"Bork," he replied, as if he understood every word.

Avery kept her fingers looped in his collar. Unsure if she could walk him across the park without losing him, considering her clumsy footwear, she hesitated. Then a voice came from over her shoulder.

"Look who I found. Elf Two. I heard you were back in town." A man's hand reached forward to grasp Maguire's collar, and she let go. He clipped a leash to the ring.

Avery's heart beat excitedly.

"Brad May," she said. "Was that you on the phone?" She swallowed down her nerves to observe him more closely.

Brad bent to adjust Mayor Maguire's bandanna, so she took the moment to have a good look at her teenage on-again, off-again boyfriend.

A few years older, his face had lost the young kid look. His chin was strong and angular. Blue eyes the color of an overcast sky. He'd always been cute. But now he was more. Much more.

The last time, she'd used him, of course. Like she did most people. Her eyes were on Logan, and she'd pretended to like Brad to stir up some jealousy. It worked in the end. Afterward she went home without a backward glance. Mission accomplished, she thought then, giving Logan that delicious kiss goodbye.

But now here he was. Brad May in the flesh. Tall, muscular, and definitely more confident. He'd grown up. And he was a hunk, no one could deny it. LA hunky. Someone you'd take a second glance at if you saw him on Rodeo Drive.

"He found me," Avery explained, pointing to Maguire.

"Yep," Brad answered. "I thought I recognized your voice. Sad situation with Stella. But now I've got to deliver the mayor to his constituents. Come on, Maguire. The parade's about to start."

# CHAPTER FIVE

Avery waved at three people hanging off the last float who held a Lily Rock Brew Pub banner. "What about Arlo. Does he still run the pub?" Avery turned to Olivia standing next to her on the curb.

A softness came over Olivia's face. "That's a long story for another time," she said. "Right now I'm wondering if you wouldn't like supper. It's been quite a day."

"Will the mayor be joining us?" Avery asked.

"Up to him," Olivia answered. "I saw him greet you from across the street and I think he's a fan."

"I knew him when he was a puppy," she explained. "That Christmas he kept escaping and getting picked up by animal control. Meadow was in a such a state. That's when Michael came up with the great idea of calling him the mayor. Giving him special authority. The little rule breaker." The last bit was said with a sense of pride for the town's politician.

Olivia nodded. "Sounds like you have very clear memories of your holidays in Lily Rock. Do you think of them often?"

"One reason I wanted to plan my hike around a long weekend here was to, you know, remember those good times." She knew that was only part of the reason, but she didn't have the energy to tell Olivia the entire truth. That whenever she needed to calm herself or bring herself back from feeling low, she'd conjure memories of Lily Rock.

The snow. Meadow's hospitality. The feeling of having a family even though hers had never bothered much.

"There you are!" Janis Jets interrupted her thoughts. Hands on hips, she stopped to glare at Avery. "I got a disturbing-the-peace call. I want you two to accompany me. I need Olivia, and I don't want you wandering all willy-nilly without supervision."

Avery had hoped she was done with Janis for the day. But obviously that wasn't the case. "Don't you need me to make a statement or something?"

"Like I said, that can wait. I need this one"—she pointed to Olivia—"to come along and do her thing. But I don't want her to leave you. So don't drag your feet, Backpack Betty. Everyone in the truck. Hurry up!"

Avery hated being treated as an extra. It reminded her of when she was small and dragged along by her parents. One stage set after another. A bunch of strangers that chucked her chin and called her pretty but forgot her name the next day. Actors, she was told, only had memories for their craft. Not the names of children.

"What if I don't want to go?" Avery nearly cringed, her voice sounding childish and defiant.

Janis's eyebrow lifted. She took on a mocking tone. "What if I don't wanna go. Please, how old are you? Don't forget you're a suspect in a murder. I had to postpone your interview because of the July whoop-de-doo. That was against my better judgment. But I've got my eye on you now." She used two fingers to point to her eyes and then to Avery's.

Avery kicked her foot in the dirt and then immediately regretted it. One big toe throbbed inside her oversized sneaker. "Ouch! Okay, but it better not be far. I can't walk in these things." She gestured to her shoes.

Jets grinned. "You can sit in the truck. Plus, this is going to be a good one. A neighbor called in a group of folks acting up in their hot tub. All wrinkly and disgusting. Yelling with loud music. So get a move on."

"What about the fireworks?" Avery looked up to the sky blanketing the world above the pines. The truth was she didn't like the sound of fireworks. She preferred to stay indoors to watch the display.

"They won't happen." Olivia turned to Avery. "Against the Lily Rock regulations due to the fire hazard in the mountains. We didn't get much rain this year. Hardly any snow. That wouldn't even matter. Droughts are a permanent condition."

"You don't have to give her a weather report," Jets abruptly snapped. "She's coming with us, like it or not."

By the time Avery scuffled her way to Janis's truck, the crowd had thinned and street traffic had returned to normal. "Give me a minute," Janis told them, hurrying toward the back exit of the constabulary.

"Did she forget her purse?" Avery mumbled.

Olivia laughed. "Just you wait. Slide in the back. You'll find out soon enough."

Janis returned with both arms around a squirming gray bundle shaped like a baked potato. The opposite-side back door opened, followed by a thump. "There you go, Tater."

Janis used a coaxing voice. "Stay away from my suspect. She may be a bad influence."

Avery leaned closer. "Hey, fella." She held out her fingers for the French bulldog to sniff. "Is this a pure-bred Frenchie?" she asked.

Janis ignored her question as she leaned in to buckle the seat belt through the dog's safety harness. "This is Tater Tot. I refuse to start the car until he's safely buckled in."

Avery glanced at Olivia.

"Don't ask!" Olivia warned. "Tater's pedigree is a touchy subject."

"A story for another time..." Avery said.

Jets got into the driver's seat and threw the truck in reverse, grunting.

The dog sniffed Avery's fingers. He looked at her with pleading eyes.

Avery checked Janis. Her eyes were on the road. So she reached over and released the dog's seat belt. He blinked his appreciation and then inched his way across the seat to climb into her lap.

Tater Tot spun twice and sat down, resting his sizable square-shaped head on her leg. His soulful big eyes stared up into her face. Then he lowered his flat nose to poke at her hand.

Avery inched her fingers along his back to his stubby tail. *Well hello to you too. Very cute.* The truck came to a screeching halt as Janis leaned over to grab him. "Did you let him out?" she growled.

Tater Tot squirmed out of her reach, remaining in Avery's lap.

"Stop that, Tater!" Janis insisted.

She hopped out of the truck and opened the back door. Tater ducked his head down to Avery's legs, his rump in the air. *I don't blame ya, fella. She's a bit much,* Avery thought, chuckling.

"Come here, sweetiekins," Janis coaxed. She grabbed his collar and pulled, the dog resisting with a growl.

Avery reached to smooth the fur on Tater's back. She gave him a knowing glance right as Jets once again secured him in the seat.

"Is Tater Tot a police dog?" Avery asked Jets, who now sat behind the wheel.

"Not on your life. He's family. Cooks and I have raised and trained him to be our lifetime companion; we'd never expect him to earn a living."

Avery held back a smirk. "So no Rin Tin Tin, then."

Olivia chuckled, turning in her seat and raising an eyebrow.

"Buckle up, Backpack Betty." Jets shifted the truck, screeching forward, while the cars behind honked their irritation.

"They obviously don't know I'm a cop," she said.

Avery leaned closer to Tater Tot. He pushed against his restraints.

She sniffed. "Your dog is one mean farting machine," she called to Janis. The back window opened as Janis took another curve in the road.

Tater Tot gave a side-eye to Avery, his tongue touching his bottom lip.

Janis glanced in her rearview. "It's okay, baby," she soothed. "This won't take long. Then back to Daddy for some din-din and Netflix."

It was Olivia's turn to roll her eyes at Avery.

As Janis took the truck down a bumpy dirt road, Avery stared out the open window. Another little free library came into view. constructed to appear like a log cabin with a chimney, Avery could easily imagine smoke rising in spirals toward the dark sky.

At the end of the drive, there was an actual cabin, this one with a front deck. To the far side, a path leading to a steaming hot tub held four people. The little library was in better shape than both the cabin and the railing around the hot tub.

Janis brought her truck to a halt to the sound of the Mick Jagger singing, "You Can't Always Get What You Want". Amped to loud decibels on outdoor speakers, Avery grinned right as the selection changed to "Back in the U.S.A." by Chuck Berry, performed by Linda Ronstadt. Old school rock and roll brought Avery joy.

Four heads poked above the steaming water. Built with redwood siding, this was no spa. It looked as if it had been there since the sixties. The revelers bobbed up and down to the music, naked shoulders glistening. Beer bottles were strewn in the dirt surrounding the tub. There was a half-open cooler but no towels anywhere.

Jets gave a nod to Olivia. "You come with me." She turned her head. "You stay with Tater Tot. We won't be long."

"Roll down both windows," Avery told Jets. "Because of...you know." She pointed to Tater Tot. The truth was that she wanted to hear Janis and Olivia and the hot tub people face off.

Jets pushed the button right as Tater yipped.

"He has to pee," Avery explained.

"Just keep him inside." Jets slammed the door shut.

As soon as Jets's back was turned, Avery released Tater from the harness. He leaned into her leg, waiting for a pet. *You big faker. You don't have to go*, she scolded him internally.

"I got a disturbing-the-peace call," Jets announced in a loud voice.

When no one turned their head, she yanked the cord attached to the speaker, unplugging it. "Party time is over, folks." Now everyone looked at her.

"It's the Fourth of July," muttered the older guy with the overgrown buzz cut. Spikes of gray hair stuck out over his ears.

"And you are..." Jets reached for her iPad.

"Marshall Reed," he said calmly. "I'm a Lily Rock resident. I own this property free and clear. It's good to know you actually came out on a busy night like this. I didn't expect that much from the local cops."

"Cop," Janis corrected. "I'm a one-woman operation. This here"—she used her thumb—"is Olivia Greer. She's a consultant."

"The mind reader. I heard about her." Reed's face took on an amused expression.

"I'm not a mind reader," Olivia replied tartly. "I bring a different perspective than Officer Jets. That's all."

Pulling Tater Tot to her lap, Avery leaned closer to the open window. Watching Jets at work was a lot like watching her father play a cop on a television set. This was going to be fun.

*If I had popcorn, it would be just about perfect.*

# CHAPTER SIX

Tater Tot propped his paws on the door's window frame, shoving his face next to Avery's. He gave her ear a good lick and then turned his head to stare outside.

*I guess both of us are nosy*, Avery thought.

His bat-shaped ears perked forward. *Little eaves-dropper*.

"You can stay, but no barking, got it?"

The Frenchie wrinkled his nose and gave her cheek a sniff.

*I guess that's a yes.*

Avery shifted her attention to the voices outside.

"Someone called the cops on your little party," Jets stated. She patted the back of her navy-blue blazer. *That bulge must be her weapon*, thought Avery. *Nice gesture. I wonder if she ever removes it from that holster, other than to take it out to put on her pajamas.*

Avery felt herself smile, thinking of Janis Jets in pj's.

"Well not us, we don't make a habit of calling the cops," returned the man with buzz cut.

Avery surmised that he was most likely retired military.

His bare shoulders still had a bit of definition. Clean shaven; his lips stretched thin. His head rose above the other three, which probably made him feel like the one in charge. *Or he has an abnormally long torso.*

"You don't have to answer for everyone else," Janis explained crossly. "How about you...bouffant hairstyle. What brings you to this little skinny-dipping party?"

The woman's voice purred. "This is just heaven for me. Under the stars. The water warm over my naked body. Come on in for a dip. The bar is open." Her giggle sounded fake, making Avery cringe. *Probably had too much to drink,* she concluded.

Janis waited for one of the others to speak, impatiently tapping her iPad with a forefinger. She looked up, as if asking God for patience. Then she glanced at Olivia. "Reading any minds yet, valiant consultant?"

Olivia shrugged.

"Officer, I doubt if the neighbors really care about the noise tonight. Come on." This voice, more reasonable, sounded young and female. Her brown hair had been secured on top of her head. Jets remained silent. Avery felt a tinge of admiration. The cop was good. She waited for the young woman to keep talking.

But no such luck. The woman ducked her head into the water, emerging with hair and face dripping wet, a smile on her lips.

*Ugh,* thought Avery. *Who knows how many germs just crawled into her nose, ears, and mouth. I'd never put my head underwater in a hot tub.*

The last to speak was the skinny guy with the narrow face and a long neck. "You might want to ask the neighbor instead of bugging us. We're real happy here, and now the music is off. No longer disturbing the peace." He sounded familiar, but in the dark Avery couldn't place him.

Water cascaded from his forearm as he pointed to the house next door, where the deck provided an unobstructed view of the hot tub and all the occupants. No one stood outside watching. "She's gone inside," he stated.

"The woman who called said, and I quote..." Jets looked at her iPad. ""There's trouble with the people next door. I can hear them screaming at each other. Please get over here before things get out of hand."' Jets smiled. "So what was the beef? Go ahead. You can tell me. Just so I can put it in my report."

When no one answered, Jets scowled. "That's the way it's going to be, is it? All right, no more being nice. I'll take your names and follow up later, when you're all decent." She waved her hand in the air to include everyone. "No one wants to see that!"

Avery closed her eyes. This was the boring part, getting the names. She sat back in her seat, a signal for Tater Tot to drop his paws from the door, turn in a circle, and make himself at home in her lap.

When Jets finished taking their details, she gestured to Olivia and they made their way to the truck.

Avery pretended to be asleep, her eyes closed tightly. No use in alerting the cop that she'd been eavesdropping. She stifled a yawn as Janis sat behind the steering wheel. "Boring you, am I?" Jets growled.

She turned the truck around, tires spinning on gravel. They bumped their way back to the main road.

Tater Tot, forgotten and unbuckled, remained in Avery's arms. *He smells nice*, she thought. Dipping her nose to his fur, she sniffed again. Like a cheap vanilla-scented candle. *Probably his groomer's favorite shampoo.*

When no one from the front seat spoke, Avery's curiosity got the best of her. "Don't you think it's odd that the owner of this place has a little library, just like Stella?"

Olivia nodded. "I do. And didn't you tell me that Stella mentioned a small group of people who formed a club? The Switchback Syndicate?"

Jets tapped the steering wheel. "I bet that was the Syndicate, or most of them. Good catch on the library, Backpack Betty." The words sounded awkward, nearly like a compliment.

"Don't call me that," Avery muttered.

"The name suits you. All those scratches and bruises and oversized shoes." Janis sounded amused.

"Just drop it," Avery said. "What about the little library link? A coincidence or a clue? Aren't you the cop?"

"No, you're right. That isn't just a coincidence. I did get phone numbers and addresses from all the nudies, so it wasn't a total loss. I can send my assistant to confirm the addresses tomorrow morning. By then I hope I have a toxicology report on Stella. Maybe after that, I can connect that slippery lot to her death."

Avery closed her eyes as Stella flashed in her mind. Tater Tot nosed her hand.

"Does that mean I'm no longer a person of interest?" Avery asked, patting the dog.

"Not on your life, missy!" Jets's truck came to a quick stop at the intersection. "Go home with Olivia. She'll keep her eye out. I'll let you know when you're off my list."

"You can drop us at my truck in town," Olivia said. "Hopefully it's not still overcrowded with tourists and July 4 late-night revelers."

"Will do," Jets agreed. "I hope the rest of my calls tonight will be for people with clothes on. What ever happened to common decency? Lily Rock has gone to the dogs."

"Yip." Tater Tot sat up.

"I didn't mean dogs like you, Tater." Janis's voice shifted to a soft coo. "You're my itty-bitty fur baby."

Avery rolled her eyes at Tater, who turned his head away as if embarrassed.

“It's Mayor Maguire."

Olivia pointed to her car, where the town's most affable politician waited. He wore his red, white, and blue ribbon with a gold medal hanging from his neck.

"Bork," he called, turning in circles with excitement.

By the time Avery opened the truck's back door and got out, he'd sprinted toward her, sliding to a stop at her feet, his tail waving.

Tater Tot growled.

Maguire stepped back to give him space.

"I don't have a treat," Avery explained.

"I have some at the house." Olivia looked back. "See you later, Officer Jets."

The truck rumbled away as Tater Tot barked goodbye out the back window.

In Olivia's kitchen, Avery tossed a bone-shaped dog biscuit in the air. Maguire caught it and swallowed in one gulp. He came closer, a look of expectation in his eyes.

Curious, Avery lifted another treat to her nose. "This smells people-worthy," she commented.

"From the bakery in town, Thyme Out," Olivia answered.

"Peanut butter, right?"

"Yup. Cookie Kravitz started a whole side business on those dog biscuits. He makes them in all sizes. Ships them from his website."

Avery looked thoughtful. She wanted to clarify if it was the same guy she'd already met. "So I heard about an FBI guy at the music academy. An investigation before I was a student. Is that the same one?"

"Same one. Janis's boyfriend now. Lives in town."

"The one she calls Cooks?"

"Yep. Plus, Michael and Cookie have their own side hustle. Cookie creates a special seasonal baked item, and Michael makes a coffee blend to go with it. It's like a wine pairing but with coffee."

"I never saw Michael as coffee-preneur," Avery said. "He used to dump in a lot of cream and sugar when I knew him."

Olivia stared at Avery, looking thoughtful.

"So you remember details, like how a random man takes his coffee. I think Lily Rock must have made an impression on you. Maybe that's one reason you came back."

Avery felt her face heat up. Olivia saw her clearly, and she wasn't sure she liked it. *My memories are my business*, she fumed. The fact that she thought about Lily Rock every day was private. She inhaled and corrected Olivia's assumption.

"I'm not all sentimental about Lily Rock. I'm unhoused, if you must know. My cottage burned down in the Palisades fire. The parents took off to Europe on a movie shoot. They left me with the ruins, so I decided to hike the Pacific Crest Trail.

"Don't rope me in with the cinnamon-roll give-me-a-hug crowd of...what did they call themselves? The Old Rockers?" Avery used the town's nickname for the resident longtimers who'd elevated themselves into an unofficial council.

"I actually despise the smell of cinnamon." The last part was a lie, but she added it to spice up her denial.

"I see." Olivia's eyes sparkled. "Glad you cleared that up. Sorry about being unhoused. So you're welcome to stay here as long as you like. It's just me and Maguire right now. Oh, and occasionally an overnight with Star. She's my sister's baby. My niece."

At least Olivia knew when to quit. But then Avery realized, *I played right into her hands. I confessed my living situation. Volunteered the details. Jeez, she's good.*

"How about a hot cup of tea?" Olivia suggested. "Lavender. You like that smell, right?"

"Sure," Avery said.

Olivia nodded, ignoring her clipped response. "Janis will be busy tonight. I'll put my phone on silent, and I suggest you do the same."

"Can Maguire sleep with me?" At the sound of his name the dog stood to all fours. She tossed him her last peanut butter biscuit.

"He picks his bed," Olivia commented. "I have a feeling you're the one he wants. After watching you with Tater Tot, I'm wondering if you don't have some kind of spiritual connection with dogs."

"No psychic mumbo jumbo," Avery said.

Olivia chuckled. "Now you sound like Officer Jets."

# CHAPTER SEVEN

Avery buried her face under the pillow.

"Time to wake up, sleepyhead," Olivia called from behind the closed door. Avery heard the handle turn, then soft footsteps approaching her bed. "Janis texted me and wants us to meet her at the constabulary."

Avery moaned. *Not her again. That cop is a real pain.* Every muscle tensed as she swung her legs over the bed.

"Do I have to go with you?" She blinked at Olivia, who looked far too perky this time in the morning.

"You might want to. She's one quick decision away from listing you as her number one suspect."

Avery stretched her arms over her head. "This is a first," she mumbled, bending over to touch her toes. "I've been cautioned by the cops before, but an actual suspect?"

"Recently?"

Avery glared straight at Olivia and then blinked. *She doesn't sound surprised,* Avery realized. *Probably knows everything about me due to her supposed superpower.*

"Not lately. When I was younger, I used to steal from stores. A little of this and that. Nothing valuable. Once my parents found out, they made an appointment with a therapist. When she didn't help, I was packaged up and sent to the Lily Rock Music Academy. Other kids had talent, but for me it was more of a reform school."

"Are you a musician?" Olivia sounded interested.

"Not exactly. I love music. But I'm an outsider. What else is new?"

"Okay, sad sack," Olivia said in a dismissive tone. "I have breakfast ready." She glanced around the room. "I thought the mayor would sleep with you last night."

"He did." Avery had fallen asleep running her fingers through his fur. "But he scratched at the door really early, so I let him out."

"Maybe the only politician I've heard of who gets a very early start." Olivia grinned.

"Your clean laundry is in the dryer. See you in fifteen minutes." She closed the door on her way out.

Half an hour later, they found Janis hunched over her desk, glaring at her phone like it had already ruined her day.

"'Bout time." She clicked off the screen.

Olivia pulled an extra chair from the corner. Avery sat down first. "So what's the hurry? We barely had a chance to get dressed," Avery mumbled.

"Just got the initial report from the crime scene. Turns out an ordinary firecracker blew up in Stella's face." Jets frowned.

"That sounds...bad. But also like someone tossed it at her as, what, a prank? You sure it wasn't a planted device with a timer?" Avery insisted.

"Do not second-guess me," Jets warned.

Olivia crossed her arms. "So Stella was meant to be frightened, then, not killed."

"Could have been a prank," Janis reasoned. "A mean

one, considering Stella's age. It literally scared the life out of her. She stumbled, hit her head, and the shock pushed her heart to the breaking point."

"So...not an accident." Avery wanted to make sure.

Janis's expression sharpened. "Until we know more about who tossed it, probably not intentional. Wasn't you, right?" Jets quirked an eyebrow at Avery.

Avery ignored her question. "My first guess, in case you want to know, would be the military dude." She stopped to remember the scene. "The one in the hot tub—he spoke for everyone. He has that look, you know, of an oppositional personality disorder. A kind of guy who'd do pretty near anything to make a point. Don't forget he likely has one of those little libraries. I bet he's part of the Switchback Syndicate." She sat back in her chair to revel in Janis's look of surprise.

"You gathered all this from the back seat of the truck?" Jets glared. "What's that about a disorder?"

"I was diagnosed with the same thing when I was younger," Avery admitted. "Bunch of bull. A Beverly Hills therapist wanted to medicate me, but I refused to take the drugs. Made my parents furious."

*There I am, doing it again. Confessing my past.* Avery felt any control she might have had over the situation brushed away by her own admission.

Olivia shifted uncomfortably in her chair. The side-eye she shot Avery felt like a warning. Avery bit her bottom lip.

Jets tapped her fingers on the desktop. "Tell me more about that syndicate, why don't you?"

Olivia answered, "Avery told me yesterday. About Stella and a few friends starting little libraries."

*Is she protecting me?* Avery wondered.

Olivia took another glance in her direction. Then she

leaned slightly forward. "Tell her what Stella told you. It may have something to do with our case."

Avery launched into the story, as Jets listened attentively. When she finished, Janis took out her iPad and made a note.

"Why don't we drop in on hot tub guy. Hopefully he's found his underwear. Next to you, he'd be the most likely suspect."

Avery wanted to defend herself, but Janis kept talking.

"And maybe he can tell us more about that syndicate." Janis's eyes narrowed. "Before you think you're off the hook, Backpack Betty, I still need your statement in writing. But not now. We'd better get a move on. You can sit in the car while the professionals do their job."

Olivia and Janis talked on the drive up the hill.

"Where's your noble assistant this morning?" Olivia asked.

"Brad's taking that class I told you about. Down in the desert. Got hooked up with a pie bar cutie and spends his nights with her. He barely shows up nowadays.

"That Redondo guy I told you about. The mentalist?" Janis continued. "Brad and him are thick as thieves. Along with the doula, what's her name... They're all taking the class together. He's giving me a headache, that one." Jets braked for a squirrel scurrying across the road.

"With him gone all the time, who's going to answer the phones and do my stakeouts?" she complained in a disgruntled tone.

From the back seat, Avery was able to observe their dynamic. First Olivia. She had a way of asking questions that brought down a person's reserve. Even Jets was putty in her hands.

"I wish the Old Rockers hadn't taken such an interest in

Brad," Janis said. "They made up a scholarship for him, so he had the money to further his education. He can barely do the job we pay him for, let alone any homework. Hey, wait a minute." She gave Olivia a side glance.

"You can type, right? And you have an old car. You can do surveillance. Perfect solution. Why don't I fire the kid and increase your salary a buck or two an hour?"

"Nope. Not for me. I have other ways to spend my time." Olivia didn't even apologize. "Plus, we tried that a few years ago. It didn't work, remember?"

Jets brought the truck to a halt in front of the hot tub property. She dismissed Olivia's statement with a shrug.

"Why don't we have a look around before knocking on his door. I'm curious about that little library. Right over there." She pointed.

Avery was the first to hop out of the truck. She walked closer to the little free library. *Good construction*, she thought, making a circle to see every angle. *Look at that. Tongue and groove. Double-pane glass. Now for the books.*

She opened the glass front door. "He's got all the old sci-fi classics. Vonnegut. Clarke. Heinlein. My dad used to read them to me as bedtime stories. Dad said the characters you read eventually wear grooves in your soul. Pretend long enough and one day you won't know where the mask ends and you begin. He's an actor."

Janis stood with her hands on her hips. "Did I say you could get out of the truck?" Her tone was accusatory.

"What's the guy's name?" Olivia asked. "The one we're here to interview?"

"Marshall Reed. He refused to ante up his cell number, claims he's off-the-grid. Fancies himself a survivalist. Otherwise I would have called ahead."

"A survivalist with a little library?" objected Avery.

"Look at this. A copy of *The Giving Tree*. Shel Silverstein. A children's book."

"But still a classic," Olivia commented. She opened the cover, a smile on her lips.

"We're not stopping to browse for your next read," Jets insisted. "Come on, Nancy Drew." She gave Olivia a hip bump.

She returned the book and then followed Janis up the path toward the cabin. Avery did not return to the back seat; she continued to watch as they approached the front porch.

Before Janis could knock on the door, Avery shouted, "What about me?"

"Okay, Betty. But keep your mouth shut, all right? No more chitchat about your childhood bedtime stories."

Avery jogged to catch up, then stopped in front of the porch to take in the battered, weathered cabin. Rusted tools and solar batteries were stacked like bricks to one side. A tangled hammock had seen better years. The cooler from the previous night stood upside down.

*He may have constructed the little library to match the house*, she thought, *but now the library's construction outshines the original. This place is a dump.*

A chipped enamel basin caught rainwater under the eaves. Hand-painted signs warned against trespassers, drones, and government stooges.

Before Janis could knock, the door cracked open. Marshall stood in the threshold, a towel slung around his waist, no shirt. His short gray hair flat against his skull. "What can I do for you ladies?" he drawled.

"Put on some clothes, big boy. I have a few questions." Janis pushed past him like she owned the place. "Don't mind if I do."

Olivia spoke quietly to Avery. "You can stay outside."

"Not on your life," Avery said, and followed them in.

The air smelled thick with the scent of woodsmoke and stale coffee grounds. A jumble of survivalist necessity items heaped in one corner. Avery recognized most of the gear.

People who hiked the PC trail had a similar array. Props to tell stories when they sat around the campfire at night, first-rate solar flashlights, special folding stoves. Maps. So many maps.

Shelves lined another wall, stacked with jars of preserved beans, dented coffee tins, and stacks of well-thumbed paperbacks. Avery recognized a few dog-eared science fiction books.

Marshall's eyes bored into her. "You a hiker? I think I saw you come down from the trail the other day. I hit the PCT when I can. Leave books and maps at the dead drop. There's a little library there. You know where that is?"

His questions felt like an oral exam. Avery intended to pass.

"I hike," she said, keeping her answer short.

"Do I know you?" he repeated, gaze sharpened.

Avery was used to that question. Plenty of people thought they'd met her before. She'd been told she looked just like her mother, an actress who played lots of B films. She let the thought slide. "Doubt it. If you did, you'd remember."

"Clothes, Marshall." Janis gestured to the drooping towel.

"Oh yeah, be right back." He turned, and then in an act of defiance, removed the towel for them all to see. When he crouched over a duffle bag, Avery averted her gaze.

As he dug for his clothes, she drifted toward a corkboard filled with maps. One pinned over another, the top sheet made her pause. PCT trails were traced in red marker, whole swatches of forest shaded out in black. She knew that map. It showed the dead drop locations where hikers shared small treasures, passed from one dusty hand to the next. Books. Batteries. Sometimes a left behind cell phone.

Once Marshall pulled on a shirt and worn jeans, Janis cleared her throat. "How well did you know Stella Rawlins?" She took out her iPad and waited.

"Long time now. We lost touch for years. Then I moved up here and ran into her at the market."

Avery sensed he was telling some but not all of the truth. He scratched behind his ear and looked puzzled. *His tell*, she concluded.

"So you were good buddies with Stella. Was it ever more than friendship? Were you a couple?" Jets asked.

Avery blinked rapidly. Ol' Janis didn't mind poking a man about his personal business.

"Maybe once or twice in the old days. But nothing that stuck—it was never like that with me and Stella. We had what people would call core differences. Our choice of books for reading material, for one.

"But I helped her with her little library. In fact I did a repair just the day before yesterday."

Avery knew he was lying. He definitely had a thing with Stella. He was doing his best to act calm, but that was a cover-up.

Marshall shook his head. "Can't believe the little library blew up. Probably sabotaged. One of those kids in town, out to get attention. Man, that stinks."

"More than stinks," Jets muttered.

"Big explosion?" he asked. "A pipe bomb or something?"

"Wouldn't you like to know," Jets retorted. "So, Marshall, you got anything lying around here that says you're the kind of guy who could rig up a little boom? Spare wires, fireworks stash, maybe a how-to manual under those sci-fi paperbacks...or a box of firecrackers?"

"Lady, I don't know who you think I am." He tugged at his belt, his mouth tightening.

"Oh, I think I have a pretty good idea," Jets replied.

"You'll need a warrant to look any further, and by the way, get outta my cabin." Suddenly Marshall had had enough of the pleasantries. He nodded toward the door, crossing his arms over his chest.

Once outside, the three women lingered in the front yard. Janis strolled toward the hot tub, flipped back the cover, and wrinkled her nose. "This is a cesspool of DNA," she announced. "If and when I get the warrant, I'll have them clean out the filter. And I'll need to be quick about it before he—" She jerked a thumb over her shoulder. "I bet he cleans it himself."

Right on cue, the door opened. Marshall stepped out with a fishnet slung over his shoulder. "Still here," he said flatly. "Step aside, please. Time for a little maintenance."

Janis backed off with a shrug. "Hurts to be so right all the time," she said to Olivia, just loud enough for Marshall and Avery to hear.

Back in the truck, Janis asked Olivia, "So, what did we get? Any deep reads of his personality? A lead as to why he'd toss a firecracker in an old friend's face?"

"He's blustery and defensive," Olivia said. "His place is minimal yet still crowded. I've never been inside the home of a survivalist before, so I've got no baseline for comparison. I think he was mostly truthful, except about Stella. They definitely had a thing."

"I thought so too," Jets agreed. "His place isn't exactly a Bellemare design. I've been in most of the cabins on the hill, and Reed's is one of the low-end examples. But did you see him flinch when I mentioned explosives?"

"He admitted to repairing Stella's little free library right before the explosion that killed her. That's opportunity, isn't it?" Avery's words rushed out. "Plus, I'm not buying his story. I think there was more to their relationship than he admits. He certainly doesn't mind walking around naked in front of women. That's for sure."

Jets shot her a quick nod. "Not bad, Backpack Betty. I was going to bring that up next. Marshall uses every opportunity to get under people's skin. Okay then, time to get going. But not before stopping at Thyme Out. I want you to meet my honey."

"I'm starving," Olivia sighed.

Avery didn't say she'd already met Cookie. Maybe he wouldn't remember her, and that would be embarrassing.

Still, Janis's sudden insistence felt less like a lunch break and more like another test. Once again Olivia spoke for her. "Avery and Cookie have met," she said.

"He probably won't remember," Avery added.

"Good to know."

Jets gave Avery a glare in the rearview mirror before shoving the truck into gear.

# CHAPTER EIGHT

Avery was still mulling over the informal interview with Marshall Reed when the bell over Thyme Out's door jingled. She followed Janis and Olivia inside. One step into the bakery and the scent of warm cinnamon, sugar, and strong coffee assaulted her nose. She suspected that the smell was designed to make people drop their guard and their wallets.

The place was warm in a way that felt deliberate, with sunshine brightness spilling across mismatched tables. The glass cake stands on the counter were overfilled with scones and cookies. One pie display looked like it had been curated for a magazine photo. *Staged*, she thought.

A sign over a corner shelf indicated the well-known Kravitz seasonal bake. Cozy? Absolutely. But to Avery, it felt like walking onto a stage set. Every crumb, every chalkboard menu, every polished fork in its basket, all of it too perfectly arranged, as if the place had something to prove.

"Sit over there." Jets nodded. "I want a word with the proprietor."

On the way to the empty table, she spotted a familiar

woman. Avery could swear she'd been one of those in the hot tub last night. Her shiny hair, pulled on top of her head, and the peasant top she wore, obviously new, made Avery feel self-conscious.

*The young one*, she concluded, *who dipped her head underwater.*

Once they were seated, Olivia leaned closer. "You doing okay?" she asked.

Usually Avery brushed off questions like that. People wanted her to share her feelings, and for what? To make *them* feel better. But in this case, Olivia's question felt sincere. She considered telling her that she felt terrible. That she hated looking like something the cat dragged in, for one. Especially in public. She wanted to confess that hiking the PCT had seemed like a good idea a couple of weeks ago, but now she longed to dump everything, including the backpack, the boots, and her outdoorsy persona. And finally, she felt irritable. Judging the bakery through the eyes of a cynic, instead of letting it settle over her, to soothe her back to a better self.

*Stop resisting, the therapist advised. Just let yourself be happy one time. Then two...*

Janis approached the table with Cookie in tow. He wore a chef's apron and a sheepish smile. "I tried to tell her," he began, "that we'd already met. How are you, Avery?" He extended his hand.

She took it quickly, relieved that he'd not forgotten her. Something about the warmth of his grasp gave her confidence. "I'm ready to hit the trail," she said. "But I'm under suspicion, so what can I do?" She gave a head jerk toward Janis. "Maybe you can talk sense to your cop friend."

Cookie chuckled. "That would be a first." He turned to

Janis. "Wouldn't it, honey cakes." He leaned to rub her nose with his.

Avery couldn't help it. "Ew," she said. "Aren't you too old for that?"

"Exactly," Olivia added. "They disgust everyone, so you aren't alone. I'm hungry. Was that mentioned? Maybe a sandwich for lunch?" She nodded to the menu board.

After they ordered, Cookie disappeared behind the counter. Janis brought out her notes, but Avery interrupted before she could start. "I'm curious. Why didn't you ask Marshall about the Switchback Syndicate? I thought for sure..."

"Never second-guess me," Janis said. "I don't tell you everything that's on my mind. I save the good stuff until the right time. After this one"—she gestured toward Olivia —"softens them up."

"That's not what I do," Olivia insisted. "I'm just a good listener." She turned to Avery. "Less judgy, really. I wait for people to explain. Talk about jumping to conclusions..." She glared at Janis.

"I'll jump to your conclusion," Jets retorted. "But back to the Switchback Syndicate. Here's what I'm thinking. On the one hand, Marshall must be in the gang. The name has his markings. Syndicate. That sounds off-the-grid to me. Most of those people lack trust. In law enforcement, for one.

"Plus, he admitted he had a little library that he filled with books on the dead drop. So Switchback has a hiking theme. Proof enough. That off-the-grid mountain man probably organized the group himself.

"But on the other hand..." Janis lifted her tablet. "I'm thinking we had everyone in the Syndicate right under our noses last night. That chummy bunch of naked hippies in the hot tub."

"The one woman wasn't old enough to be a hippie," Avery pointed out.

"I recognized her," Olivia said. "Naomi Wells-Duran. She lives with her wife and their daughter in a very cute gingerbread cabin." She blinked at Janis. "You know the neighborhood. Where we solved that case with the tidy influencers."

"Gag me with a spoon," Jets croaked. "Those places were all Hansel and Gretel, including the wicked witch inside."

Though Avery wanted to hear more, she needed to point out the obvious. "Okay, so Naomi must have been that younger woman in the spa. She's sitting right over there." She gestured with a nod.

Naomi chatted with two other young women. Strollers had been left against the nearby wall. Two held babies, alert and looking around. Only one child sat in the mother's lap. "Why would she be in the Syndicate? She's gotta be busy, right? Not exactly Marshall's type of co-conspirator," Avery said in a thoughtful voice.

Janis blinked at the word "conspirator." She closed her iPad right as the server arrived with their order. "Hold that thought," she commented and then reached for her roast beef on rye.

# CHAPTER NINE

Once the lunch plates were removed, a basket of cookies and a coffee carafe arrived. Olivia picked up the basket and offered it to Avery. "Sierra Snowcaps, like we had yesterday."

Avery didn't hesitate. She took her first bite and rolled her eyes in pleasure. All the cinnamon smell and cozy vibes were forgiven. This cookie was worth it.

Jets watched, a slight smile coming to the corner of her mouth. She waited for Avery to swallow. "Once we're done here, I want to check in with the older hot tub hottie. Her name's Cordelia Pratt. She's my next person of interest."

"She seemed slightly tipsy," Olivia said. "Not a reliable witness."

"Kind of," Jets admitted. "But I want to follow up on my hunch that the hot tub meetup was more than just a few folks gathering in the woods to look at the stars. That they are the Syndicate."

Avery reached for another cookie. *Might as well eat*, she thought. *Maybe take one for the road. I feel like a kid brought along for the ride.*

"Okay then." Olivia licked frosting off her finger. "But I want another batch of these to go. I'm addicted. With Michael gone, I'll snuggle up to a cookie before bed."

What, again? Reading her mind about the cookie. And how did these women manage to make her feel so awkward with all of their boyfriend talk? "Let's get going," Avery suggested. "People are waiting for our table."

Once outside, they had to sidestep a group of hikers. Backpacks were stacked at their feet, trekking poles leaned against a nearby tree. Most looked sunburned and happy, slightly less dirty than when Avery had seen them the day before.

A familiar man in his early twenties leaned on a hiking pole, talking to another hiker. Shaggy brown hair hung around his face, looking freshly washed. He glanced in their direction, his eyes resting on Avery. He sent her a slight nod.

"Friend of yours?" Jets asked lightly, already angling her head to take him in. "Wait a minute. I know that skinny neck. That's the other guy in the hot tub."

"He's a hiker, someone I knew on the trail." Avery finally knew something Jets didn't.

Olivia's brow furrowed. "Did he tell you he was local, while you were hiking?"

"He never mentioned he lived here," Avery said.

"I have an idea, Backpack Betty," Jets said. "Why don't you mosey on over and chat him up. Find out what his deal is. Olivia and I will meet you back at the constabulary. My noble assistant should have more information by then.

"Take your time. I need to do the usual dressing down," she continued. "Since Brad's always in trouble, I chew him out from habit. Unless of course..." She paused with a smirk. "You want to watch. It'll be fun. Pure entertainment."

Avery was in no hurry to see Jets in action with Brad. Plus, now was her chance to get a little space from the cop and Olivia. She didn't wait for Jets to offer again, so she quickly turned to hurry toward the group of hikers.

Theo greeted her as soon as she approached. "I thought that was you. Hanging out with the cops now?" His eyes challenged her for an explanation.

"There's a reason," she mumbled. "But not now. Where can we meet? I can't wait to tell you what happened."

He looked surprised. "Sure. I'll get my bakery order and find you. How about the park? Head on over and save us a bench." He turned back to his pal.

The park held welcome shade and a spot for Avery to think without interruption. Maybe it was the redwoods, but she felt herself breathe more deeply before sitting on a bench at the base of one of the giant trees.

Avery relished the small miracle of being alone. No Olivia circling her like a concerned aunt. No Janis sharpening her tongue with more smart remarks. Sometimes Avery wanted to clap a hand over the detective's mouth just to make her stop talking.

*Judgy much?* she thought in irritation. *That woman is the queen of leaping to conclusions.*

Sunlight filtered through the redwood branches, casting a gold slice of light over her bare arms and legs. She felt her shoulders relax, her muscles giving in to the warmth.

*I miss the trail*, she realized. The pine-scented air, the quiet rhythm of moving toward a goal. Out there, she knew where she was headed. Now? Other than putting distance between herself and Janis Jets, she wasn't sure.

The constabulary could be seen easily across the street. *I guess Jets wasn't exactly letting me out of her sight*, Avery realized. Next to the constabulary, there was the library. Avery sniffed. She'd spent hours wrapping gifts in front of Meadow's window that one Christmas. Logan on one side and Brad on the other. Maguire trading paw shakes for dog bone treats.

*Good ol' Meadow*, Avery thought. Last time she'd been here, the librarian had found her and Elf One a job and a place to stay on Christmas Eve. And those cinnamon rolls... Her mouth watered at the thought. Maybe she could forgive Meadow's nosiness after all.

"Hey, found you." Theo slid onto the bench beside her, close enough that their shoulders brushed. He held out a paper sack stamped with the Thyme Out logo.

"Can't believe I'm saying this," Avery said, smiling, "but I've had plenty of Sierra Snowcaps today. Kind of craving a good old chocolate chip. Got any of those?"

He dug into the sack and pulled out an oversized cookie. "Here you go." He handed it to her with a grin.

"So... I thought you were like me, an unhoused hiker," she said. "Do you live here?"

"Yeah. For about a year." He rubbed his thumb along the paper bag. "Got a cool place. A tree house with an outdoor shower. Big enough for me and maybe one other person." Her looked at her with a lift to one eyebrow. "Not too fussy, but air conditioned."

A little stab of envy caught her off guard. "That sounds awesome. I wish I could see it." The words were out before she could reel them back.

His head tilted just a fraction too slowly. "Really?" He leaned in, his smile warm, but his eyes... She knew there was interest and then too much interest. He was definitely doing his best to flirt, which made her fidget uncomfortably.

"That can be arranged," he continued. "Wanna stay with me until Monday? I'm back on the trail then. We could make that work."

Something about the way he said it felt rehearsed. Maybe an offer he extended to others for a quick hookup.

She gave the smallest shake of her head, forcing a neutral tone. "Maybe." She kept her gaze on the grass, letting him think what he wanted. She wasn't here to share his bed or his shower. Only to find out if he was part of the Syndicate and, if she was lucky, beat Janis Jets to an important clue that would clear her name.

It would look good for neither—Janis nor Olivia— if Avery were to slip away unaccounted for. Besides, if Jets relished chewing out Brad, what more would she do to Olivia if she let a person of interest escape?

Avery bent to pick a leaf off her shoe. When she sat back up, she inched away from Theo, providing more space between them on the bench. "By the way, weren't you the one telling me about some kind of group called the Switchback Syndicate? Had to do with books and those little libraries."

She noticed his body stiffen. His glance narrowed. "I'm pretty sure I never brought that up. Must have been someone else." With one hand, he crumpled the paper bag along with his lie into his fist. To her relief, he didn't make another offer to hang out. Instead he stood as if impatient to go.

"I heard someone died in an explosion yesterday," he said.

Avery felt the blood rush to her cheeks. "My landlady, as it turns out. Well, temporary landlady. Her name was Stella."

He nodded, his gaze moving past her, a thoughtful expression on his face.

"I didn't hear the explosion. Just found Stella in the dirt. She must have been checking her little free library. It was in shambles, books everywhere. She might have hit her head and died minutes before I showed up." Avery's voice trembled in the retelling.

"That's terrible." Theo looked away as if not sure what to say.

Annoyance pricked Avery. Was that all he could come up with? The woman was dead.

"Maybe I heard about the Syndicate from her, in one of her emails." Avery watched his expression carefully. "I remember now. She said a guy named Theo was in the group. That's where I made the connection."

Now he had no choice. Own up and admit it or double down and lie again. Avery held her breath.

"Yeah, I'm part of it," he sighed. "It was supposed to be a secret, you know. Not everyone in Lily Rock would support our beliefs. But I knew Stella. Sort of."

"What were your beliefs?"

"Bringing back the old books. Mostly kid favorites. Switching back to a time when it was safe to pick up a totally unknown story in the library without being used and abused by far left notions." There was a hint of anger in his voice.

*Now there's a clue*, Avery realized. Theo's distaste for what he labeled far left. Something she could share with Janis and Olivia. Except for one more thing.

"Were you in the hot tub last night with those other people? I thought I saw you."

"What the... Are you stalking me?!" His tight-lipped expression made her flinch. "Like I said, come on over to my place. I'll show you where I'm staying; no use in you following me everywhere." He waited, a look of expectation in his eyes. When she didn't answer right away, he reached to touch a chain at his neck, fingering it anxiously.

Avery felt her stomach twist. Theo's unintentional confirmation came at a certain expense. He didn't seem nearly as upset about her being a potential stalker as his accusation let on. *I better get going...*

"I'd like to meet up. Just not now. I've got things to do." She quickly rose and walked away without glancing back. With the constabulary straight ahead, he might get the hint. Maybe she'd report him.

His eyes bored into her back, sending a shiver down her spine.

She changed course and walked toward the library instead. Meadow McCloud stood in her window looking out. The librarian smiled and gestured, welcoming her inside.

# CHAPTER TEN

The air inside the library felt cool and smelled faintly lemony from furniture polish. Meadow stood behind the counter, talking to a small woman wearing a loose linen jacket. The woman spoke in a quiet, insistent voice. Her fingers curled over the edge of the counter as if she needed it for balance. Her bouffant hairstyle looked familiar.

Avery lingered by the display of new arrivals to give them a chance to finish their conversation. She pretended to take interest in a novel with a couple swooning on the cover. Meadow and the stranger kept murmuring. There was something about that hairstyle that niggled Avery. But before she could place her, the door swished open.

Naomi juggled an iced coffee and pushed a stroller. On the move, she exuded the energy of a caffeinated young mother. Avery felt the earlier twinge of envy. Put together to be noticed, Naomi's ponytail bounced with a sense of purpose as she made her way to the Children's Book Nook.

Other mothers and children held books, chatting with each other. Naomi greeted them one by one, bestowing her smile on each. She had that sense of self-satisfaction that Avery admired. One she'd never possessed.

She glanced down at her worn shorts and stained tee. Clean from Olivia's washer and dryer, but still shabby. She sighed, thoughts returning to the young mother. Naomi was a real protector of her small kingdom. Good mothers had to be on guard. One never knew these days.

Naomi stopped her stroller to look around. Her gaze landed on Avery, and she dipped her chin in a greeting. Then she spun in a hurry, pushing the stroller around the Children's Book Nook and examining the shelves.

*Did she recognize me from Thyme Out?* Avery wondered.

Returning her attention to the front desk, she saw Meadow smile over the other woman's head. Her gaze wide, begging to be rescued.

"And I told Stella she was wrong," the woman said, her voice sharp with judgment. "It wasn't trash. It was a statement. But she wouldn't listen."

Meadow looked away and then reached across the counter to pull Avery closer. "Cordelia, this is an old student from the Music Academy, Avery Denning. She's—"

"Yes, yes, one of those PCTers." Cordelia's gaze settled on Avery, unblinking. "I heard one of you was supposed to stay with Stella." She tilted her head, as if carefully considering her next words. "She and I were close," Cordelia continued. "Unfortunately her taste in books was entirely inappropriate. Even Meadow would disapprove." She cast a glance in the librarian's direction.

Avery lowered her eyes. She didn't want to be dragged into this conversation. She had no idea what were Stella's favorites, or Cordelia's for that matter. But to be so judgy about a few books...

There was a battered tote bag at Cordelia's feet. A coil of red ribbon peeked out beside the corner of a paperback. Cordelia caught her looking. "I checked those out," she explained.

Meadow frowned. "I don't want to hold you up any longer, dear. Nice to see you." She motioned for Avery to come around the counter. "Avery and I have a lot to catch up on. We can talk later."

Cordelia took her tote. She gave a quick wave, heading to the nearby exit. Avery watched as she walked across the street toward the park before turning back to Meadow. Moments later the librarian's arms circled her body in a warm embrace.

"I heard from Olivia that you're staying in town," Meadow said. "She was a bit lonely with Michael gone. My goodness, you've gotten taller." She stood back to take in Avery's appearance.

A look of concern came over her face. "But you're also tired. Too much hiking. Well it's a good thing you've stayed an extra few days. This is the perfect time to rest and get back on your feet. So awful finding Stella that way.

"I'll get you a few books to read. Good for the warm evenings and to calm your mind." Meadow was in her element. She was known for picking out just the right book.

"You can sit outside on Olivia and Michael's patio. Sip tea. Take naps. I'm sure the mayor would love to stay with you as you recuperate. One minute, dear. I have just the thing."

Meadow slid an old copy of *The Hidden Staircase* across the desk. "Just came back. I bet you read these as a youngster. Nancy Drew is everyone's favorite. And how about this? Judy Bolton. Less popular, but I love that girl. Two Midwestern amateur sleuths."

Avery wondered if Meadow remembered how old she was, past the age of children's fiction. *But maybe librarians don't care much about that. A good book is a good book.*

Once Meadow was done, she had three more titles stacked on the counter, all mysteries. Mostly genre fiction that she called cozies.

"And now for something more contemporary," Meadow said.

Before Avery could object, Meadow pulled out a library tote bag with Mayor Maguire's smiling face on the front. She slipped the books inside and then turned to the rolling cart. "Oh, this one is perfect," she said.

By the time Avery said goodbye, she'd acquired a new tote and enough books to anchor a small boat. She walked into the constabulary, feeling slightly giddy at Meadow's attention. But she stopped short. Brad May sat behind the desk, his head bent over the computer.

A quick smile of recognition accompanied a glint in his eye. He'd apparently survived Janis's reprimand. In the old days, he would have hung his head and been embarrassed at the slightest criticism. It might have taken days for him to recover. That was back when Brad's idea of "responsible" meant showing up an hour late to exchange weed for cash.

Now he looked like the kind of guy who might actually pass a background check. Who would listen with clear eyes, not taking anything Jets had to offer as personal.

Their gaze locked. She felt her face flush.

"Looks like you've been to see Meadow," he said dryly, nodding to the tote. "The boss is expecting you. I'll buzz you in." He tapped in a code, and the door slid back with a soft click.

"How are you?" Avery asked.

"Great. Really great." His tone was even, but his fingers

hovered over the keyboard. "Gotta get back to work," he explained, chin dropping. "I messaged the boss you're on your way."

She stepped into the constabulary hallway, the door closing behind her. Maybe Brad was taken, but that didn't stop her from looking. Her interest surprised her. She thought she'd gotten over him years ago.

"Come on in," Jets's voice called down the hallway.

Avery slid into the chair beside Olivia. Janis didn't bother with small talk. "So, what've you got? That Theo guy part of the Syndicate?"

"He was one of them. But I've got something better than that." Avery leaned back, basking in the attention. "I overheard another hot tub alum. The lady with the bubble helmet hair." She paused to watch Janis's expression. Nothing showed on her face.

"Name's Cordelia. Friends with Meadow McCloud. She didn't like Stella much, though she admitted to being part of the Syndicate."

Janis's eyebrows went up. "Go on."

Avery laid out the conversation, how Cordelia sounded annoyed with the victim.

When she finished, Janis said, "So now we've identified all four of the bobbing heads, or as you called them, the hot tub alum." She paused to give Avery a wink.

"We have their admission they'd formed something called the Switchback Syndicate. Would Stella have fit, bathing in her birthday suit, had she been alive?"

"Physically, it would have be quite chummy," Olivia said. "Crowded though."

Jets persisted. "Maybe they already knew she was dead. More like a job well done kinda thing, the meetup. One of those *Murder on the Orient Express* deals, where every suspect had a small part."

As Janis and Olivia discussed that possibility, Avery realized she was no longer needed. *What happened to my pat on the back?* she wondered. The "you're on the team, Avery," speech Lily Rock was known for.

She looked away, pretending to be impatient while Janis and Olivia continued to talk.

# CHAPTER ELEVEN

Avery opened her eyes the next morning. She'd slept in late and had to admit she felt less crabby. That time on her own, chatting with Theo had revived her spirits. Even Meadow's solicitous book selections felt welcome. Who knows, she might even read a couple in the evening. Meadow had chosen well. Mysteries were a favorite.

Avery followed the smell of brewed coffee to the outdoor patio.

"How did you sleep last night?" Olivia put a mug of coffee on the table and slid it closer.

"I slept much better." She reached for her mug. "Your guest room is surprisingly comfortable. I didn't think it would be, so modern and everything. Nice." She took a sip. Olivia swallowed hard, making Avery freeze. Sometimes she talked like her parents, condescendingly so, and this was one of them. "Sorry," she mumbled under her breath.

"The whole house has been unexpected," Olivia admitted. "It took me a while to get used to this latest Bellemare creation. But now I'm all-in. I think there's a sense of calm in the contrasts. You know, the glass and the wood and the steel. The light paint and the darker floors. But what do I know, I'm not an interior decorator." She laughed as if she'd made the same joke on any number of occasions.

"Me neither," Avery agreed. "So are you as tired of dragging me along as I am of being dragged?" *Might as well put it out there*, Avery thought. Olivia would know anyway.

"What do you mean?" Olivia looked amused but hardly surprised.

"I know I'm an assignment. That Janis is convinced I have something to do with Stella's death. Makes it awkward, doesn't it? You being her consultant and all."

Olivia nodded thoughtfully. "It's Officer Jets's job to be suspicious. Comes naturally to her. Sometimes to a fault. I think that's why she finally hired me.

"She teases about my special gift, but we balance each other out. At least I tell myself that every time she makes another snarky remark that hurts my feelings."

Avery felt a pang of surprise. Olivia never looked as if her feelings were hurt, no matter how barbed Janis's remarks.

*I'm sensitive to criticism*, Avery thought. She sat with Olivia's admission and her own experience for a moment, wondering if Olivia were mirroring for her so that she'd see something in herself she didn't want to admit. She'd heard of people who did the same, how empaths had that skill. *I'm gonna try it myself*, Avery decided.

"How are your feelings now?" She used a playful tone, hoping to amuse Olivia.

"Perfect," Olivia said, looking toward the creek. "It doesn't get much better. Good company. The sound of the crows above and the stream below. The early morning blessing of Lily Rock." She turned to Avery. "And you. I like you a lot. I'm enjoying your energy with this investigation."

Avery flushed. She couldn't remember when anyone had expressed their appreciation to her face with such sincerity. To her credit, Olivia didn't seem to expect a response. She kept her gaze on the mountain range in the distance, reminding her of a forty-something Zen master.

Feeling at a loss for words, Avery picked up her cell phone to look for messages. One came from Theo. She immediately regretted giving him her number that night on the trail.

Let's meet up for a coffee.

Though she didn't welcome his company, she wanted to claim her freedom from Olivia. She could make an excuse, go on foot.

She wiggled her toes. *They're healing,* she thought. *I could hike into town.* Her early morning optimism returned. Theo was a person of interest. If she could get more out of him, she could report back to Jets.

Not only that but the story behind Stella's death mattered more than she'd initially wanted to admit. Surprisingly so. If she could just get Theo to push aside any romantic ideas... *I can change his mind. Mirror like Olivia. Then he'll be more inclined to spill his guts.*

"A text from a boyfriend?" Olivia asked. "I heard the ping."

Avery placed the phone in her lap to figure out her next move. "Somebody from LA," she said offhandedly. "Wanted to know when I'd be coming back to town." The lie felt stale on her tongue. She swallowed hard.

*I can sneak away or I can just tell her where I'm going.*

Olivia no longer looked in her direction. It was as if she didn't want to know.

*Sneak it is.* Avery answered Theo's text.

What time?

9 or so

Make it 10.

Thyme Out

She sent a thumbs-up emoji.

"I have to take my backpack to the repair place," she explained. "You ready to come with?" *Fake it, Avery. Try hard to make your voice sound like you really want her to come.*

"Sure. How are you doing with those sneakers?" Olivia pointed to her feet.

"I'm ready to put my boots back on. The toes are healing," she said.

"Let me take a shower and get dressed. Then I can drive you into town." Olivia stood. "Done with your coffee?"

"Thank you." Avery looked away as she took her mug.

When she heard Olivia shut off the kitchen faucet, she waited. Once Olivia headed to her room, Avery took off her clunky shoes and tiptoed her way back inside. *Move it, Avery. You'll be gone by the time she gets back.*

Hair in a messy bun, she tugged her sweater over her sweatpants. The worn hiking boots with socks felt confining. Her toes could barely wiggle.

The backpack, buried in the closet, took longer. She hauled it out by its one surviving strap, slung it over her shoulder, and headed toward the hallway. *Still no sign of Olivia.*

Up the stairs, across the wide expanse of floor, and out

the door, she crossed the bridge at a jog. Once she stepped onto the road, she took a deeper breath.

Determined to outdistance Olivia, her pace quickened. At the first opportunity, she cut into the woods, where Olivia would be less likely to spot her, should she drive past.

A few feet into the woods, the dried brush and mesquite trees made for good cover. Sighting a boulder next to a pine stump, she slid the backpack off her shoulder and stuffed it under a log, obscured from view. Avery kicked dirt over the top.

A car's motor rumbled past. Olivia's old Ford came into view. Avery ducked into the shadows and held her breath.

As soon as the Ford's tailpipe disappeared around the corner, she exhaled and made her way on the inner path toward town.

Twenty minutes later, the murmur of patrons rumbled inside Thyme Out. One server went from table to table filling orders. The remaining customers lined up at the counter to place their order, impatient but willing to wait.

Hikers swapped stories. Packs had been shoved under tables. Avery skirted the line of customers at the counter but she couldn't spot Theo. *Maybe he's on the patio.*

She found him outside, sitting at one of the mismatched chairs near the rose arbor. He lifted a hand to wave her over. From a distance, she detected a wariness. *Maybe he's calculating how to lure me to his tree house.* She pushed that thought to the back of her mind.

When she sat down, Theo looked away. *What's going on?* she thought. *He texted me. Put out some charm, bro. I could turn around, grab a coffee at the counter, and head back to Olivia's if I wanted.* Avery felt her jaw tighten. She hated being the victim of someone's mixed messages.

"Did you order anything to eat?" He eyed her empty hands.

"You invited me, remember? I figured you were paying." Avery let a smirk play at her lips. She wanted to keep it friendly.

He sighed, already pulling out his phone. "Fine. I'll order on my app. Coffee and a chocolate chip muffin?"

"Perfect." Avery smiled. He'd remembered she liked chocolate chip. If she weren't so uncomfortable with his wavering advances, she might not have minded going back to his place. He was kind of attractive, in that lost boy kind of way.

Once he tapped Send, he leaned forward, eyes fixed on hers. "Word is you're crashing at the Bellemare place. Pretty fancy, I've heard. All glass, steel, and wood."

She resisted the urge to defend the house. "My original plan didn't quite work out." She sent him a what-are-you-stupid glare.

He blushed. "Right. Stella's room. You were supposed to stay there."

A server appeared with a tray, sliding two muffins onto the table. "Coffee's on the way," she said, before moving away.

Avery felt her shoulders loosen. Despite her misgivings about the staged vibe, the coffee and food were superior. *My turn to ask him a few questions.* "So have you actually seen the crime scene? Or just caught the gossip?"

Theo glanced over his shoulder. He leaned in. "I went by when I first heard about the death. Didn't get too close."

"I see," she said, feeling a surge of excitement. "I'm kinda curious about the house, are you?"

"I am. We could check it out together." Theo's cheeks flushed.

"Not the worst idea," Avery said slowly. "I wouldn't mind the distraction. I'm trapped in Lily Rock until the cop gets my written statement. I even had trouble slipping out of Olivia's sight this morning. A 24-7 bodyguard." She looked up to see his expression.

"Really?" he said, biting his lower lip. Perspiration formed on his upper lip. *He's really excited about visiting Stella's place*, she realized. *Maybe too excited...*

"So if we go together to check out the scene, we have to keep under the cop's radar. Or else." She mimed a cutting her throat. "Goodbye, freedom. She might even arrest us both."

Theo's eyes lit up. Apparently he didn't mind courting a little danger. "Hurry up and eat," he said. "Then we'll slip out the back."

# CHAPTER TWELVE

Avery and Theo neared Stella's house. *No patrol car*, Avery thought. Just the sagging yellow tape twisted over what was left of the little free library. She glanced toward the back of the lot, where another strip of tape had been tied to the posts that supported the stairs to the front deck.

"Want me to look around the house?" Theo asked, sounding eager.

"Sure. Be my guest. I'm curious about the little library." She focused her attention on the wreckage, keeping her voice casual.

As he drifted toward the porch, Avery inspected the boxy remains. Charred on the edges, the glass front hung open. It looked much the same as the first day, only there was no basket and no books strewn on the ground...and no body.

Her eyes stopped on a paper wedged between two slats on the side panel. She plucked it out to have a closer look. The edges were scorched, brittle in her fingers. Could be a bookmark. Could be an old flyer. She held in gingerly in her hand.

The front read: “How to Be Saved and Know It.” A flyer, she decided. The cramped print began: “If you should die today, where would you spend eternity?” Her stomach turned. *Not exactly a comforting thought. Am I holding a mini sermon?*

She flipped it over gently. The boldface type on the back, the message, gave her a shiver. A scripture reference to Ephesians followed by a warning that confession of sins and surrender to Jesus as savior was the only way to guarantee eternal life.

Avery's first impulse was to crush it like a venomous spider. Questions flooded her mind. Who would slip this into a little free library? Surely not Stella.

"Hey," Theo called out from the porch. He held up a small object pinched between his fingers. "Key. Cops must have missed it. I bet it opens the front door."

Avery put the paper back in the library and then brushed the soot off her hands and approached the porch. Stella had sent her a key in the mail. So Theo's had to be another spare.

He stood on the second porch step, waiting for her to catch up.

"Where did you find that exactly?" she asked.

"I have deduction skills," he snapped.

"Seriously, you just knew?"

"I can show you." He leaned over to pick up a pot of geraniums. Using his boot, he tapped the board underneath. "Right here. Obvious, right? The cops must be small-town idiots to have missed that.

"Can I see?" she asked.

He handed it over. "Lucky guess. People hide keys in dumb places."

Her brows rose. "Guess you're psychic now."

Theo smirked. "Just observant."

She handed back the key.

The cops had been all over his place and they'd missed it. Either Theo had the best instincts on the Pacific Crest Trail...or Stella Rawlins knew him well enough to tell him where to find it.

And if that was true, maybe Theo knew more about Stella than he was letting on.

He slid the key into the lock, and the door opened easily. He stepped inside. "We don't want to be seen," he reminded in a mock whisper, as if making fun of their earlier conversation.

Once she stepped over the threshold and closed the door, Theo announced, "I'm going to use the toilet."

Avery glanced toward the floor where a wicker basket under the entry table had been stacked neatly with white towels and one washcloth. On top, a card with her name printed in bold made Avery's throat catch.

Blinking warded off tears. It seemed Stella was ready for her weekend boarder. A red, white, and blue ribbon was tied around the towel bundle, making it look festive. *She wanted me to feel welcome.*

The sound of the toilet followed by water made her swallow hard to get her feelings in check. Theo stepped back into the room. He took one look around, inhaling deeply. "She was expecting you," he said. "Everything's tidy and the place has been aired out."

"I know. I might have mentioned we connected on email a couple of months ago," she explained. She picked up the note with her name.

Sunflowers blazed on the front of a small card. Stella had written in bright blue ink: "Just a reminder that if you forget your key while you're staying here, I left an extra under the geranium. I'm so happy to finally see you face to face and give you a hug."

The note was signed *xoxo*.

Her breath caught. "These were for me," she confirmed.

Theo turned toward the kitchen as if no longer interested. She watched as he opened one cupboard, then another, his movements quiet and deliberate. "She was a nice lady," he said over his shoulder.

Avery didn't answer. Her sadness was too big. The email correspondence with Stella had been a constant, every morning, without fail. She'd get a cup of coffee and read, anticipating their chat.

Somewhere along the way, she'd grown to care about the woman she'd never met. And then there was that nagging feeling that she wanted to return to Lily Rock once again. As Theo continued to inspect the kitchen, Avery caught sight of another basket at the foot of the stairs. This one looked familiar and worse for wear. The handle was frayed, the basket stacked with books.

This time Avery had no interest. Touching the handpicked books that Stella had selected felt too personal, or maybe she wasn't ready for the emotional impact. Either way, she moved to the hallway.

Pushing open the last door, she paused, the scent of pine and freshly laundered sheets spilling into the air. Stella's spare room. The one she'd planned on renting to Avery.

Not a modern guest room like Olivia's but more cozy, with minimalist charm. She'd assessed Stella correctly, that she was that kind of woman—organized, someone who thought less was more. The room reflected her personality.

There was no quilt, no mismatched pillows. Just a double bed with a firm mattress, a white comforter pulled smooth, a single pillow. On the nightstand sat one fresh sunflower in a plain vase next to a singing bowl made of copper, that when struck with a mallet produced a resonant tone. An unscented beeswax votive candle sat nearby.

The room felt intentional, prepared. Very calm.

Avery pulled open the top dresser drawer. Empty. Every drawer in the dresser was the same: lined with clean white paper, not a speck of dust. A pine luggage rack stood under the window. Gauze curtains, pushed to each side, added to the simple charm. As did the view into the backyard and the woods beyond.

*Enchanting*, Avery thought. She could have stayed here. And maybe she and Stella would have been friends. Her chest tightened.

Turning away from the window, she found Theo lingering in the doorway. He leaned one shoulder against the frame, his eyes unreadable in the dim light.

For a moment neither of them spoke.

Then he smiled just a little. "Get what you came for?" he asked.

She wanted to say she hadn't come for anything, but there was something about his question that made her pull in. *You don't have to explain, Avery. Be like Olivia. Enigmatic.*

# CHAPTER THIRTEEN

Theo locked the front door while she waited on the porch. He turned and placed the key back under the geranium pot.

She followed him to his car, feeling slightly sad but also relieved. It wasn't easy looking at the home of the recently deceased. She knew Stella was dead, but it was as if the house hadn't gotten the message.

As he drove back to town, she told him about the flyer, then asked, "Ever see anything like that before?"

His jaw tightened. "Can't say that I have."

"Are you sure? You seem agitated."

"Religious stuff makes me cringe." This time she knew he was lying. Something about the way he gripped the steering wheel and the tone of his voice. He pulled alongside the road.

"Time for you to check in with your jailer," he said.

*Apparently I'm not getting that invite back to the tree house*, she thought. *I wonder what changed his mind...*

Within minutes he pulled into a parking place. Once he stopped the engine, she hopped onto the pavement without a goodbye. Without a backward glance toward town, she made her way toward Olivia's.

This time taking the main road. She retrieved her backpack on the way, slinging it over her shoulder.

Olivia's car came into view, parked out front. Avery trudged over the bridge, sweat prickling along her neck.

Olivia sat on the front patio, bare feet propped on a hand-carved tree stump. A paperback book was open in her lap. She looked up and smiled. "Have a nice getaway?" Her tone was warm, almost amused. "Looks like you still have your backpack."

"I'm sorry," Avery said, dropping into the chair across from her. "I was feeling stir-crazy being watched all the time. I hope you don't mind. Did my escape get you in trouble with Janis?"

"What Janis doesn't know won't hurt her." Olivia's sly smile filled her with relief.

"But my understanding comes with a price," Olivia warned. "You have to tell me everything. That way, if she asks, I can lie with conviction." She closed the book and leaned forward. "So, what have you been up to?"

Avery's smile became a full-on grin. "I met up with Theo. We, uh, got into Stella's house. He knew where she kept a spare key."

Olivia's eyes flickered, the smile tightening for just a second before she covered it with mock horror. "You violated a crime scene! Well that's it. Certain jail time. No more mayoral meet-and-greets. And forget fries with your burger. If she's really mad, you'll be banned from Thyme Out. No cookies for you!"

Avery laughed. "So goodbye Sierra Snowcaps, then."

"Only if I tell."

"I thought you took Officer Jets more seriously than that."

"I used to," Olivia said, shrugging. "But then she hired me, actually pays me money. And now I've lost my kid-gloves approach to the world's most caustic small-town cop. If you don't push her back, she'll run all over you."

"She—Stella, I mean—left me a card and a basket full of fluffy towels," Avery said quietly. "I saw my room too. All made up and ready. I just wish I'd gotten to meet her." She felt her eyes prickle.

Olivia stood. "Why don't we head to the kitchen and fix some lunch. You can tell me more about how that felt, to be in Stella's home. But now we need sustenance. Did you find anything else that might be a clue?"

"I found something really odd in Stella's little library."

Avery trailed behind Olivia into the sleek and modern kitchen. Everything gleamed, every line was sharp. “Kind of the opposite of Stella's,” she muttered. She hadn’t meant to say that out loud.

"I know," Olivia said softy. "Not like a cottage. Takes getting used to. But now I love it here. It's so Michael. Come on. I'll make us sandwiches and we can talk about what you found while we eat."

Avery leaned over the sink to wash her hands. "I'll help," she said, surprising herself. Up until now, her idea of help had been staying out of the way.

After a brief scramble to assemble the ingredients, they worked together to make two ham sandwiches worthy of deli stardom. Slices of ham, cheddar cheese, lettuce, and tomato nestled between homemade bread.

"Meadow bakes three times a week," Olivia answered her unspoken question. "The bread is hearty and delicious. Matches her personality."

"It didn't feel like it would come from Thyme Out," Avery replied. "Cookie's more of a dessert chef."

Olivia smiled. "You are very intuitive, you know."

"Why would you say that?" Avery felt surprise. Being called a spoiled brat all of her life, no one ever mentioned anything about intuition.

"I was taught by the best how to interpret people. I'd always known I was different, but it took another person to point it out to me. Right here in Lily Rock." Olivia handed her a plate. "Let's sit at the counter. You can tell me about what you saw in Stella's little library, and we can consider our next step."

"Don't we need to tell Officer Jets first.?" Avery asked.

Olivia shook her head slowly, a mischievous twinkle in her eye. "Better to apologize later."

# CHAPTER FOURTEEN

During lunch, Olivia and Avery discussed who would rise to the top of their person of interest list. Once they numbered the suspects, they headed to the Ford, and Olivia held to her conviction that they needed to take the initiative while Janis was busy.

"It's best not to go alone," Olivia said, turning the key in the ignition. "I'm relieved that you agree."

Rumbling up a steep incline in the old Ford, Olivia stopped beneath the dappled shade of a red oak. The engine hiccupped and then shut down.

*Why are we stopping here?*

"Okay," Olivia said, resting both hands on the wheel. "What's our excuse again, for dropping in on Cordelia? Don't forget, without Janis, we don't have the official cop to show her badge."

"Haven't you done this before?" Avery asked. "Interviewed someone by yourself?"

Olivia shot her a quick glance. "Never with you. That's its own adventure."

"Well, I was going to ask her straight up if she put the leaflet in the little library," Avery said.

Olivia folded her hands in her lap, thinking. "Now that I have a minute... Maybe that would be too direct. She'd slam the door on us. I bet she'd call the constabulary before we drove away." She tapped her fingers on the steering wheel. "I know! Cordelia Pratt is a romance author. I saw one of her books in the library."

"Oh." Avery wrinkled her nose. "I've read some romance, but not by Pratt."

Olivia gave her a quizzical glance. "I read a few out of politeness," she explained. "Meadow had a special display a year ago, so I tried them. Not my deal. The covers were kinda dated. I did hear they were popular in the eighties. Flew off the shelf at the same time as the royal wedding, when Charles married Diana. But they're not in demand now."

"Why don't we say we're fans?" Avery's eyes brightened. "Got her address and that we both want an autograph."

Olivia twisted the key in the ignition. After a few gasps, the engine turned over. "I'm in," she said, steering past the intersection.

Cordelia Pratt answered her door wearing a bright red tunic over black workout leggings. Her gray highlighted hair was pulled back from her face by a matching red bandanna. She was still catching her breath.

"I'm not religious," she said, attempting to close the door.

"We're not either," Avery instantly replied, sticking her foot in the gap. "You're Cordelia Pratt, aren't you? I recognized you in the library the other day. Didn't get a chance to say I'm a huge fan!"

Cordelia's face lit up with a delighted smile. "Oh my goodness, I'm so happy to meet you." Her gaze shifted to

Olivia. "And you, of course. Wait, you're that musician. What's the name of your band... Sweet Four O'Clock? I saw you at the pub the last time you played."

Avery's head swiveled toward Olivia. *Musician. In a band. Well she certainly kept that to herself.*

"That's me," Olivia said. "No one forgets an autoharp player." She extended her hand. "I'm also a fan."

"We were wondering..." Avery began.

"Yes?" Cordelia said quickly, patting the perspiration from her brow with the hem of her shirt. The flicker of expectation in her eyes tugged at Avery's heart. *She's so desperate for attention, kinda sad.*

"Could we get your autograph?" Olivia finished.

"Of course!" Cordelia swung the door open wide.

Once inside, Avery looked up at the vaulted ceiling and the high windows. But as soon as she looked down, she sneezed. Dust and clutter made the room feel claustrophobic. "My allergies," she explained.

A dark green velvet loveseat sat to one side. Two end tables flanking it. The coffee table in front held stacks of hardcover books. The wall behind the sofa looked like an old movie theater, with several framed posters of book covers. Bare-chested men and women with plump bosoms.

Avery stepped closer to scrutinize. The woman on each cover might have been Cordelia in her youth. The man reminded her of a commercial for aftershave that she'd seen during a late-night sitcom.

The posters showed covers that exuded pure romance. Lush gowns, windswept hair, men with chiseled jaws. She sneezed again, glaring at the cause, a layer of dust on each poster frame. Avery used her fingertip to straighten the largest poster, titled *The Red Ribbon Room.*

"Please, sit," Cordelia called from another room. "I'll just be a moment!"

Olivia slid onto the loveseat, crossing her legs neatly. Avery perched on the edge of an armchair, her eyes still skimming two bookshelves. One middle shelf was stacked with leaflets advertising a library talk that was dated a year ago. Next to it was an old clipping with a photo of Cordelia. She was appearing at the Riverside County fair down the hill, who knew how long ago.

Olivia's expression was unreadable. Finally she said, "She's trying to remind herself of who she was."

The sound of drawers opening and closing caught Avery's attention. Then Cordelia's voice, talking to herself. "Now where did I put that pen?"

*Living alone I suspect... She probably talks to herself a lot*, Avery noted. Her gaze shifted to a half-empty mug of tea sitting beside a spiral notebook with an expensive-looking fountain pen laid across it. The page beneath was filled with looping cursive. Maybe lines for her next story. She was tempted to alert Cordelia to the pen, but was interrupted.

"Found it!" Cordelia swept back into the room carrying a leather-bound address book.

"I thought you were looking for a pen," Avery said lightly.

Cordelia blinked at her, then glanced down at the book in her hands. "Oh, silly me. I must have been thinking of something else." She gave a quick laugh, the kind meant to smooth over a slip. "Anyway, where were we?"

"You were going to sign something for us," Olivia prompted.

"Of course. Do you have a copy of *The Red Ribbon Room* with you? That's my most famous."

Avery shook her head. "I wasn't sure you'd answer the door, so..."

Cordelia set the address book on the coffee table and crossed to the bookshelf. Her fingers drifted along the spines. "Now, I know it's here somewhere..." She pulled down *The Silver Moon Affair*, then stared at the cover as though seeing it for the first time. "No, that's not it," she muttered.

Olivia and Avery exchanged a quick glance.

Finally, after more tries, she produced two copies of *The Red Ribbon Room*. She carried them back to the coffee table, flipping one open to the title page. Instead of signing, she began to read to herself, a slight smile on her lips.

Avery leaned forward. "Maybe you could sign right here on the title page?" she suggested gently.

Cordelia looked down, startled, then laughed. "Oh, yes. I don't know where my head is today." She scrawled her name, ending with a flourish. Tapping the book and smiling, she handed it to Avery. "There you go. A first edition. It will be valuable one day."

"Thank you," Avery said.

"Anything for my readers," Cordelia replied, her gaze drifting past them, as if her mind had taken her somewhere else.

# CHAPTER FIFTEEN

Olivia and Avery drove away in silence, two signed copies of *The Red Ribbon Room* resting on the console between them.

"She's a bit loopy, right? Or did I just imagine that?" Avery asked.

"You didn't," Olivia sighed. "Disturbing. For you too?"

Avery turned her gaze to the passing trees. "It's beautiful here. Sometimes, when I can't sleep, I think about Lily Rock. The academy days. Christmases. Like pressing play on an old movie."

She'd deliberately changed the topic to avoid the little voice in her head that chided, *How can you lie to a woman who's losing her mind?*

"Lily Rock gets under your skin." Olivia slowed as she approached the gravel turnout. "At least it did for me. I told everyone at the time, I never planned on coming back. But one thing led to another."

"She makes me sad," Avery blurted. "Cordelia, I mean. Losing her author fame and her memory piece by piece? I can't imagine."

"It happens," Olivia said softly. She reached over and squeezed Avery's shoulder. "Sadness is part of life. You let it in, stay with it, then let it move through you. That's why living in the present is so important. There's nothing we can do about what we've left behind."

Avery stared into the forest, the smell of rich earth drifting past the open window. "If you say so."

Her jaw tightened. *Why doesn't she say something more comforting, make it better.* Avery had trouble when other people were sad. It made her wonder if she'd be blamed. That seemed to happen often enough in her childhood.

When she turned away from the window, Olivia looked at her with compassionate eyes. "Okay then. Where are we in our investigation?"

Avery pulled out her phone. Now she wanted to avoid Olivia's signature warm gaze. *I'm not gonna spill my guts*, she reminded herself.

Avery tapped on her cell screen. "I listed our people of interest right here. Cordelia, Meadow's friend. At least I assume they're pals. A similar age. Both love books. But we didn't come away with anything important from her. The next on our list is Theo, the hiker. Then Marshall Reed, the guy who prefers his birthday suit to clothes. And Naomi Wells-Duran."

Olivia frowned. "Naomi, a new mother. That feels iffy."

"Yeah. The one with the kid," Avery agreed. "You must have seen her in town. She has a bag slung over one shoulder, toddler clamped on her hip like she's auditioning for a parenting commercial. Those kind of moms think everyone is looking."

Olivia gave her a sidelong glance. "You seem to have lots of opinions about mothers." She left the comment in the air, which Avery had no intention of picking up.

"You'd think that Naomi would have better things to do than sit in a hot tub with a bunch of retirees," Avery grumbled.

"I have an idea. Paws and Pines is hosting a meet-and-greet tomorrow. A fundraiser where kids pet goats and ponies, parents adopt cats and dogs. Mayor Maguire will be there."

"Perfect," Avery said. "I assume you're thinking what I'm thinking—that Miss Ideal Mom will show up with her ideal kid. Probably with a backpack full of organic snacks and a gallon of hand sanitizer, just to prove she's raising the next president."

Olivia chuckled. She lifted an eyebrow at the sound of her phone buzzing, then pressed speaker.

"Where are you?" Jets's outrage spilled into the front seat.

"Taking in the scenery with my houseguest." Olivia winked at Avery.

"That's dumb. She's been here before. Is she listening?"

"On speaker. We're about to plan dinner."

Avery's head swiveled. *Really? Dinner?* There had been no mention of food.

Jets's laughed crackled. "So, Avery, what's to eat? I'm coming over to see with my own eyes. Better make enough for three."

"Not tonight," Olivia hastily added. "Give us a chance to settle in first. Maybe tomorrow."

"Have it your way," Jets mumbled. *Click.* The line went dead.

Olivia explained, "I'll get dinner tonight. You can help tomorrow. This has been quite an ordeal, the past couple of days. Take advantage of my good nature and say yes."

The last thing Avery wanted to do was to serve Janis

Jets a meal. She'd be tempted to poison the cop, given half the chance.

The next morning Olivia sat at the kitchen counter. She put down her coffee mug with a smile. "Ready for Paws and Pines?"

"I was wondering..." Avery began, walking toward the coffeepot to serve herself. "Is Sparkles still there?"

"You mean Janis's Shetland?" Olivia sounded surprised. "Or as she would say, the unemployed eat-her-out-of-house-and-home adoptee?"

Avery chuckled. "The last time I was here, Sparkles and I kind of..." She searched for the right word. "Bonded. Any chance I can see her at Paws and Pines?"

"I keep forgetting you were here before. Yes, Sparkles is still at Paws and Pines. Has her own stall at the back of the barn. Once in a while she allows people to saddle her up, but so far she refuses to let any children ride her.

"Of course, adults are too big. Speaking of fond memories, my sister Sage still talks about walking Sparkles through the woods on Christmas Eve with Brad. How from a distance they were mistaken for Mary and Joseph."

"That's what I remember!" Avery said. She felt herself flush when Olivia mentioned Brad. "Did you say sister? Does that mean you and Sage are related?"

"Oh yes." Olivia grinned. "And I'm an auntie. Star is the baby of our family."

"How did all of that happen? There was no mention of Sage having a sister when I was here."

Olivia didn't look surprised. "I'll tell you sometime. When Michael gets home. He's due to arrive in a few days and loves to talk about the baby."

"He's a good guy," Avery added. "I remember that part at least."

"He's the real reason I stayed in Lily Rock." Olivia's eyes glittered. "A very persuasive man."

Ten minutes later they parked at Paws and Pines, already crowded with children and family members eager to pet the animals. The main corral held sheep and goats, ducking behind bundles of straw. Eager children waited to be let inside.

Across from the barn was a horse circle with three small horses. Children clutched saddle horns, a volunteer walking alongside. Avery looked toward the barn right as Janis Jets strode up.

"About time," she grumbled. "Did Backpack Betty have a little sleep-in this morning? Or did you two stay up late last night, jibber-jabbering about girl stuff? I was disappointed when you didn't have me over for dinner," she grumbled as an afterthought. When neither Avery nor Olivia spoke, her eyes narrowed.

"You're both late!" Jets insisted, loud enough to turn a couple of heads.

Olivia chuckled. "I'd say you're not the boss of me, but that, of course, is no longer true. Why don't I put it this way: on the one hand you get to tell me what time, but on the other hand? I don't always agree. Other priorities."

Avery barely repressed a laugh. "I want to see Sparkles," she said, hoping to keep Jets off-balance.

"Do not get me started on that sad excuse for a horse!" Jets mumbled. She turned to look around. "I'll take you for a cuddle with the world's most useless pony later. For now I've got a job to do. Isn't that what's her name?" Jets gave a quick nod to a woman standing near the pony corral.

"Naomi Wells-Duran," Olivia said.

"What's her wife's name?" Avery asked.

"Fran Wells-Duran," Jets replied crisply. "She's standing a bit to the side."

Fran carried a tote bag slung over her arm. Printed on the outside in bold letters it read: *Ask me about my little free library.* She was tall and thin, dressed in jeans and a black tee. Her hair was dark brown, clipped short.

Olivia caught Avery staring. "Fran is a nice quiet woman. Soft-spoken. Good with their baby. The child's name is Nancy."

"I wonder why she wasn't in the hot tub that night?" Jets mused. "According to her tote, she has one of those little libraries."

"Probably babysitting," Olivia said in a reasonable voice. "Giving Naomi a night off."

Jets scoffed. "I guess." She turned to Avery. "Hey, Backpack Betty. Why don't you make yourself useful. Mosey on over and talk to them. We'll watch from here."

Avery didn't need another invitation. She made her way toward the pony ring. "Hello. Mind if I look at your baby?" She bent down to glance at Nancy in the stroller. "I just love children."

*Big fat liar*, Avery scolded herself. *I actually can't stand children. But you gotta do what you gotta do.*

"I'm Fran," the woman said, moving between the stroller and Avery. "That's my wife. And this is Nancy. She's three months old, needs lots of naps." Fran's eyes were warm brown, her gaze direct. Avery felt an instant connection.

"I'll wait until she's awake." Avery backed away. "How long have you lived in Lily Rock?" The introduction banter felt awkward, but she pushed through, forcing an interested expression. Before she could explain there was an interruption.

Naomi interjected to extend a hand. "I'm Naomi, by the way. I saw you at the library." She took hold of the stroller bar. "I want to take a photo of Nancy's first pony ride."

Fran shrugged, sending Avery a look of embarrassment. "Now you know who's in charge in our family. We've lived here a couple of years. Got a cottage off the main road. Why don't you come along with us to the pony ride?"

"I'd love to see Nancy with a pony," Avery agreed. She glanced at the tote. "Do you have a little free library?" She directed the question at Fran as the three women walked.

Naomi answered. "Yes, we do. Would you like a bookmark with our address?" She reached into the bag. "You can stop by and visit anytime. It's one of our pet projects. We keep excellent copies and preferred books for children."

She handed over a strip of cardboard that read "Little Free Library." On the back it said, "Stop by for a selection of classic children's books."

There was something in Naomi's tone, the way she interrupted the conversation to speak for her wife, that annoyed Avery. *Kind of controlling*, she thought. *A pet peeve of mine.*

"I don't have kids," Avery said with her brightest possible voice. No use pretending she wanted any either, or that she envied the two women. Nancy represented a lot of work to Avery. She had no sentimental ideas to the contrary.

As they approached the pony corral, she glanced at the bookmark and then slipped it into her back pocket. "I just remembered. I promised to meet someone by the barn. Have fun with Nancy. I gotta go." She moved away before they could say goodbye.

# CHAPTER SIXTEEN

*There's something about Naomi that puts me off.* Avery felt the need to justify her feelings. She stepped quickly toward the barn when a man blocked her path. She recognized him instantly—Brad May.

"Excuse me." She moved past.

Her heart gave a startled flutter, and before she could talk herself out of it, she changed her mind and turned around. "Hey there. This feels familiar. Back at Paws and Pines."

His brow furrowed, then recognition dawned. "Right. I almost forgot. We used to meet here. Sit on that rail and—"

"Smoke weed," she finished, grinning.

"Until Sage caught us," he chuckled.

"So, no longer the Lily Rock dealer?" she teased.

"Nah. Too busy. Besides, I get tested now that I'm in the deputy program. If I want a shot at the academy, maybe even the force someday, I've gotta stay clean and sober."

She studied his face, lingering on his mouth. "You're looking..." She exhaled quickly. "Great."

His eyes met hers. Steady, familiar, and she thought she saw the ghost of a flicker before he looked away.

"You've got a girlfriend now?" she asked, hoping he'd tell her more.

"I do," he said without hesitation. "In the desert. Her name's Mia. We met when I was on a case. At first I thought she was a suspect, but she was just helping out an old guy." His smile warmed, genuine. "She's...important to me."

"When you say you were on a case, do you mean you and Janis?"

"Nope. Redondo and Rose," he said with quiet pride. "They're my partners. We run a PI firm called Neighbors in Crime. Pretty under the radar. Very elite clientele." He tried to hold back his self-satisfaction, but his voice gave him away.

Avery knew his tell. A blush crept up his cheeks and he looked away. To her surprise she didn't mind. Brad's seriousness, the way he'd grown into himself, made him more attractive than she expected. Plus he wouldn't bother to exaggerate if he didn't want to impress her.

"Maybe we could get a beer sometime. Later this evening?" Avery suggested.

He shook his head, though his eyes lingered on her face. "I can't, I use my nights to study. Plus you're a person of interest." His voice softened, a flicker of regret slipping through. "Maybe once you're cleared, for old times' sake."

Old times' sake. Avery didn't like the sound of old times. Reminded her of Cordelia. How sad she was. *I don't want to be like her!*

Brad watched her expression closely, then added with a firm tone, "Take care, Avery."

She wasn't used to being turned down. As he walked away, she felt defeated. As if she'd missed an opportunity.

Because he'd changed and grown, and somehow she felt just the same.

Yet that flicker in his eyes left her wondering. *I should have stayed in touch with him*, she thought. *Only I didn't know he'd turn out so...I don't know, interesting.*

A sense of despondency settled over her. Something else to make her feel bad. But then a weight slammed into her knees, shoving her off-balance. Avery yelped. She looked down and burst into laughter.

A curly-haired labradoodle leaned hard against her legs, tail wagging.

"Mayor Maguire to the rescue!" She bent to give him a pat.

The dog licked her chin, sat on his haunches, and barked one loud, "Bork."

*The same old trick*, she thought. *He's asking for a dog treat.*

"Still working the crowd, huh?" She ruffled his fur, grinning despite herself. "At least you haven't changed."

Maguire spun in a circle, then bounded a few steps toward the barn. He paused, looking back over his shoulder.

"I'm supposed to follow you."

It seemed that Lily Rock's four-legged politician had a plan. And today that included her.

Avery already felt better. *Who cares about Brad May? Or Naomi and her baby. I want to see Sparkles.* She trusted animals more than she did people.

Once inside the barn, she found Janis and Olivia leaning over the half door to a double-sized stall. The smell of fresh hay brought back good memories for Avery. She approached the stall quietly, watching as Janis held out a carrot. "Come on, you oversized comfort animal. Take a bite. I dare ya!"

"Hello," Avery greeted them.

A low whinny came from the stall.

"See?" Jets said. "She won't even take food from me."

Olivia moved aside for Avery to have a look.

Sparkles the circus pony. Avery's heart fluttered. She let her eyes take in the former star of the Baubles the Clown show. As she looked past her flanks to her long tail and back to her eyes, the Shetland raised her head and gave a slight nod.

*She remembers me,* Avery realized. *Just like I remember her.*

The pony took two steps forward. She shifted her gaze to Jets and snorted. "Why don't you step back," Avery suggested.

"Whatever," Jets mumbled.

Avery felt the connection strongly. An invisible bond between them. It had started that Christmas. When she realized she was more similar to the Shetland than she was to any person. Sparkles didn't trust humans, and neither did she. Sparkles had a salty personality and didn't like children. Neither did she. Plus, once Baubles died, Sparkles had no interest in being anyone else's trick pony. That was why Avery respected her.

"Crabby little hay-burner. She eats but is otherwise useless," muttered Janis. "Seems to like you though."

Avery lifted the latch on the half door of the stall. She slowly approached Sparkles, not taking the pony's interest for granted.

"Hey, Sparks, remember me?" She used a quiet, low voice.

Sparkles flicked an ear, gave her a sidelong glance, then let out a low whinny.

Avery took the carrot from Janis, who watched with

fascination. She reached toward the pony and opened her palm for Sparkles. "Come on. Just a step closer. Then it's yours." Avery knew that first step would be crucial.

To her delight, the pony didn't hesitate. She snorted and came right over, dipped her nose to her hand and snapped up the carrot. The loud crunching of the vegetable made Avery's heart leap. "Sparkles is still a good judge of character, don't you agree, Officer Jets?" she called over her shoulder, keeping her gaze on the pony.

"Yeah, yeah. She's a regular saint when you're around. With me, she's the devil in a mane."

Olivia's laugh broke the tension. "Looks like Sparkles remembers her old friend."

Avery stroked the Shetland's soft nose, warmth spreading through her chest. *Not just an old friend*, she thought. *But a tried and true forever pal. You and me.*

Avery leaned closer to whisper in the pony's ear. "Hey there."

While the pony sniffed her hand for another carrot, Jets began to talk. "Did you get that interview with the moms?"

Avery nodded. "A little bit."

Jets pulled out her iPad and made a note. "You can visit Sparkles any time, Backpack Betty. On the house, no charge," she muttered. "When you're done there, you can tell Olivia what you talked about with the moms. She'll tell me. Have a nice day."

On the drive home, Avery sniffed her hand. Smelled like horse. She loved that smell. It had been hard to say goodbye to Sparkles, and it seemed to her like the pony had felt the same. She wondered when she'd see Sparkles again.

Now Avery's thoughts returned to Stella. She'd managed to push away the image of her body lying in the dirt with that blank-eyed stare. How the dark blood formed a puddle next to her head.

"So I was wondering," Avery began.

"What's that?" Olivia asked.

"Did Officer Jets tell you anything, any more details about how Stella died?"

"I'm not supposed to share details of an ongoing investigation," Olivia reminded her. Then she shrugged. "But since you've been unofficially drafted into the role of sleuth, I suppose I'll break another rule."

Avery chuckled. "You must drive her crazy. The way you nod along like you agree, then do exactly as you please."

"The British have a phrase for that," Olivia admitted. "I watch a lot of shows. *Miss Marple*, other period dramas. They'd call me a 'needs must' kind of woman."

"Which means?"

"If there's a strong enough need, then one must bend a rule or two," she said. "Anyway, Jets got a preliminary report from Forensics. Stella died from a heart attack. She fell and hit her head, which explains the blood. She was older, maybe unsteady on her feet."

Olivia paused. "But they also found bits of a firecracker underneath the little library. That explains the damage. Plus there were traces of chemical residue on Stella's blouse. The conclusion is that the firecracker went off close to her face."

Avery shuddered. She'd never even been fond of firework displays. In her childhood, she'd hide with the family dogs inside and turn up the TV to avoid them.

"So am I still a suspect?"

"Not according to me," Olivia assured her. "But Janis is playing it safe." She cast a quick glance in her direction. "So what are you up to? I can tell you're thinking about something."

Avery reached into her pocket. "I introduced myself to Fran and Naomi. Nancy was sleeping."

"And..." Olivia pulled her Ford to a halt in front of the house.

"Look at this." Avery held up the bookmark. "She has a little library with the theme of children's classics."

Olivia took it from her hand. "Is that a connection with the Syndicate?"

"I'm not sure," Avery said. "Turn it over."

Olivia sounded surprised. "The tote and this... Like she's concerned about her own brand. I didn't know little libraries did that. Naomi's pretty ambitious for a new mom. DIY projects take time.

"Do you think that makes Naomi a genuine suspect? A mom who has a little library filled with children's books?" Olivia handed the bookmark back, her tone skeptical.

"But would she be willing to kill to protect her kid?" Avery reasoned.

Olivia opened the car door. "Could be," she said, not sounding entirely convinced. Before she could close the door, Avery interjected one more thing.

"Why don't we leave the suspect list and take a tour of all the little libraries in Lily Rock. Maybe the books will give us clues. What do you think?"

Olivia looked away.

"And when I say us, I mean me. That way no one will suspect we're investigating," Avery added. "If anyone asks, I could say I'm staying over in Lily Rock and wanted to read a book. That I found the library on one of my 'walks'." She used her fingers to air quote walks.

"Good idea," Olivia hesitantly agreed.

"According to you," muttered Avery. "I bet Officer Jets would disagree."

"Needs must," Olivia replied.

# CHAPTER SEVENTEEN

Wearing her worn boots, her backpack slung over her shoulder, Avery made her way to the main road. She didn't say goodbye to Olivia this time, relieved to get out on her own.

"Tacquitz Road," she said aloud, thinking it had to be a Native American name. Her map app confirmed the address for Naomi and Fran's house. With the small thrill of independence, she quickened her pace.

It felt good to stretch her legs, to push past the low burn of Brad refusing her offer to get together and, of course, her feelings on Stella's death. Although Sparkles had cleared the air the moment she took the carrot from Avery's palm, movement helped her lingering feelings melt away.

After a few minutes she lengthened her stride, her muscles beginning to warm. Her calves burned with the incline, but she refused to slow. She looked up, spotting Lily Rock towering above her like a silent sentinel.

A sharp blast of a horn yanked her attention back to the road. She stepped aside just in time as a pickup roared past.

Avery caught his face in profile. *Theo*.

He didn't stop. Didn't wave. Just barreled on, leaving a cloud of dust in his wake.

"He's in a hurry," she said under her breath, huffing low in her chest.

When she reached the crest, Avery slowed, brushing sweat from her forehead. The houses in this area were older, tucked beneath sagging pines. The heat of summer brought out the smell of brush and mesquite. All of the scrubs next to the road had turned brown.

She checked the address. Naomi and Fran's gingerbread cabin was easy to spot. A modest A-frame, surrounded by a jumble of summer sunflowers nodding over a white picket fence.

Off to the side, the little free library stood in the shade, its painted blue door slightly ajar. Avery drew closer. Her glance stopped on a piece of trash, a paper caught under a nearby boulder. She bent down. Not just paper. A familiar brochure. The title shouted in bold block letters: "How To Be Saved and Know It."

She scanned the lines about sin and confession. The same cheap print, the same urgent tone as the leaflet she'd found at Stella's library.

A chill prickled her skin.

Could this be why Theo was in such a hurry?

Theo's truck. Theo's face. And now Theo's handiwork. Was he the one spreading the fear?

Avery straightened, eyes sweeping the empty street. The quiet pressed close, broken only by the faint creak of the library door swaying in the breeze. A crow cawed overhead. The sound carried on the slight wind, sounding eerie, making Avery's spine tingle. A warning. But of what?

She pulled the little door wider and reached for the first book that caught her eye. *Are You My Mother?* The cover was worn soft from use, several pages torn off at the edges. She flipped it open. Another thin leaflet fell free, releasing the doomsday promise.

She slid the book back and tried another. Then another. By the fifth book, she'd found five leaflets, each tucked neatly inside, waiting for the next unsuspecting reader.

The library looked harmless enough from the outside. But now it felt tainted, as if disguising something sinister. An unexpected reminder to the reader that they'd be punished and die. Not exactly a message for children. Did Naomi and Fran know that their library and the carefully selected children's literature was being used to spread hell-fire and damnation? Avery shut the door quickly, turning the latch.

She backed away a step, wanting distance. Not just from the little box but from the words themselves. Threats dressed as salvation had left a sour taste in her mouth.

She glanced at the ground. A heel mark pressed deep where someone had pivoted in a hurry. Beside it, the clean outline of a fresh boot print. The tread was sharp, not yet softened by dust or time. Maybe Theo's...

Avery crouched, brushing her fingers lightly across the impression. Bigger than her foot. And recent. She reached for her cell and took a photo. *I might need this later. Theo's truck spotted on my hike, Theo's footprint... Is he the one who peppered the libraries with the leaflets?*

She straightened, scanning the quiet street. No sight of him and nobody at home. *Maybe the moms decided to linger at Paws and Pines until Nancy woke up.*

Making her way back to the road, Avery broke into a slow run.

. . .

"I need to see Janis Jets." Avery pushed through the front door of Olivia's house, breath still ragged from the hike back. "I found something."

Olivia glanced up from her phone. "Do you want to show me?"

"I want to show you both," Avery insisted. She didn't bother pulling the crumpled leaflet from her pocket. Nor did she mention the photo. Something told her the evidence would carry more weight if Janis and Olivia saw it at the same time.

"Then let's head to town," Olivia said, rising. Her gaze swept Avery up and down.

"I know I'm a mess." She felt her cheeks flush.

"I didn't want to say anything," Olivia admitted. "But that's not a problem. It's that you seem really intent on this investigation. You realize that it's Janis's problem, right?"

Avery felt her intensity leave her, as if Olivia had used a soft cloth to wipe her fears away.

"How about I distract you," Olivia began. "There's a great salon in Lily Rock. On the way to speak to Janis, I can drop you at The Hair Parlor while I catch up with Meadow. Then we can go to see Janis together." Olivia looked hopeful.

When Avery didn't answer right away, she added, "Don't worry, I'll pay for the salon."

Avery bristled. "I can pay for myself," she shot back. "I have money, you know." She no longer felt Olivia's kindness. Offering to pay reduced her to feeling like a child.

Olivia blinked, most likely caught off guard at her tone. "Actually, I didn't know. I thought you were between houses and out of cash."

"Credit card." Avery pulled it from her pocket and held

it up as proof of her dignity. Avery had her own trust fund, handed over on her twenty-first birthday.

She no longer felt the need to talk to anyone, now that Olivia had suggested the salon. It was as if her feelings weren't her own. At least the angry and intense ones.

By the time they reached town, any lingering annoyance had dulled into indifference. She was the first to push open the car door.

"The Hair Parlor's across the street," Olivia called after her. "Upstairs at The Fort. Meet me when you're done. I'll be at the library."

She felt the discouragement, her legs heavy with the strain of the earlier hike. She'd been excited about the discovery in Naomi's little library. But Olivia had dismissed her, sending her to get her hair done. Olivia was like everyone else in her life. No one wanted to listen.

*Might as well get my hair trimmed; I'm looking kinda trail worn*, she thought.

Up the stairs, she paused at the landing. Old Toy Trains had been transformed into a bookstore. Beside it, Lady of the Rock looked the same. On the other side, she found The Hair Parlor. The logo included the image of an oversized lop bunny.

For a moment, Avery stood motionless, memories pressing in, accompanied by other emotions. Christmas. Belonging. A sense of home. And then that giant nutcracker outside of Old Toy Trains rose up in her mind.

She blinked away the fear, only to find Theo. He stood at the corner of the building like an apparition. His arms folded, his gaze pinned on her. He didn't look away. Then his head tipped the slightest fraction, as if weighing her or sending some wordless message.

Her breath caught. Was he trying to warn her? Or was

it something darker? A dare, maybe, or a reminder that he was one step ahead?

The faintest smile ghosted his lips.

She shuddered.

A crow cawed from the rooftop, sharp and sudden, the sound making her look up. *I hear you*, she told him in her mind. Then a swoop as the bird flew away, his wings flapping into the distance.

Avery turned for the salon door, her pulse unsteady. Each step heavier than the last. She felt Theo's unwavering stare. His eyes still watching.

# CHAPTER EIGHTEEN

At first glance, Avery thought she'd stepped backward a few decades, into the sort of hair salon her grandma might have frequented. The wooden counter by the door displayed jars of hard candy and a little ceramic owl stuffed with business cards. The air smelled faintly of perm solution, mixed with flowery-scented hairspray.

She almost dismissed the place as old-fashioned until her gaze shifted to the shelves along one wall, which held rows of sleek, trendy products with labels she recognized from her Rodeo Drive salon in LA. *I could use a moisturizing shampoo,* she thought.

The row of stylist chairs gleamed with chrome footrests and vinyl seats that had probably been around since the Reagan years. But they were spotless, lovingly polished. The stylists themselves had a unique feel; they seemed equally out of sync with the "cutting edge" image Avery had come to expect.

No tattoo sleeves, nose rings, or spiky pixie cuts. Instead, women in jeans and soft T-shirts moved comfortably between chairs, their personal hairstyles simple but confident.

Avery studied the woman in the first chair. Lots of bright highlights, sure, but the ponytail was nothing fancy. Just a casual pulled-back mass that looked artfully messy without screaming for attention. It wasn't what Avery would've called trending, but somehow it worked.

And that, she realized, was the point. This wasn't a place for reinvention or trend-chasing. The Hair Parlor was about maintenance, reassurance, and maybe a little comfort, including some mountain-town touch of chic.

"Right on time." The receptionist greeted her. "Olivia called over for your appointment."

Avery looked up and smiled. Fran. This time alone, without her wife. Then it hit her. Olivia made this happen, not just to distract her or as a comment on her appearance. *No wonder she brought it up.*

"Fran, right?" Avery glanced around the salon. "Did you leave Nancy and your wife at Paws and Pines?"

Fran's shoulders sagged in mock exhaustion. "I did. And honestly, I'm glad to be here today. Sometimes the two of them can be a bit much." The twinkle in her eyes softened the complaint, the tone more affectionate than exasperated.

"I'll be styling all the drop-ins today. My chair's at the very back." Fran's voice was easy, as if she had no trouble with last-minute appointments.

It had been a long while since Avery stared at her reflection in a salon mirror. *I do look a mess*, she thought. Her arms were dry and scratched from trail life, her face parched, chafed by the wind.

Fran swept a plastic cape over her shoulders and snapped it neatly at the neck, her hands efficient but not rushed. "So, what can I do for you today?" She tugged gently at the elastic holding Avery's ponytail, letting her hair spill down before running practiced fingers through the dry strands. "Are we thinking a new style or just a trim? I love the color. You're a natural blond, right?"

Avery sank deeper into the chair, a rare moment of surrender. "Yes, I am. I like to leave all that up to the artist," she said quietly.

Fran's grin spread wide. "Careful. You might walk out of here with something we'll both regret."

Their eyes met in the mirror's reflection, steady, not judgy. "I don't think so," Avery murmured. "I brought a credit card, so have at it."

"Yes, ma'am." Fran shared a playful little salute. "Be right back. I've got to mix some colors. Don't run off while I'm gone."

"Have you owned this place long?" Avery asked after Fran returned and tugged a strip of foil from the box.

"Just over a year," the stylist said. "We came up to get out of the city. When the old salon manager retired, I bought the place and did a few renovations. Business is steady now. Lots of locals, a few tourists, plenty of PCHers drop in on their way through."

Avery watched Fran in the mirror as she smoothed color cream onto a strand of hair and folded the foil with crisp efficiency.

In Lily Rock, that question *how long have you lived here* was more than small talk. It was a way of placing yourself, of proving you belonged. People wore their years like a prize ribbon.

Avery never did figure out how to answer that question. Her Lily Rock roots here were real, but shallow in places, pulled up too soon. *It doesn't matter*, she thought. *All this will be a memory once I leave again.*

Fran glanced at Avery's reflection, tilting her head to the side. "Don't drift off on me," she said lightly, folding another strand into foil. "This part takes focus, or you'll walk out with stripes instead of highlights."

Avery smiled faintly, grateful for the excuse to shake off her thoughts.

"I'll be back when it's time to rinse. You can close your eyes now."

When the alarm dinged, she followed Fran to the shampoo bowls. Fran peeled away the foils while Avery enjoyed the sound of customers murmuring in the salon. Warm water washed over her scalp as Fran's fingers worked in steady circles, kneading away stored fatigue and frustration.

"You said you guys have a little free library at your house?" Avery asked, not mentioning she'd already walked over and seen it for herself.

"Sure do." Fran squirted shampoo onto her scalp, the scent of citrus and eucalyptus tickling Avery's nose. "We're part of the Switchback Syndicate. You heard of it?"

Avery's eyes flicked open, her heart giving a little jump. "I have. So you're a member?"

"I've been to a couple of their meetings." Fran shut off the water, running her fingers through Avery's hair to chase away the excess moisture. "I think you're gonna like the highlights," she added with a smile. "Lean forward so I can dry your hair."

Back at their station, Fran smoothed the towel around Avery's head one more time as she continued to chat while giving Avery's hair a quick trim. "My wife, Naomi, she's got strong feelings about what's appropriate for Nancy. So she uses the library to promote books without, you know... sexual content."

"Like *Julián Is a Mermaid*?" Avery remembered seeing a copy in the children's section when she visited the library. "I haven't read it, but I assumed it was about gender fluidity."

Fran's lips thinned, but her voice stayed even. "Yep. Beautiful book, in my opinion. I'd have no trouble reading it to Nancy. But Naomi takes every copy that shows up in our library and gets rid of it. Throws them in the trash. She thinks it's dangerous."

"So you two disagree? About what goes in your library?"

Fran gave a small shake of her head. "Oh no. I stay out of it. I'm busy here most days anyway. Naomi's the one at every town council meeting, two mom groups—she's always running around from one committee to another. I'm the backup babysitter, cook, whatever she needs." She gave a quick shrug. "Somebody's gotta keep the trains running."

A chime sounded at the front desk. Fran turned toward the door. None of the other stylists looked up. "Be right with you!" she called to the next customer. Then softer to Avery, "Excuse me a minute. Gotta settle them in a chair."

As Fran walked away, Avery sat quietly, rubbing her fingers against the towel at her neck. There was a tone in Fran's voice she couldn't quite name. Something practical, resigned, maybe even weary.

It struck Avery that the weariness wasn't necessarily about the long hours or childcare responsibilities. Maybe it had something to do with Naomi's strong opinions.

*Kids aren't my thing, I don't know the first thing about the experience of being a mother*, Avery reminded herself. *I may have this all wrong...*

Yet her brain continued to look for more. *Fran. She's older, steadier, less caught up in the whirlwind of parenting politics. The practical one*, Avery decided. *The one who keeps things from tipping over, at least in her family.*

Fran returned, carrying a blow dryer and a styling brush. Once she finished, she swept away the cape and gave Avery a mirror to look at the back.

Her hair fell past her shoulders in soft waves. Avery sighed with satisfaction. The blend of highlights made her feel more like herself.

"See you up front," Fran said, and walked away.

Avery made her way to the counter, where Fran handed her an electronic bill. Avery added a tip before tapping her credit card.

"Want to schedule another appointment? Maybe in eight weeks?" Fran asked.

Before Avery could answer, the bell over the door jingled. She inhaled sharply as Marshall Reed stepped inside, tugging off his baseball cap to reveal flattened hair.

"Got time for a trim?" he asked Fran.

"Give me a sec," she replied.

"I don't know how long I'll be in town." Avery picked up their conversation. She turned to Marshall.

"How are you doing?"

His brow furrowed. "You're the one who found Stella."

"I'm the tagalong with Officer Jets and Olivia Greer. Until the case is solved," she explained.

"The case? Nah. Don't make such a big deal out of it. Stella died of natural causes." He sounded very sure of himself.

"I'm just a tagalong," she explained again. "I have no idea about cop business. Found the body. That's the extent of my involvement."

"Oh, yeah." Marshall smiled, a touch uncertain. "Good to see you again."

Then his gaze lifted upward. His next comment was directed at Fran. "Camera still working?"

"No problems," Fran said. "We've got a feed and recordings for up to ten days. I'm a satisfied customer."

Avery followed his glance. The lens pointed straight toward the entrance and the reception desk.

"You install cameras?" she asked.

"One of my many jobs," Marshall said easily. "You need one?"

"Not me," Avery said quickly. "But maybe a friend."

"Ask at the hardware store. They'll contact me."

Fran gave a quick wave. "Nice talkin' to ya," she told Avery. "Give me a call if your plans change about that next appointment."

Outside, Avery looked for Theo. He'd gone. No sign of him anywhere.

*It's time to head to the library*, she thought. She looked at her phone to find a text from Olivia.

> Go ahead without me. I'll catch up. Got more errands.

Avery took a deep breath to prepare herself. She wasn't sure she wanted to face the cop by herself.

# CHAPTER NINETEEN

Janis stared at her with hard eyes and a frown. "Well, don't you look spiffy. No more Backpack Betty. All fluffed up with curls."

Avery sat down and dropped her gaze. She wasn't quite ready for the usual repartee with the cop. She fluffed the hair on the back of her neck, giving herself a moment to adjust.

"So whatcha got?" Jets prodded.

Before she could answer, Olivia stepped quietly into the room. She nodded to Avery and took the empty chair next to her.

Avery slid the leaflet out of her tote onto the desk and smoothed it flat with her palm. "I found this in two little libraries. Stella's was the first. I didn't keep it because it crumbled when I touched it. But this one." She held it up. "It was in Naomi and Fran's little library. I think every single book—at least all the ones I checked—had one tucked inside. Children's books. Scaring parents and kids shouldn't be allowed."

"That's your opinion. Very noble." Janis took the paper

to study. With one eyebrow cocked, she said, "And quite interesting. Anything more?"

Avery hesitated. The footprint and the image of Theo leaning against the side of the building... She wanted to tell the cop, but she also wanted credit, not to be dismissed in that way Jets trivialized everything. Her name. Her hair. Her... She wasn't ready to hand it over.

Before she could reconsider, the door swung open and Brad May stuck his head in.

"Hey, boss." His eyes flicked to Avery, widening. "Oh, I didn't recognize you. The hair. You got it done. Nice." With a shrug, he turned his attention to Jets. "Another complaint. There's a guy up the road says someone's been dropping threatening notes in his little library. Wants you to check it out."

Jets sighed, leaning back in her chair with a scowl. "I'd like to take the whole lot of little libraries and the books and leave them in someone else's town."

Avery wasn't surprised. Another leaflet sighting. *Interesting.*

If it was Theo, as she suspected, he'd been all over town and could have put them anywhere. She wondered who'd complained but didn't wait for anyone else to ask. She looked back at Brad. "Was the guy who complained named Marshall?"

His eyes widened with appreciation. "As a matter of fact, yes it was."

"Thought so." She nodded with satisfaction.

Jets flicked the leaflet back onto the desk. "Nobody believes this religious stuff anymore. Junk mail, that's what it is."

Olivia watched quietly, her expression unreadable.

Brad closed the door.

Avery pressed her lips together. She could almost feel the weight of Theo's gaze, his intentions not quite clear. If she mentioned him now, Jets would snatch the lead away and forget who gave it to her.

No. This one was hers.

"That's all I've got," she said, holding both palms up with a submissive grin.

The officer snorted. She reached for the phone. "Why don't you get outta here. See you at dinner. Can't wait to find out what's on the menu tonight."

Avery made her way to the door. She had no idea what to make for dinner. But if it turned out that Theo was behind the distribution of those leaflets, then she'd be the first to call him out.

# CHAPTER TWENTY

"You seem awfully quiet," Olivia said, as they drove the winding road back to her house.

"Getting my hair done, I've gotta admit, I feel more relaxed." Avery rubbed her palm over her arm. "Now if I could just make my skin less itchy. I'm dried out. Like one of those bundles in an herb shop."

Olivia chuckled. "You're welcome to take a long bath when we get home. Add some scented oil. That might help." She pulled into the driveway and yanked the hand brake. "But don't forget you're making dinner."

Avery sighed, staring out the window. "I haven't forgotten. What time do you want to eat?"

"You're the cook. Just let Janis and me know the plan." Olivia slammed her door and headed inside.

Avery stared through the windshield. Tracking down a killer was thrilling. Making dinner, not so much. For one thing, she felt like her guest status was being revoked.

"Perfect," she muttered, dragging herself out of the car. "Next they'll be making special requests. Salmon on a plank. Fresh salad with avocado and radicchio." She pasted on a cheery grin to no one in particular. "Five-star dining, coming right up. Chef Microwave at your service."

She skipped the bath, washed her hands, and rummaged through the fridge. Containers were stacked across two shelves: Mexican, Italian, skewered meat, and rice with sweet-and-sour shrimp. *Olivia eats out a lot. Maybe that's why she wanted me to cook.*

As she placed containers on the counter, Avery's thoughts drifted back to Naomi and Fran. *Opposites*, she decided. *One quiet and self-effacing, the other bossy and sure of herself. Interesting pair.* She wondered which one Nancy took after, or if Nancy was even a biological child. And that mermaid book... She'd have to ask Meadow if she could check it out. What was the big deal, anyway?

Avery opened the lid of each takeout box and stared inside. Her stomach lurched, queasy. Mexican, Italian, Chinese, all bleeding into each other. If Janis or Olivia complained, she'd point them to the peanut butter jar. She looked over her shoulder at the cupboards. *I wonder if she has any strawberry jam. That would be my favorite.* She picked up her phone to text them both.

Dinner. One hour. Don't be late.

Her phone buzzed a few seconds later. Avery half expected Janis's excuse, but the name flashing on the screen wasn't hers; it was Theo's.

Come on by now. I'll show you my place.

She froze. This was her chance to confront him about the leaflets.

She tried to talk herself into saying yes. What was the

harm in showing up? If nothing else, she could hear him out and be back before the others noticed. Maybe he'd reveal himself as Stella's killer. A half smile came over her lips. That would be sweet. She texted Theo.

The tree house?

A walking map dropped into her messages, a blue trail winding through the trees.

Thanks for the map. If I disappear in the woods, you're the prime suspect.

Suck it up.

Guess I'll risk it, but only because I'm bored.

Then she added...

Hope you're not luring me into a Lifetime movie.

She bundled all the food back into the refrigerator and then reached for a sweatshirt. *Better hurry, before Olivia asks questions.* Out the door and over the bridge, she headed to the main road, taking brisk strides.

With the house behind her, she stopped to text Olivia and Janis.

One hour later. I have to prepare my feast.

She chuckled as she pressed Send.

Halfway to Theo's, she checked her phone again. Her heart raced when she saw his text.

Where are you?

Avery didn't answer. His impatience made her wary. She lengthened her stride. Then a bark came from deep in the woods. She stopped.

"Maguire?"

The labradoodle bounded out of the underbrush, tail wagging. He trotted closer, circled her once, sat on his haunches, then pressed his shoulder into her leg. The nudge of possession made her smile. She felt a lot better. He'd make a good bodyguard. She started again and he matched her step.

Another phone ping brought her to a halt. "What is it this time," she grumbled, checking her phone and seeing Theo's text.

Hurry up. I've got something to tell you about Stella. You're still coming, right?

The mention of the dead woman felt like a hook. Like he was afraid she'd change her mind and wouldn't make it. Or did he want to lure her into a trap?

She shot back a thumbs-up and pocketed the phone, along with any more misgivings.

Avery finally reached the end of the road. Mayor Maguire sprinted ahead, ears flopping, and disappeared around the bend. "Bork!" he called, as if hurrying her along.

Avery quickened her pace, lungs burning, her breath coming in short gasps. Rounding the corner, she found Maguire. He stood with tail waving, waiting for her to catch up.

Her eyes lifted. The tree house loomed straight ahead.

This wasn't some cobbled-together kid's fort, hammered up as a secret hiding place. This was a tree house reimagined for adults. She remembered thinking the same when she'd first seen photos of it on the PCT rental site.

A broad window of glass opened to a room. Only the ceiling beams could be seen from the road. The window made the best of the view. Lily Rock sat in the distance.

*Spectacular*, she thought.

The deck that surrounded the tree house held an air conditioner and a generator. *Maybe the main source of power*, she concluded. Off to the corner was the outdoor shower, complete with a curtain that fluttered in the breeze.

The tree house felt unique. Out of place. And yet, somehow exactly what she'd expected from Theo. It was rated the most popular rental on the PCT site, and she could now see why. Terribly inconvenient. Stella's room, for example, would feel more accessible and comforting. But not this place. The rope stairs alone would make coming and going on a whim difficult.

Avery squinted, shading her eyes. For a second, she thought she saw movement. A blur of a shadow slipping past the window.

A sharp crack, then the crunch of wood made her step backward. She saw a body hurl from the deck, landing with a loud thump in the dirt. Avery felt her hands tremble.

Maguire's ears shot up. He barked once, sharp like a warning.

"Wait," Avery called, her heart lurching.

Maguire hesitated, just long enough for her to grab his collar. She held him in place.

The silence pressed in, broken only by the hum of the air conditioner and the flap of the shower curtain above.

Avery craned her neck. She called Theo's name. No answer. She and Maguire took steps to close the gap. She looked overhead.

A length of broken board, a hole wide enough for a body to fall through.

"Theo," she whispered, though his name stuck in her throat.

Maguire pulled, lunging toward the body. Her fingers slipped and he broke away. She saw Theo, his mouth half open, one arm underneath his body, bent at the wrong angle. He was fully clothed.

*So he wasn't taking a shower, getting ready for me to come over. Maybe he was standing near the shower, leaning over the rail, looking for me to come up the road.*

The last thought made her shiver.

Covering her mouth with her hand, a metallic tang rose on her tongue. She reached for her phone. "911. I have an emergency."

# CHAPTER TWENTY-ONE

Avery watched from the front seat of Jets's truck as paramedics moved with grim efficiency. One EMT pulled open the double-wide doors of the ambulance, while the other rolled the stretcher with Theo's body inside.

Jets had arrived minutes after Avery's call, driving like a bat out of hell. Her truck bounced over the dirt lot surrounding the tree house. As soon as she scrambled out of the truck, she began to give orders, insisting that Avery make herself scarce.

"Move on, Backpack," she'd insisted, though not in her usual dismissive way. Her tone had an undercurrent that Avery wasn't used to. As if she cared.

Avery's glance drifted past the truck's windshield toward the tree house. The rope ladder swung lazily in the cool night air, as if it had no care in the world. Jets stood nearby. She cast a glance to the truck, then back to the paramedic who seemed to be giving a report. Avery couldn't hear what he said. But Janis's stony expression made her uneasy.

Curiosity, more than anything else, made Avery reach

for the door handle. Her hand paused as she reconsidered, but that didn't take much time. Janis was preoccupied with the details of the crime scene; this was Avery's opportunity.

She left the door ajar, not wanting to attract attention when it closed. Scurrying to the back of the truck, she crouched behind the bumper right as headlights from Olivia's Ford illuminated her whereabouts.

Avery dove to the dirt, making herself flat, fingers crossed. To her relief, Olivia hurried past, calling out to Janis.

Jets greeted her consultant. Neither glanced her way.

*Close call.* She stood and made her way toward the rope ladder. Hiding, she watched Janis and Olivia. As the two women continued to speak, heads close together, she made her next move.

Part pulling and part lifting, she legged it up the rope. As soon as both feet hit the deck, she ducked to one side to stay out of sight. Her breath came in gasps.

Avery reached for the handle on the sliding glass door. One tug and she slipped inside. *What a mess*, she thought, quietly closing the slider. A shiver ran down her spine. Unless Theo was a terrible housekeeper, this place had been trashed.

A narrow bed frame leaned at an angle, a leg snapped clean through, the mattress half slid to the floor. Blankets and a quilt were tangled in a heap, stained with dirt and boot prints. Shelves that had once held canned and boxed food had been swept clean, their contents scattered across the floor.

One of the double-paned windows over the small kitchen sink was cracked from the inside. Generator cables snaked through the holes in the wall.

Theo's work desk had been overturned, papers spilling

to the floor. A familiar children's book lay among the papers: *Are You My Mother?* by P.D. Eastman. Avery's throat tightened. She remembered a lady in the library reading it to her when she was a kid. The same cover as Theo's book, with the little bird and the mom wearing a kerchief.

Beside it was *The Giving Tree*, Shel Silverstein's ode to unconditional devotion. Avery frowned. The book made her furious the first time it had been read to her. She learned early that attention came with strings attached, that affection had to be earned. And so the idea of being loved just as she was...felt almost impossible to believe.

Tucked under the book, she noticed several familiar leaflets. The same salvation pamphlets like the others. Their connection to Theo felt obvious.

Stepping over the books, she kneeled to inspect a familiar hiking map, scribbled over in a bold distinctive hand. Avery shoved it into her back pocket right as Jets's voice came from outside.

"Of course I told her to stay in the truck. Does she ever obey orders?"

Avery assumed a stance of nonchalance as Jets and Olivia came into view. Suspicion was written all over Janis's face. The door slid open.

"And what do we have here, Backpack Betty? You're snooping at the scene of another dead body. We know you called it in. Brad recognized your voice." Hands on hips, she glared at Avery.

Olivia nudged her way past Janis, her tone more measured. "Before you think about arresting her, Officer Jets..." She paused, mouth twitching into a half smile. "You might want to consider our dinner plans. Avery's cooking."

Olivia's effort to shift the mood hung in the air. Avery wanted to jump in and declare her innocence. Explain about the books and leaflets. She opened her mouth just as Olivia gave a slight shake of her head. Instead, she clamped her lips shut.

Jets mumbled a response under her breath right as a uniformed cop joined them.

"We're here to bag up the evidence," he stated curtly.

"Got cuffs on ya?" Jets asked, directing a side-eye at Avery.

As he reached for his pocket, Olivia spoke, using a very firm voice. "Come on. Let's talk to Avery over dinner. No use jumping to conclusions. You know I'm right."

Jets bit her bottom lip. She turned to glare at Avery. "Even you have to realize that you're neck deep in this mess. Now I have a contaminated crime scene because you couldn't just follow simple directions and stay in the truck!"

Avery's chin dropped and she stared at the floor. Somehow Olivia's defense had touched a nerve. And for once in her life, she wanted to admit she regretted what she'd done.

Empty containers of reheated leftovers cluttered the table. Jets took a long swallow of water, then coughed. "Okay. We've eaten. Now for a few questions."

Avery licked peanut butter from her finger. Somehow the old habit from childhood brought her comfort. Scooping peanut butter from the jar.

"Those children's books. Did you see them? Why would Theo want to keep them?" Avery's voice came out in a burst.

Olivia blinked. "Children's books?"

"I need to rinse my hands, be right back," she said.

Jets and Olivia talking in hushed, muffled voices made

her mad. She didn't like it when people talked behind her back. A hangover from high school.

Seated back at the table, she began. "Theo was part of the Switchback Syndicate. Those old titles—I remember them from my childhood. Maybe he had a niece or something."

"Maybe he's just a single guy who loved children's books," Jets countered. "Look at you, licking peanut butter from your finger like a kid. It brings comfort, right? So does reading old books." Jets wasn't convinced. She tapped the table with her finger. "It doesn't add up, though, him not having a little library. If he was in the Syndicate, that could be an issue. I'll let my guys comb the evidence before I say more."

Olivia reached to pat Avery's arm. "You've got peanut butter on your lip." She licked her own to show where.

Avery felt more like a kid than ever.

"Do you think," she addressed Janis, "that Theo killed Stella and then someone killed him?"

"Nah, I'm not getting that thought at all," Jets said. "What are you saying, there's some kind of little free library serial killer on the loose in Lily Rock? We've had our share of murders, I'll give you that. But I'm still thinking you're the common denominator." Jets sounded quite certain.

Avery's stomach began a slow churn. "What about the mess? Who would do that? Were they looking for something?" Her questions came quickly.

"Whoever killed Theo probably tossed his place. I don't know if it was before or after. The timing will have to be figured out." Jets had a thoughtful tone. "On the one hand, they might have been looking for something; on the other hand, it feels like revenge to me. Messing things up because you're filled with rage and have to take it out on the other guy."

Olivia leaned forward. "Unless you have actual evidence that links Avery, besides being a good citizen and reporting the bodies, then she deserves to know if she's under suspicion so that she can hire a lawyer."

Avery's pulse quickened. She'd always known she was innocent. Up until now, she thought Jets was just being difficult. But Olivia's sudden concern made her wonder, *Am I really a suspect?*

Her parents had a family friend, a lawyer. She wasn't sure if he'd ever taken a criminal case. Her voice came out faint. "I can call my family's attorney. If you think I need to." She blinked at Olivia, waiting for confirmation.

Jets held up a palm. "What are you talking about? I'm not gonna arrest you, Backpack Betty. You may have been at the wrong place at the wrong time yet again, which is suspicious. But I had to push you. Part of the gig. Just to see if I could squeeze any more toothpaste out of the tube."

Avery didn't like being compared to toothpaste. Before she could object, Olivia spoke. "She has nothing to confess, Janis. Isn't that obvious? She basically lives on peanut butter and black coffee. Not serial killer material, not by a long shot."

Avery's eyes burned. She'd never been defended by anyone before, so Olivia's support made her feel oddly emotional. "I'm going to my room," she mumbled. Her chair clattered across the floor as she bolted away.

*Let the two professionals sort it out*, she thought, huffing up the stairs.

# CHAPTER TWENTY-TWO

Avery lay in bed, eyes open, staring at the ceiling. Neither Janis nor Olivia had followed her. Now that she felt certain the conversation was over, she had trouble falling asleep.

Her head sank deeper into her pillow. A shaky breath escaped her lips, right as her phone pinged a message.

She stared at the unfamiliar number and then read the text aloud.

> You're cordially invited to the next meeting of the Switchback Syndicate. Tell no one. Add this number to your contacts to receive further communication of day and time.

She tapped the screen with a reluctant finger and added the number to her contacts. *The plot thickens*, she thought. *But why me? Why would they invite a stranger to one of the meetings?* She lifted the phone to text back.

> Who is this?

She waited. But there was no response. With the phone in her hand she looked away, her attention shifting. Theo's map. She'd taken it from the crime scene before Jets showed up. *I'm going to figure this out on my own. No use dragging those two in. If I come out alive, maybe I'll get credit for my investigation. If not... No point thinking about that now.*

She closed the screen and then rolled over to sleep on her stomach, the pillow cool on her cheek.

The next day, Avery tugged on the strap of her backpack and started up the trail. The morning air smelled of pine and dust, feeling sharp against her skin. With the map she'd taken from Theo's folded in her pocket, she had a clear goal. One she hadn't mentioned to Olivia over breakfast.

"More coffee?" Olivia had asked as they sat outside, sliding the carafe across the table.

"Sure," Avery said, forcing a smile.

"Did you sleep well?" Olivia's voice had dropped into that low, confiding tone she used when she read Avery's energy. *Too accurately*, she thought.

"Not really." Avery had hidden behind her noncommittal response. Keeping her eyes averted helped maintain her boundaries. She watched the sunlight climb over Lily Rock.

"Any plans for today?" Olivia questioned.

Avery took a sip of coffee. Despite Olivia's sincerity, she'd felt the same as she did the night before. Better to leave her and Janis out of it. The only way to make that happen was to avoid being taken in by Olivia's mesmerizing way of pulling down her emotional defenses.

. . .

A rustle came from behind a low shrub, bringing her back to the present. Mayor Maguire bounded toward her, his tongue lolling. He circled and darted back to the woods. Avery grinned. *He wants to play hide and seek.*

"Don't rat me out," she warned him. Then he came back in a rush, tail waving. When she ignored him, he trotted alongside.

As much as she appreciated his company, she was concerned she'd be noticed. The mayor was very popular. "Shoo," she told him with a wave of the hand.

He paid no attention.

The climb was harder than she expected. The altitude and the rest weren't helping her stamina. The one thing that spurred her on was the decision to take charge.

Halfway up the steep trail she stopped for a quick drink. What would Janis call her if she knew what she was up to? Avery grinned. She liked getting under the cop's skin. She could hear the accusations in her head. Reckless and stubborn, Jets would yell. Then she'd roll her eyes and call her Backpack Betty for the hundredth time.

Avery screwed the cap on the bottle. "Well, this Betty has work to do," she muttered, and pushed on.

The trail leveled at a junction marked by a weathered signpost. And there, bolted crookedly to a post, she found what she was looking for: a little free library. Hikers called it a dead drop. *Looks like it's both,* she reasoned.

Orange paint peeled off the sides, the plexiglass window heavily smudged with fingerprints and dust. Maguire lowered his nose to sniff the post.

Avery inched the door open. Inside, there was a lopsided stack of paperbacks. One Danielle Steele novel, a dog-eared copy of a Tom Clancy bestseller, and a bundle of outdated hiking magazines. She was about to close the door when her fingers brushed a familiar green spine.

*The Giving Tree.*

Her chest tightened. She eased the book out and opened it. Sure enough, tucked in the middle was a leaflet. Plus the smell of mildew wafted from the book. She turned her head to sneeze.

Once she'd stuffed the leaflet into her pocket, she placed *The Giving Tree* back on the shelf.

Maguire looked up, one ear lifted. Then he uttered a low whine, pivoting quickly to look toward the woods. He ran ahead, disappearing behind a row of trees.

Avery let out a sigh of exasperation. She yanked the strap of her pack tight. *He must have seen a squirrel*, she thought. *I'll hike back myself.*

# CHAPTER TWENTY-THREE

The bell over the door at Thyme Out chimed Avery's arrival. She found a free table and swung her backpack underneath. The display menu no longer advertised Sierra Snowcaps. They'd been replaced by lemon thyme cookies.

"I'll take half a dozen," she told Cookie Kravitz, who stood at her table, a slight smile on his lips. "And a mug of the daily flavored coffee," she added.

"Cream and sugar with that?" He grinned.

"Just black." Avery liked Janis's boyfriend more than she liked Janis, truth be told. "I'm surprised you stayed in Lily Rock." She wondered if that was his original plan.

"I did. Janis and I live together over in the cove. Great place."

"I guess," Avery said.

"I'll bring your coffee as soon as it's brewed." Cookie looked over his shoulder at another table.

Once he'd left, Avery unfolded her map, smoothing the creases with the flat of her hand. Hiking to the little library hadn't been a wild hunch. It was because she remembered.

The first time she'd spotted the unusual dead drop was

when she was with Theo. "What's that?" she'd asked, pointing toward the odd little dilapidated wooden box.

Theo shaded his eyes. His voice warmed, almost possessive. "Oh, that's a little free library."

"My map says it's a dead drop." She'd been curious. At the time, he'd not mentioned that he stocked the little library, nor that he lived in Lily Rock.

"Lily Rock people do the darnedest things," he said with a flicker of pride. "Don't knock it. I found a couple of good books in there. Why don't you have a look?"

She'd laughed, bending to tie her boot. "I'm too busy bandaging my troll feet to read."

"Your loss," he'd said, his voice childlike with disappointment.

Avery blinked back to the present. She hadn't thought much of it then, too wrapped up in her blisters and banter. But now the conversation felt revealing, like there was something hidden by Theo.

She folded up the map as the bell above the door chimed. A short, stocky woman in a wide-brimmed hat drifted in. She was dressed in athletic gear, a yoga mat hanging over her shoulder.

"Well, well, well," she purred, making a straight path to Avery's table. "Haven't we met before?"

Avery's jaw dropped. Apparently Cordelia didn't remember that time in the library or in her own living room. Unsure what to do, she pretended they hadn't met. "Hello." She used a noncommittal tone. She waited for Cordelia to search her memory and come up with a name.

The romance writer plunked one of her paperbacks on the table. "I keep the little free libraries stocked in Lily Rock. My specialty is the romance genre."

*Okay then, I guess we're starting from scratch.* Avery

decided she wasn't going to correct Cordelia. It would make their conversation even longer.

"Romance must never die, don't you agree?" Cordelia gave her a beady stare beneath the flutter of lashes.

Avery felt pinned. *I have to pick up the book and act interested.*

She wondered if everyone in Lily Rock, when presented with one of Cordelia's old books, felt impatient, not wanting to be impolite and refuse. Especially to an absentminded woman who may be memory compromised and not checking all of her boxes.

"Now where did I put my pen to sign your copy," Cordelia murmured. She rummaged in her oversized purse. "Ah, I remember. I left it at the last book signing. An admirer must have kept it as a keepsake." She chuckled, then tapped the novel she'd placed on the table.

"Keep it. I'll sign it the next time we meet. Stories find their readers sooner or later." To Avery's relief, Cordelia drifted away from her table, toward the counter.

She stared into her mug, listening to the din of customer voices, picking up short snippets of conversation. The usual banter, nothing caught her attention. The hiss of the espresso machine punctuated a burst of laughter from a group of women in the corner. She looked up.

Naomi, holding Nancy in her lap, spoke loudly enough to be heard across the cafe. "Did you actually read the book, or do you only come for the gossip?" When people spoke that loudly, Avery narrowed her eyes.

Avery turned her gaze away. She needed to focus on Theo, not on Naomi's need for attention. Maybe Theo killed Stella. He certainly had a secret. She shuddered. She couldn't imagine him being that violent, but even though he was dead, she needed to consider him as a possible suspect.

Maybe he tossed the firecracker as a prank. Maybe the explosion had been meant as a warning. If he were the one distributing those scary religious leaflets all over town, maybe he targeted Stella and wanted to get under her skin.

Some people were like that. *Here's another maybe,* Avery thought. *A big one. Maybe Theo felt personally responsible for Stella's soul. He wanted to make her confess her sins, so that she could get to heaven.*

But what about his tree house studio? It had been tossed. That was a clue as to a person of interest, wasn't it?

*What about Marshall Reed?* Avery's mind turned. *He'd have no trouble tossing a firecracker at someone. Or a room, if he thought there was something he needed.* She felt quite certain. For one reason, he carried that air of someone who colored outside the lines.

Off-the-grid, an extremist in waiting. Even his choice of reading material. All that old-school science fiction stuff, with apocalyptic undertones, appealed to unstable people with an ax to grind. Or so she'd heard.

Those leaflets. The sharp-edged religious pamphlets screaming about doom and salvation. Like jagged little blades disguised as scripture. Marshall could have killed both Stella and Theo. A regular crusader. Made the deaths look like accidents.

She glanced over at the book group.

Naomi paused mid-sentence to look back. Avery forced a sheepish half smile. Her stomach knotted, a bitter taste at the back of her throat. The young mother nodded, then turned back to her friends.

Avery picked up her phone. She'd expected to hear from the Syndicate by now. Instead there were two texts from Olivia. Both wanted to know if she was coming home soon. She responded.

Done hiking. Be there in a while.

# CHAPTER TWENTY-FOUR

She reached for her backpack and slung it over her shoulder. As the door to Thyme Out swung open, Avery bumped smack into Brad May.

"'Scuse me," he said, catching her backpack to steady her.

Heat rushed to her face. She ducked her head. He made her feel self-conscious, she realized. And uneasy.

"Leaving us already?" He pointed to the pack. There was something almost wistful in his tone, but she forced herself to answer briskly.

"Just a morning hike. Trying to get in shape after a few days off. Then I'll be out of your hair."

His eyes studied her face. "It's good seeing you around," he said, as if explaining his interest. Then, too casually, "Been back to check on Sparkles?"

"No time to talk, Olivia's waiting for me."

Before he could reply, she adjusted her pack strap and strode away, boots striking the sidewalk with more determined force than she felt. She kept her head held high, eyes fixed forward, convinced that turning back would make her look weak.

Whatever his interest had stirred up, she wasn't about to let him see.

She quickened her pace, thinking, *I'm clearing my name and finding Stella and Theo's killer. No time for a detour into old mistakes with Brad May.*

Avery slowed as she passed Village Hardware's storefront. She looked inside right as Marshall Reed turned away from the counter holding a paper bag.

She deliberately waited for him to leave the hardware store, hoping to speak with him.

He noticed her immediately. "Hello," he called, his chin lifting in a stiff nod.

"How are you?" Avery answered, forcing brightness into her voice. She fell into step beside him. "Stocking up?"

"There's always something that needs fixing." He looked around, his gaze never quite landing on her.

Avery let a moment pass. "Stella's little free library...you built it, didn't you?"

He glanced over, eyes narrowing just slightly. "Yeah. She asked, I obliged. I used to drop in for maintenance now and then. Why?"

"Oh, just..." Avery hesitated and then blurted, "I saw the blown-up version, but the construction looked solid to me. Thought it must've taken some know-how."

Marshall's mouth twitched, something between pride and irritation. "It's just wood and screws. Anyone could manage it." He shifted the bag against his hip. "Shame about Stella."

The words were flat, final, but Avery caught a tightening in his jaw. "You must've been proud of what you built," she pressed. "She said the little library was special."

Marshall stopped at the curb. His eyes, dark under the brim of his cap, now looked directly at her. "You hardly knew Stella." His voice dropped low, almost casual. But the edge in it made her skin prickle.

When she didn't protest, he gave a short, humorless laugh. "Like I said, it's just a box with books. That's all." He stepped off the curb. Avery stared after him, still feeling unsettled.

If he'd built the library, he would know every hinge, every weakness. Maybe he'd add his own books to her collection, take out other ones he didn't approve of.

Maybe Stella challenged his taste and he'd had enough.

Thought he'd make her think twice. Change her mind. Give her a little scare.

Avery crossed the street to sit down on a nearby bench. A woman and a dog played catch with a tennis ball nearby. Her mind was a muddle of possibilities, especially when it came to Marshall.

*I could investigate more efficiently if I had a car*, she ruminated. *Hiking everywhere is so slow. I'm also stuck with that thing*. She kicked her backpack.

*Olivia needs to wait*, she concluded.

*There's that shop where other hikers drop their gear for repair, what is the name again? Actually, why not just wander in and have a chat with the proprietor?* Maybe she'd get lucky and make a few inquiries too.

At the corner of Circle Drive and Main Street, she found the place. Carry On Outfitters. As a PCT hiker left through the front, he waved but didn't stop to talk. She stepped inside.

The shop was narrow but deep, a long aisle flanked by pegboard walls. Used and repaired packs lined the floor alongside stacked trekking poles. Rows of boots, looking worse for wear, stood against the connecting wall.

A chalkboard leaned against the counter. Today's message, sprawled in bold white chalk: *Not all who wander are lost.* Avery sniffed. *Easy for J.R.R. Tolkien to say. He didn't lose his house in a fire or discover two dead bodies.*

Behind the counter, a scarred wooden workbench overflowed with tools. Needle kits, strips of leather, spools of heavy thread were spread across the surface. An industrial-sized sewing machine hummed, its light on, waiting for the operator.

A woman came from the back. "Hello there. Avery, isn't it? Meadow said you were in town."

"You know me?" Avery blinked and then squinted, trying to remember.

"I'm a friend of Sage and Meadow's. I was here that Christmas you did the wrapping station, but we didn't get introduced." She held out a rough hand to shake.

"Your name?" Avery gripped her hand.

"Melinda Abernathy. Been a resident for ten years now. I sew for the PCTers when they're in town. What can I do you for?"

Avery held up her backpack. "I've got a problem here," she explained, fingering the broken strap.

"You're carrying too much of a load. But you probably already know that." Melinda slid the pack toward her. "Let me see what I can do."

As she bent over the stitching, Avery leaned on the counter. "Lots of people come in here," she remarked, trying to get the woman talking. "Mostly hikers?"

"Not just hikers." Melinda gave a tug to the zipper, testing its bite.

Avery nodded toward the chalkboard. "I saw the quote."

Melinda glanced up, a corner of her mouth twitching. "A classic. Marshall put that up there. He's the kind of guy who marches to his own drummer. And if he doesn't like you for some reason... He'll never agree to a job, no matter how much you offer to pay."

"The guy up the hill?" Avery's pulse quickened.

Melinda's hands stalled for a moment. "That's right. He likes to act like he's some kind of mountain man. Repairs gear for folks for cheap. But half the time it's just glue and duct tape. Says it'll outlast the trail. That's his excuse for poor workmanship."

Her voice dipped lower. "And for some reason, people believe him. Like I said, the mountain man vibe."

Avery felt a moment of satisfaction. Now she'd heard another opinion of Marshall that she mostly agreed with. *Investigations are just nudging people toward their natural inclination to make conversation about their neighbors*, she concluded.

"I might need him," she said. "For a project. I'm staying a little longer in Lily Rock than I expected. Do you have his card?"

Melinda reached into a drawer. "Here you go. Remember, I warned you." Then her eyes narrowed. "But tell him I sent you. I can use the goodwill."

Avery scribbled her cell number on a scrap of paper and slid it toward Melinda.

"I'll call when it's done." Melinda didn't look up, her machine already stitching.

Out the door, Avery took a deep breath, relishing the sudden freedom of leaving the backpack and, if lucky, her nickname behind. She crossed the street and caught sight of Meadow McCloud framed in the library window. Her silver braid hung over the front of her denim jumper. Avery made the quick decision to drop in and ask her about Marshall.

"Good morning, dear." Meadow's voice sounded both kind and precise. "Something I can help you with?"

Avery stepped up to the counter and leaned across, her tone expectant. "What do you know about Marshall Reed? He seems kinda...sketchy to me."

Meadow's eyes widened a fraction, then narrowed. She studied Avery's expression. "Now that's an interesting assumption. How well do you know him?"

Avery explained about the quote on the board. And then Melinda's disparaging remark.

Meadow's eyes brightened. "Ah, yes. 'Not all who wander are lost.' I do like a good quote to start my day."

Avery shrugged, trying to hide her impatience. "But what about him? Marshall?"

Meadow folded her hands on the counter. "He comes into the library nearly every week. Most of the time he checks out the same authors. Bradbury, Heinlein, Clarke. He's loyal to the classics."

"I got that," Avery interjected, hoping for more. "What I want to know is his reputation as a handyman. He told me he built Stella's little library. Said he does repairs all the time."

The librarian's lips pressed into a straight line. "Avery Denning, does Officer Jets know you're conducting your own investigation?" Her tone was firm, almost motherly.

"Not exactly..." Avery mumbled.

Meadow lowered her voice. "Why don't you come around to my office for a bit? We'll talk where we won't be overheard."

# CHAPTER TWENTY-FIVE

The library's public spaces were neat and orderly, but Meadow's office was something else entirely. Books teetered in stacks on the floor. Her desk was strewn with papers. A faded quilt hung across the back of her chair. A vase of fresh lemon lilies sat on the windowsill, their fragrance filling the air.

"Sit down." Meadow gestured to a chair. She shut the door firmly.

Avery perched on the edge, hands gripping her knees. "Sorry if I was too abrupt. I just need answers."

Meadow folded her glasses into their case and placed them on the desk. "Bluntness has its place, dear. But so does discretion. Especially in a small town."

Avery held in a sigh of impatience. "I don't think Marshall Reed is as harmless as everyone makes him out to be. People just accept he's the eccentric guy who does repairs. Lily Rock was always like that, taking in strays."

Meadow tried to hold back a smirk. "If you say so, dear. You should know, being such a pillar of convention yourself.

Before you finish that thought, remember. Speculation is a dangerous companion. Marshall has called Lily Rock his home for years. Some people think of him as eccentric, yes. But he's also useful. Folks overlook a lot when someone fixes their broken steps or hammers a nail without asking for payment."

"That's just it," Avery pressed. "Why would he do all that for free? Doesn't it seem odd?"

Meadow studied her for a long moment, her eyes almost wistful. "Odd doesn't always mean dangerous. Sometimes it just means lonely. And loneliness makes people find ways to be needed."

Avery shifted, unsettled. "So you trust him?"

"I didn't say that." Meadow's mouth curved into a thin smile. "I watch through my window. And I listen. I notice patterns. And I'll tell you this much: Marshall Reed likes to keep his personal life to himself. That alone would give you pause if you were, let's say, Officer Janis Jets or her capable intuitive consultant, Olivia Greer."

Avery felt Meadow had effectively managed to put her in her place, just like a book that got returned to the shelf. She felt chastised for judging Marshall and stepping into territory that didn't belong to her. She had also been reduced to amateur status with the mention of Olivia and Janis.

As much as she wanted to share about the anonymous text, Meadow wasn't the one. She'd most likely call Janis before Avery could get out the door.

Avery thanked the librarian politely, though her cheeks burned. She hated being looked after and told what was best. For most of her life, she'd gotten along with little advice, since her parents rarely gave her the time of day.

Meadow had all but told her to leave the sleuthing to

the professionals. *Not gonna happen*, she fumed, walking out the library door.

The cool mountain air settled over her, clearing away her anger, making her more determined. She might not be an officer or Olivia Greer with her "intuitive gifts," but she was the one who kept asking questions, who kept stumbling into dead bodies, for whatever that was worth.

The thought steadied her. If Marshall Reed was hiding something, she'd find it. And she didn't need Meadow's permission to look.

Passing the local market, Avery slowed. If she was stuck playing "dinner girl" again tonight, she might as well do it properly. *Baked chicken. I can manage that*, she decided, ducking inside.

A few minutes later, she emerged with a tray of chicken thighs wrapped in plastic and a bundle of fresh asparagus in a mesh produce bag. She'd bought the bag at checkout. Feeling quite eco-friendly and determined, she hung the bag over her arm. *Not a bad meal*, she told herself, feeling pleased. *Better than leftovers*.

Back at the house, she slid the food into the refrigerator, then snagged an apple from the fruit bowl to take outside. She sank her teeth into the fruit, the mountain air crisp against her skin.

*Olivia must have gotten tired of waiting for me*, Avery concluded. She savored both the quiet and the satisfaction of piecing things together by herself. Fewer distractions and unwanted opinions that way.

Right now, if anyone bothered to ask, she felt convinced Marshall Reed knew more than he was saying about both murders. It was time to piece together his motive. She already had opportunity and weapon.

*That's how all the cop shows work.*

She'd have to pin down the exact timing, of course, but she had no problem imagining him standing at a distance and pitching a firecracker in Stella's direction, sliding away without being seen.

Did he stay to watch Stella crumple to the ground, frightened at what he'd done? Had he run into the woods or back to his truck? She wondered if Lily Rock had closed-circuit cameras along the main streets. That might reveal the truth.

But what about Theo? She took another bite.

Maybe Marshall set up a meeting with Theo to bond over books. Theo certainly had his own strong opinions. They could have disagreed. Maybe Marshall was tired of listening to him, tired of the Syndicate meetings too.

So he planned to hit him on the head and drag him to the edge of the tree house platform. Stage the weak boards and then make it look like an accident.

A dead drop, all right...the ugliest kind.

The first death felt unintentional. But Theo? Maybe Marshall had planned that one. Though killing a person over a book... Avery shook her head and tossed the apple core into a nearby bush. *Natural compost*, she told herself. *I bet John Muir would approve.*

*Okay, so I need a front-row seat to Marshall Reed in action. How he talks, how he moves, what he avoids saying. Maybe then his motivation for killing would become clear. Accident or revenge.* Either way, the thought made Avery want to know more.

*I don't have a car to follow him around town. I can't do it on foot, waiting for impromptu meetups.*

The answer popped into her head so suddenly, she laughed aloud. Of course. Build another little library. *I can instigate that. I'll commission him right away.*

She'd tell him it was Olivia's birthday. A little free library would fit right in on her road. Kind of quirky, wholesome, a bit of mountain-like charm. And if it wasn't exactly Olivia's dream project... Well, she'd forgive it once she saw how cute it looked by the bridge entrance. Convenient too. People could drive by and stop to chat.

Avery could hover close while Marshall worked. She'd offer him drinks of water and chitchat. Act all interested in his process. Old guys liked that. She'd learned the hard way. Her parents would leave her to her own devices on set; talking to the crew was her only way to keep busy.

She grinned, already picturing a brand-new little library, a perfect alibi for her nosiness. Marshall Reed with a hammer in hand, unaware he was under investigation. *I'll give you amateur*, she seethed.

Avery lifted her phone and dialed his number, getting his voicemail. "This is Avery Denning," she began. Her breath caught. She cleared her throat. "I'd like your help in designing a very special little free library. For someone's birthday," she added, using a bright voice. "Would you call me back so we can get started?"

*Should I have left my address?* she wondered, pocketing the phone.

*Not if he's a stone-cold killer, Avery.* She snorted at herself, half amused, half serious. *I'll tell him I want it to be a surprise. That way we can do the work at his place, in his workshop. I don't need to give an address, then.* Suddenly her plan fell into place.

She lifted her chin, eyes searching for Lily Rock. There was a touch of snow dusting the mountain range, despite the heat below. A scrub jay darted from branch to branch. The air smelled faintly of dust and pine. Avery felt secure with her plan. Now to get started.

"Gonna be a hot one," she murmured, squinting into the midday sun. Then a grin tugged at her mouth. "A good day to catch a murderer."

# CHAPTER TWENTY-SIX

Avery rested on the patio, her feet balanced against the tree stump table.

"You outside?" came Olivia's voice. She dangled her car keys in one hand. "When I get back, we can catch up?"

Avery gave a quick nod and then glued her eyes to her screen.

"Okay then," Olivia said, walking toward the bridge.

Minutes later, her phone buzzed. Marshall Reed's name flashed on her screen. She froze a moment, heart giving an odd little skip, before swiping to answer.

"Hello," she said, a little breathless.

"I got your message," he began. His voice was warm, even friendly. The timbre of it caught her off guard, slipping past her defenses. For a split second, she was reminded of her father on one of those rare occasions when he'd been in a good mood.

"Do you have time to construct a new little library?" she asked.

"I do," he chuckled. "I can start today. I've got my own book of designs if you want to stop over."

Avery stared at the flowerpots lining Olivia's patio. Her heart thumped in her chest; he'd taken the bait.

*I could make an excuse and hang up,* she thought, nerves getting the better of her. She gulped and took the plunge anyway. "Okay, that would be fine," she managed. "My friend's home is modern, so not like a gingerbread cottage, if you know what I mean."

"I do know," Marshall said, humor in his tone. "Like I mentioned, I have plenty of design plans to look at in my workshop. Come on by. That way you can narrow down the options to figure out what you want."

*He played right into my hands.* Excitement tingled in her chest. *I must be really good at this investigating thing,* she concluded. *He has no clue.*

"Do you know where I live?" came his next question.

"I've been there before, if you recall," she added brightly.

"Oh, that's right. With the two cops."

"One's a consultant," she corrected.

"I'll text the address anyway," Marshall said.

A niggle of warning returned. *Don't forget, if he's the guy, you could be his next victim...*

Avery pushed away her inner voice to settle on a time with Marshall. As soon as she hung up, she caught sight of Olivia walking across the bridge, carrying a bag of groceries. "I'll have lunch ready in fifteen minutes," she assured Avery. "Kinda late. I'm hungry."

"Okay. Thanks," Avery agreed. But she suspected her lunch would come with a side of lecture, Olivia style. She looked toward the mountain range to calm her nerves. Thoughts of her ultimate demise gave way to the distracting chatter of two squirrels arguing.

The sound of dishes clattering and the run of the faucet caught her attention. Putting her phone in her pocket, she made her way inside. She found toasted bread and sliced tomatoes set on a platter.

"The tomatoes smell fresh." Avery leaned closer to sniff.

Olivia assembled sandwiches with the same neat precision she brought to everything.

"Can I help?" Avery asked.

"I've got this. While I finish up, tell me what you've been up to. Looks like you went on an early morning hike. It must have been a good one, you were gone so long."

Avery moved to the sink, scrubbing her hands under the cool water. "Yeah, just up the ridge. The weather was perfect. I lingered longer than I expected to." She kept her tone breezy, recounting only the safe details: the hike, the blue sky. She left out the rest about Marshall and Meadow.

Drying her hands on a kitchen towel, she turned to Olivia with casual brightness. "When is your birthday, by the way? Inquiring minds and all that."

Most of the conversation over lunch was about Olivia's house, when Michael was due home, and how much they both loved Mayor Maguire.

"He's gone off again," Olivia said, looking toward the dog's usual spot at the front door.

Avery tapped her foot beneath the table. "Want help cleaning up?"

"Don't worry about it, I'll do it." Olivia rose, sliding plates into the sink. "You have other plans for the afternoon?"

"I'm going back into town." Avery kept her tone light. "Thought I'd get some cash from the ATM and shop around a bit." She glanced down at her trail-worn shorts. "Maybe find another pair of shorts."

"Good idea," Olivia said. She didn't look the least bit suspicious.

Avery made her way outside, exhaling with relief. It wasn't easy deceiving Olivia, and she felt guilty. Her host's intentions were so pure, anything less than completely honest felt like a slap to her face. But what had she said before? *Needs must.* Avery needed to keep Olivia in her own business. So she came up with a plan to block her out. She pretended to be normal and breezy, avoiding any questions about her feelings and telling half-truths where necessary.

The walk to Marshall's gave her time to clear her head and prepare for the next step of her investigation. Without Olivia and Janis hovering, micromanaging, and taking over, Avery felt free to use whatever was needed to get answers.

A waft of dust scattered dry leaves along the road. She looked down to avoid being blinded by the sun and quickened her pace.

The narrow lane to Marshall's home included a row of sagging mailboxes along one side. His cabin waited at the end of the path. The single-story house hardly felt welcoming. The weathered cedar siding looked ages old and in need of paint. Flashes of afternoon sun bounced off the tin roof.

*If I had a cabin like this, I'd make good use of that porch,* she thought, eyeing the wraparound redwood structure. A broom was braced against a rail close to the hot tub. She noted a new vinyl cover and a lever to lift the lid. A couple of faded towels hung over a branch, most likely left to dry.

*Marshall's workshop must be there.* She glanced toward an outbuilding, built to look like a wood-sided barn. The wide doors had been propped open.

Avery caught the scent of freshly cut lumber, noting a

table saw and a stack of boards. Marshall must have been busy already today.

A squirrel popped down from a branch, scurrying toward a tray filled with peanuts. He took one between his front paws and began to nibble. She watched with fascination the animal's precise way of shelling the outside to get to the good part. *Kinda like what I'm doing with my investigation,* she thought.

The screen door creaked open, and Avery spun around. Marshall stepped onto the deck, wiping his hands on a rag. His face lit when he spotted her. A genuine smile. Not what she expected. The squirrel chattered loudly from his branch. Finished with his nut, he looked around with wide eyes. *Maybe checking for a predator...*

"Well now," Marshall said, a chuckle underlying his tone. "It is you. I never know when I'm on the phone who I'm actually talking to. Where's your pack?" He pointed.

"Getting repaired," she said. "The cop calls me Backpack Betty. So I thought I'd get rid of the visual reminder. Melinda said to tell you hi," she added as an afterthought.

Marshall's eyes narrowed. "Never trust police," he said. "I can see you already know that. Good call."

She felt her connection with him, their mutual suspicion of authority. That did feel genuine.

"Come on then. I'll show you my workshop." Marshall gestured to the outbuilding.

The air inside was cool. "This is like a man cave," she commented.

He paused to consider her words. "My property is one giant man cave. Like in the old days, before men were marginalized by females who used their spare time to flood the economy and to overdecorate."

Now Avery knew they were connected. Not because

she necessarily agreed, but because he felt free to tell her his feelings.

"I bet you're one of those guys who keeps nuts and bolts in old coffee cans." She watched him closely.

"No use wasting anything," he grumbled. But his tone wasn't defensive.

Avery glanced at his workbench. Blueprints and sketches, randomly tacked to a corkboard, caught her attention. A birdhouse and a child-sized chair had been shoved to the far side of the bench. *Maybe projects waiting to be finished later*, she thought. *Making room for my request.*

"You'll have to excuse the mess," Marshall said. He gestured toward a three-ring binder propped against the wall. "That's my design catalog. Everything I've built in the past ten years is in there. Take a look, see what jumps out."

Her inner voice spoke up. *Hopefully not a firecracker, exploding in your face...*

Avery reached for the notebook and opened it slowly, giving herself a chance to slightly raise her gaze to take in the contents of a shelf. She wanted a clue, anything that would link him to Stella and Theo. Something that would explain why Marshall would go to such extremes to attack two of his neighbors.

Nothing of interest on the shelf. Just more screws and odd bits and pieces of electrical wires and switches from other projects.

He glanced her way, so she dropped her gaze.

"This is impressive," she said, flipping over another notebook page. She turned them slowly, giving herself a moment to consider her next move. *Play it cool*, she thought. *You're just another customer, commissioning a little library.*

One photo showed a cheerful red library with scalloped trim. Too cute. Olivia would hate that in front of her house.

Another displayed a sleek glass-fronted box. *That one's modern enough, with the black roof.*

She felt like Goldilocks, looking for the just right bowl of porridge. Avery chuckled under her breath. *Pick one already. It doesn't have to be "just right."* She forced a smile, pretending to study the book carefully. She felt him look toward her again.

He leaned against the bench, arms folded. "They're more than just boxes for books," he said. "They're a way of leaving a mark on your community. A sign you were here, that you care enough to build something that lasts. Your friend will appreciate the gift, I guarantee."

Avery ignored the prickle inching its way up her neck. "How about this one?" She pointed to the house with the glass front and the black roof. "It looks modern. Would you paint the post black too, or another color?"

Marshall's gaze narrowed. "Without seeing your friend's home, I won't be able to make that decision. Who is she, by the way? I can drive past her place, take a look, and let you know."

The air in the workshop shifted, heavy with sawdust and silence. Avery's heart gave a painful squeeze. Sooner or later she'd have to give up Olivia's address. But the thought of Marshall Reed pulling up outside her home made Avery's skin crawl.

*Careful, Avery,* she told herself. *Whatever you say next, it better be right.*

# CHAPTER TWENTY-SEVEN

Avery pasted on a thoughtful smile. "Maybe you should wait before you do a drive-by. I want to save the surprise. She might notice."

Marshall tilted his head, studying her for a moment, then gave a small shrug as if to say fair enough.

Avery leaned back against the workbench and tapped the page in the open binder. "I didn't realize that you were a legit carpenter, until I asked the librarian. Meadow told me. Oh, and she also mentioned your reading preferences since she knows I like sci-fi. Old-school science fiction like Bradbury, Heinlein, and Clarke."

"I guess the town librarian isn't a confidential source. So it's okay. What else did Meadow tell you?" An eyebrow rose.

"That you're the go-to for small jobs and little free libraries. That's why you were my first call." She tried to make her interest in him sound authentic, but she had to admit, to her ears she sounded like a nosy twit.

Before he could respond, she continued, "My dad used to read sci-fi out loud to me when I was a kid. Kind of our version of bedtime stories." She gave a small laugh. "Most girls were listening to fairy tales, I was hearing about rocket ships and strange new worlds. And then I started picking up my own books. *All American Boys* was a favorite. I read it over and over." She held her breath and waited for his response.

Marshall's expression warmed, the stern lines at his mouth giving way to a small smile. "That so? I'm not a fan of that one, but Heinlein... Not many people your age talk about the classics anymore. Everything's newer, flashier." His eyes drifted toward a stack of dog-eared paperbacks on another shelf. "There's something about those old stories. They made you think. Not just about the future but about who we are as humans."

"Exactly. My dad said they were a way of testing human character. Put people in strange situations, see what comes out."

Marshall chuckled softly, his hand brushing his mouth. "That's right. Strip away the ordinary, and you learn what people are really made of."

Though she kept her smile steady, she wasn't quite sure of his meaning. Was he talking about his books or about his distrust of other people?

She lifted a battered copy of *Fahrenheit 451* from the shelf. "I remember this one." Thumbing through the pages, she half hoped she'd find one of those ominous leaflets tucked inside. Not even a scrap of paper, not a bookmark. She slid it back with an inward groan.

Marshall bent his head to put away a few tools. He picked up a hand saw, then a screwdriver, inspecting each with a craftsman's patience. "I can get on this project right away if you'd like."

"Won't your other customers get impatient, the ones

before me?" She glanced toward the end of the bench, the child-sized chair half refinished.

He gave her a knowing smile. "I run on my own schedule. Making a little library from scratch takes precedence. Maybe someday I'll make one in the style of Bellemare. The architect up the hill. I'm sure it would be popular."

Avery's stomach tightened. *Does he know I'm staying with Olivia?*

She kept her tone deliberately flat. "I knew Michael Bellemare a while back. Haven't seen him since I returned to town." That much was true. She'd basically listened to Olivia on the phone talking to him but not actually set her eyes on the guy.

"That so?" Surprise flickered across his face.

"I was at the music academy," she quickly added, tossing the explanation out like a decoy. "Long story."

"Don't want to pry." His voice dropped as he turned back to his tools. The saw rasped against the wood as he shifted it into place, measuring and marking with careful precision.

Avery felt that his window of interest was closing, and that her opportunity for learning and finding clues might be over. She had one more question. "I was wondering..." She coughed in her hand. "I've been seeing these doomsday leaflets in town. Have you found any in your little library? My friend would hate that."

Marshall's hands froze. The change in him was sharp, like a push against her chest. He set down the pencil and met her eyes with a flat stare. "Not a church man," he said, his mouth twisting into a scowl. "An atheist. I don't believe in anything. Not heaven, not hell."

She instinctively stepped back, putting a few inches of

distance between them. "Oh, sorry. I didn't mean to upset you."

"Not upsetting me," he said, tone clipped but a notch calmer. "Just not my thing."

He didn't have to ask her to leave. The message was clear in the way he turned his back to her, shoulders hunched over the workbench. Each precise line that he drew on the board made her shudder. There was an anger underneath his moves. The tense body, the quick slash of the pencil. She suspected his anger could turn to fury in a quick second.

She cleared her throat. "Well, I'll let you get back to your work, then. Thanks for showing me the designs."

"Anytime," he said, not bothering to turn around.

"Do you need a down payment?" she asked.

He didn't look up. "When it's finished, I'll collect."

The dismissal stung, even though she told herself she didn't care. She eased toward the door, her footsteps muffled by the sawdust on the floor. The air outside hit her in a full rush of dry heat. She drew in a deep breath, grateful to leave.

On the walk down the drive, her pulse steadied. By the time she reached the road, she felt convinced. She'd come dangerously close to triggering Marshall's deeply held resentment. Next time, she'd have to be smarter.

# CHAPTER TWENTY-EIGHT

The steady hike back to Olivia's gave Avery a chance to assess what she'd learned. She knew she'd been right to keep Olivia's identity from Marshall. He was far too eager. And then his withdrawal when she brought up the doomsday leaflets spoke for itself.

*He had strong feelings about religion. That's for sure. Or did he resent me digging into him with more questions, no matter what they were? Maybe...*

Marshall was a reluctant survivalist, she concluded. He wanted to look like a guy who lived on the edge of society, but there was still a part of him that yearned for company. That smile when he first saw her felt genuine. He wasn't quite the loner he wanted people to think he was.

She felt her phone buzz. Avery tugged it from her back pocket. Another anonymous text. She read it, her hand shaking.

> Freedom isn't free, Avery. Bring a book worth fighting for.

She jammed the phone back into her pocket. *Whoever's*

*writing these wants me dangling on a string. And what book? Something from the library? One from Olivia's house?* The text unsettled her, especially coming right after her visit with Marshall.

*I have to pick a title*, she thought. *I need to be ready.* Without access to her own shelves, she felt lost. They'd been burned in the fire. The librarian might be willing to help her select one. But she didn't want to reveal the ominous texts and explain. She had to quell Meadow's persistent need to know for the sake of her own investigation.

At the fork in the path, Avery hesitated. The shortcut through the woods would drop her back at Olivia's door in no time. But town was her next stop. She sighed. Her legs carried her forward, past the pines and toward the main road.

The sun beat down on her shoulders, the heat pushing her onward. All she could think about was when she'd get the final summons to meet with the Syndicate. *Better get a book. No time to waste.*

The library was far from quiet. Unselfconscious laughter spilled from the children's section. Avery sidestepped as a woman maneuvered a stroller, nearly over her foot.

"Excuse me," Naomi Wells-Duran said briskly. "We're late for story hour." She rolled past without a glance back.

"Children." Meadow's voice carried above the bustle, calm but firm. "And caregivers. Please lower your voices. Take a seat over there." She pointed toward a semicircle of plastic child-sized chairs. Naomi drew the stroller close and folded herself into a chair with an audible sigh.

"I have a wonderful story for you this morning,"

Meadow said, her smile wide as she faced the group. The chatter softened into silence. She lowered herself into another child-sized chair, her denim jumper falling over her legs.

Meadow held up a picture book, its glossy cover shimmering in the light. "This is about a boy named Julián who knew he was a mermaid. Have any of you ever wished to be a mermaid?"

Tiny hands shot up, giggles breaking the hush before dissolving into expectant stillness. Meadow opened the book with reverence, her voice lilting as she explained, "The story is written by Jessica Love." She paused to scan her small audience. "And what do we call someone who writes a book?"

From her spot near the stacks, Avery's gaze drifted past the cheerful scene to the adults gathered. All were mothers, their faces softened by the moment, eyes following their children. Except for Naomi. Her lips were pursed, her gaze narrowed, suspicion etched deeply in her lined forehead. Naomi watched Meadow McCloud, her body leaning forward, ready to pounce.

Avery leaned against the end of a bookshelf. Questions pricked her mind. *What is Naomi's problem? Is it personal with Meadow? Or about the book she's reading?*

When Meadow finished the story she closed the book with a satisfied smile. "Now you can pick a book yourselves."

Naomi was already on her feet. She stepped past her stroller, the eyes of all the parents and children directed toward her.

"I'll take that," she said, plucking the book from Meadow's hands.

The librarian's mouth opened, caught by surprise.

Avery blinked. The children, who only moments before had been leaning in wide-eyed, let out a collective gasp. One little girl frowned and tugged on her mother's sleeve.

Naomi held *Julián Is a Mermaid* at arm's length, pinched between forefinger and thumb like a soiled rag. She glanced around the room, scanning the corners as if searching for a trash can.

Avery's mouth tightened. *It's the book. She wants it gone.*

Meadow's smile didn't waver. She reached to rescue the book from Naomi's grasp. "Ms. Wells-Duran," she said gently, her voice carrying just enough steel to quiet the room. "This book belongs to the library's collection. It's here for the children and parents, and it will remain available to them."

A hush fell, the children's curious eyes darting from Meadow to Naomi and back to Meadow. She shifted her gaze to them, her tone softening. "And of course, anyone is welcome to borrow it properly. The way we do with all of our books."

Meadow turned to her cart. Her fingers lingered for a moment on the bright cover. Then she slid the book on the top shelf. Hands smoothed her jumper as she continued, her tone nearly a whisper. "Stories are for everyone," she said. "And this one especially deserves to be shared."

Naomi's mouth tightened, but she didn't argue. She leaned over the stroller to check on her sleeping child.

*Is she embarrassed?* Avery wondered. *I would be.*

Avery felt a ripple of admiration for Meadow. How she'd stood her ground, firm and professional without raising her voice.

Avery lingered near the shelves as Meadow took a

moment to wander among the children and parents. She'd stop to point to a book. In some cases she'd ask a question about the story.

Those who weren't looking at books worked diligently on paper coloring sheets. Tiny chairs scraped across the floor, the murmur of parents rose and fell. A few books lay abandoned on the carpet.

Once Meadow answered the last trickle of questions with her usual patience, the children's section emptied. Only then did the librarian acknowledge Avery with a tired but genuine smile.

"Hello, dear. Quite the kerfuffle, wasn't it? All over such a beautiful book." She stacked the last of the chairs with practiced ease. "My job as librarian has taken on new meaning in these turbulent times. Everyone wants our shelves filled only with the stories they personally approve. I have to be very careful. Emotions fly when I least expect them."

She gave a little wave to the final mother rolling a stroller toward the exit, then scanned the quiet room as if reassuring herself the storm had passed for now.

Avery repeated Meadow's words again in her mind. *"Everyone wants our shelves filled only with the stories they personally approve."*

*That text,* Avery thought, her pulse quickening. *Freedom isn't free. Bring a book worth fighting for.*

Was there a connection?

She cleared her throat. "You handled that really well," she said, keeping her tone casual. "Naomi didn't seem thrilled about mermaids."

Meadow's smile flickered, then steadied. "No, she didn't. But it isn't my job to filter the world into tidy little boxes.

Children are smarter than most people give them credit for." She began gathering the stray picture books, stacking them with care.

Avery followed her to the cart, lowering her voice. "What about the adults who don't want certain books available in the local library? Do you ever feel like you're..." She hesitated, searching for the right word. "Fighting for something bigger than story hour?"

Meadow's hands paused on the stack, her expression unreadable. For a heartbeat, Avery thought she'd overstepped again, like with Marshall.

Finally Meadow said softly, "There are always people who believe freedom is theirs to define. That's when other people have to step in and remind them it belongs to everyone."

Avery's breath caught. *Freedom. There it is again. The same word as the text.*

"So," she continued, "if a group of folks wanted to form, let's say, a secret club talking about books, would you be concerned?"

Meadow's eyes lifted to hers, sharp now, a hint of something cautious and knowing. She didn't answer the question right away. Instead she slid more books onto the cart. "That would depend," she said quietly. "I know there's a secret syndicate in Lily Rock. They're very exclusive; they invite people with a formal invitation." She stared into Avery's eyes. The unspoken question lay between them. *Meadow wants to know if I've been invited.*

Avery reached into her pocket and pulled out her phone, holding the screen toward Meadow. "Like this one, maybe?" she said softly.

Meadow gasped and her eyes widened. She pressed a

hand briefly to her throat, then gave a small, firm nod of her head. "Yes. I think you've received a formal invitation by text."

The gesture and words were enough. No explanation, no elaboration. All Avery could feel in the moment was Meadow's concern for her safety.

# CHAPTER TWENTY-NINE

Avery lingered outside the library, still hearing the echo of Meadow's sharp gasp in her ears. She didn't select her book, wanting to get away before the librarian asked any more questions.

One step into the street and she felt a chill up her spine. There was a commotion in the redwood park. She hurried across, watching paramedics in white jumpsuits gather in front of a bench.

A red-and-white ambulance was parked nearby. No lights, no siren. Janis Jets's voice barked, "Stand back, everyone. Police business." Arms folded, she watched the EMTs do their job.

From a distance, Avery saw a woman seated on a bench, her torso bent forward, head between her knees. Her silver-streaked curls spilled loosely around her hands. One paramedic crouched low, speaking gently, while another checked her pulse. Avery strained to hear but caught nothing above the traffic hum.

At last the woman lifted her face, eyes blinking.

Avery's pulse quickened. *That's Cordelia. What now? Another accident, another victim?*

She crossed the street to stand next to a giant sequoia. The romance author wobbled to her feet, while both paramedics took an elbow. Jets continued to observe, her eyes falling on Avery. She gave a quick shake of her head as if to warn her off.

*I guess she doesn't want me to come any closer*, Avery thought. *Fat chance.*

She glanced around and spotted an unoccupied bench. Once seated, she'd be able to catch most of what Cordelia and the paramedics talked about. She leaned her back against the bench slats, trying to look casual, one leg crossed over the other.

"Ma'am, can you tell me your name?" A paramedic asked.

Cordelia's hand fluttered at the neck of her shirt. "My name... Oh, it's right there, just at the tip of my tongue." Her voice trembled.

Everything about Cordelia reminded Avery of a faded flower. Not in her prime, but unwilling to let go of the last bloom.

"Do you know where you are?" the other paramedic prodded.

Cordelia squinted up at the trees, then toward the horizon. "A church picnic?" she guessed, a little laugh escaping. "No, no, that's not right. Silly me. My daughter will be worried that I'm late."

Avery frowned. *Daughter? That's news...*

Janis's voice came next. "Cordelia, it's Janis Jets. You were seen dancing and twirling in the middle of the street. Blocking traffic. Do you remember that?"

"Oh, really?" She turned her head away as if searching

for an answer. Finally she spoke. "That doesn't sound like me. I must have been consumed by my muse. I lose track of time and space when that happens. Must mean a new book is coming soon. I'm an author, you know." She reached into the tote bag and held up a book. "I'm leaving this one with Meadow McCloud. They're very popular."

The paramedics exchanged a glance, murmuring too softly for Avery to catch their words.

Cordelia looked so small compared to the bulky first responders. So frail and bewildered. And yet something about the scene didn't add up for Avery. The quick shift in Cordelia's voice, the way she seemed to pull herself back into focus when it came to her book sales. To Avery, when she held up the book, she'd looked calculating and very focused.

*Is dementia like that?* Avery wondered. *In one minute, out the next?*

She didn't envy Cordelia. She felt concern and a tingle of pity. If the romance author was losing her mind to her muse, that was one thing. But to forget where she was and dance in the middle of a busy street... Maybe there were no more books in her future. And that would be hard to accept for a previously well-known author who made a living writing and selling.

Avery sat still, arms folded tight, watching the paramedics help the older woman to her feet. Somewhere above, a crow gave a harsh scolding cry.

Avery tipped her head back. The dark silhouette of a black bird darted from branch to branch. The sound, the caw, unsettled her, as if the crow warned her: Mind your own business.

. . .

Avery left the scene without a backward glance. She made it to Olivia's and walked the footbridge, her boots scuffing against the wood planks. The smell of rosemary and lemon drifted from the kitchen. Her stomach rumbled as she stepped inside.

Olivia stood at the stove, apron dusted with flour, humming softly as she stirred a pan. "Perfect timing," she said without turning. "I was about to call you. Dinner's almost ready."

Avery moved toward the counter, reaching automatically for the spoon. "Want me to finish that?" she offered.

Olivia slid the spoon deftly out of reach, her tone brisk but not unkind. "No, no. You've been gone all day. Sit. I've got this."

"I picked up groceries. I wanted to do dinner," Avery said.

"I saw the chicken. I used it as the main dish."

Avery forced a smile and slid into a chair. What a day. The texts. Meadow's response to them. Marshall's barely disguised anger, Cordelia's frail body bent over on the bench.

"You've been baking." Avery kept her voice light.

"Roasted chicken, biscuits, and rosemary potatoes." Olivia lifted the pan from the burner, setting it on a trivet. Then she glanced over her shoulder, her eyes a little too knowing. "Janis called me. Said she saw you in town this afternoon. Lurking in the trees to watch the paramedics."

Avery's pulse skipped. She laced her fingers together on the table. "Yeah," she said carefully. "It has been a long day."

# CHAPTER THIRTY

Dinner ended with the soft clatter of forks and a comfortable lull in conversation. When the dishes were stacked to dry, Olivia's phone buzzed. She glanced at the screen, her face brightening.

"It's Michael," she said, lifting the phone to her ear. "I'll take it in the other room." Her smile carried both an apology and obvious delight.

Avery felt a prick of envy at the sound of Olivia's hushed laughter. She was happy for her, truly. Olivia was the best. But the idea of her so effortlessly paired off with a perfect partner left a quick, uninvited pang of jealousy. *If only I had someone like Michael...*

For a moment, she allowed herself to think about Brad. His crooked grin, the way he'd steadied her backpack that time. Avery exhaled sharply, annoyed. She wasn't ready for that kind of connection, she reminded herself. A relationship like Olivia's and Michael's. Good for them, but that wasn't for her—not right now.

What she felt was longing for something that symbolized a grown-up life. But she wanted hers to be solo. Not dependent on another person's expectations.

When Olivia's voice dropped to a low whisper, Avery stopped listening to give them privacy. She took her mug of tea and settled outside in one of the barrel chairs. The mountains stood dark and jagged against the sky, scattered with early stars. Crickets rasped from the shrubs, their rhythm both soothing and insistent.

It had not escaped her notice that since her arrival, she felt more attuned to nature. Birds and squirrels. More frequent glances toward the mountains and Lily Rock. She sipped slowly, welcoming the calm of the evening that settled over her rough skin and frayed nerves. *Is observing nature a skill or just something that comes with the welcome-to-Lily-Rock package?*

She didn't have an answer, mostly because other thoughts took over as soon as she asked. *Freedom isn't free, Avery. Bring a book worth fighting for.*

She ran one finger over the rim of the mug. *What book would I even choose? And why does it feel like the choice matters to me?*

Then Olivia's laugh floated out to the patio, warm and easy. *Michael must have said something funny*, she thought. Tilting her head back to see the stars, she felt a pang of loneliness, something she rarely faced.

Between the safety of Olivia's house and the darkness filling the night sky, she wondered, *Do people couple up just to avoid being alone?*

The sound of Olivia's bright laughter came as an answer.

*People couple up because they belong. They're better together than apart.*

She blinked. The book. An obvious choice. She'd just

been talking about it. Pushing away her thoughts about Michael and Olivia, she tried to recollect when she'd first heard about that particular story.

One summer at the beach, one very long hot summer. A friend recommended it, her high school boyfriend. "There are two authors," he explained, running a finger down her arm, staring toward the waves.

Avery shivered. His touch had felt amazing. But back to the book. *What were the authors' names?* She frowned, thinking of Meadow asking the children what we call someone who writes a book.

Jason Reynolds and...Brendan Kiely. They were co-authors of *All American Boys*. A *New York Times* bestseller. The first time she'd read it, long after breaking up with the boyfriend, it felt like a gut punch.

A year later, she read it again. This time it left her unsettled for weeks.

A story about a white kid, a bystander who saw his best friend's older brother beating a Black classmate senseless. The protagonist recorded it on his phone instead of stepping in.

Quinn was forced to ask himself an important life-altering question, one Avery could still hear echoing in her mind: *What side of history do I want to stand on?*

She drew in a slow breath. Her copy of *All American Boys* had burned in the Palos Verdes fire. But her memory of how unsettled she'd felt by that question still lingered.

By the time Olivia joined her, Avery had a huge smile on her face.

"Michael says hi," Olivia said, settling into the other barrel chair. "He wanted to know if you still answer to Elf Two."

"Did you tell him I've graduated? I'm now Backpack Betty. I bet he cracked up."

"Actually," Olivia said, her voice light, "he said he couldn't imagine you backpacking. Not the teen he used to know. He thought you'd be, at the very least, an actress on television. What with your connections. And your parents."

"Did he really?" She hadn't realized she'd ever given off that vibe. Her jaw tightened. "I'm no nepo baby," she said, sharper than she intended.

Olivia chuckled softly, unbothered. "Apparently not. He'll be home soon to see for himself. You can tell him then."

Avery dropped her gaze to the tea mug, aware of an old irritation. As if the shadow of her parents followed her everywhere. Inescapable reminders of their public lives. They'd wanted a different daughter. One who was polished. Who delivered effortless performances, a daughter who mirrored their ambitions.

*Not in my lifetime.* She felt a painful lump in her throat.

But what surprised her was the return of anger at Michael's words. He saw her as someone she'd tried desperately not to be. Some pampered kid with a safety net. *Do I give off that vibe?*

Avery glanced at Olivia, who was sipping her tea, looking toward the mountains. *She's beautiful*, Avery realized. *No wonder Michael loves her. Thoughtful. Scary insightful. Generous. Willing to open her home to a complete stranger*.

"Backpack Betty suits me better than Elf Two," she said with a small smile. But what she didn't add, what pressed just beneath her ribs, was that she was ready to make a few changes. Even if she didn't quite know where to start.

. . .

The next morning, Avery sat at the kitchen counter, sipping her second cup of coffee. A sharp rap came from the front door.

She half expected to see Olivia, back from her morning errands. But when she opened the door, she found Janis Jets, arms crossed, her uniform freshly pressed. At her side, Mayor Maguire was like a picture-perfect labradoodle, sitting at her knee, tail waving in the air with a greeting.

"I have a few questions for you, Backpack Betty." Janis strode inside without being invited. Maguire trotted behind, then made a quick turn, as if he'd forgotten something. He circled and leaned into Avery's leg.

She patted his head, confused by him and by Jets's early morning momentum.

"What were you doing in the park yesterday?" Janis demanded. "Lurking behind trees like some kind of *Harriet the Spy*."

Avery smoothed Maguire's curls, stalling. "I was resting after a long hike. Isn't that what parks are for?"

The dog looked up. She knew instantly why he'd changed his mind. *He's protecting me from the cop.*

Janis's eyes narrowed. "Isn't it obvious that you need to stay away when paramedics are hovering, and the town's constable doesn't want you hanging around? Have you no sense?"

Avery forced a smile. The Maguire magic worked. No longer nervous, she changed the subject. "Who's *Harriet the Spy* anyway?"

"She was a fictional character and a personal favorite when I was young." Janis's eyes softened. "She had this notebook..." A slight nostalgic smile came to the cop's lips. "Wrote down everything about everyone in her neighborhood. No detail was too small. If Mrs. Plumber wore two different shoes to the corner store, Harriet had it logged by noon."

Avery chuckled. "I never take notes. Not even in school. I remember everything." She tapped the side of her head with her forefinger.

Jets scoffed, eyes narrowed with skepticism.

Avery continued. "Plus it sounds like Harriet was bored. She needed a hobby or to join an after-school sports team."

"Snooping *was* her hobby," Janis said, defending her heroine. "And she was good at it. A real inspiration for girls like me who didn't...quite fit in."

Avery felt surprise. Jets seemed so confident. For one brief second, she identified with the cop—the not fitting in part.

Jets nodded and smiled, making Avery fidget. *Is she actually showing me her vulnerable side?*

Then the cop cleared her throat. "Harriet was trouble just like you. Now that I think about it, she was always turning up when she wasn't supposed to, asking questions and noticing things that other people missed." Her eyes narrowed again, this time as if she was thinking.

Avery shifted from foot to foot. She preferred the crusty side of Janis, that was much easier to deal with. "Don't forget I wouldn't be caught dead with a notebook. Someone might think I was introspective. So not me!"

She waved her palms in front of her face as if shooing away flies.

"You don't carry a notebook *yet*," Jets speculated. She gave Avery a once-over. "Yeah, that's it. I have you pegged now. You're Harriet 2.0. All the nosiness, none of the stationery."

Avery laughed despite herself. "I'm not sure if that's flattering or insulting."

"Take it however you want. But stay away next time. Read the room already."

"You mean the outdoor public park where I can linger whenever I want," Avery corrected.

"You know what I'm saying," grumbled Jets. She took a deep breath. "Olivia usually feeds the mutt when he shows up. Why don't you get to that." She pointed to Maguire. "Is she around?" Jets glanced over her shoulder.

"I think she went for a walk. Can I give her a message?" Avery looked Jets over, realizing this wasn't a friendly visit. "Did something come up on the case?"

Maguire gave a short impatient bark. He trotted toward the walk-in pantry and sat down, his nose aimed at the handle.

"Good morning." Olivia walked into the kitchen wearing Bermuda-length shorts and a bright red T-shirt with a logo that said "Trouble" in bold black letters. She patted Maguire on the head. "Hey, buddy. I'll be right with you."

"I was just going to feed the mayor," Avery said. "Nice shirt."

"Long story," Olivia answered. Then she nodded at Janis. "The fancy Frenchie people left town without clearing out their warehouse. Lots of shirts were auctioned at Paws and Pines. I can get you one if you'd like."

"I need to talk to you," Janis interjected.

"Go ahead," Olivia said. "There isn't anything Avery doesn't already know. It's about the case, right? Have you heard from Forensics?"

"That's right." Jets sat down at the counter. "While

Avery over there makes me coffee, I'll tell you the details." She scrolled on her phone as Olivia smiled. She turned her back to Janis to catch Avery's eye. Lowering her chin, she pointed to her shirt.

Both women laughed. Trouble about summed it up.

# CHAPTER THIRTY-ONE

Jets slid her coffee mug across the counter toward Avery. "Your turn to fill me up," she said dryly.

Avery topped it off and set it back down.

Jets had not revealed the reason for her visit yet. Finally she cleared her throat. "I've got some information. Stella, like I suspected, died of a heart attack. According to Forensics, her unfortunate demise was a result of a wrong place, wrong time kinda thing. She had no reason to believe a firecracker would go off near her little library, so there's that."

"Just a coincidence?" Avery asked.

"Not relevant," Jets replied flatly. "Dodgy ticker. Her doctor confirmed it. Wouldn't have taken much."

Olivia leaned in. "And Theo? Any connection between him and Stella?"

"Not that we could find." Jets took a sip of hot coffee. "We did a search history on his computer. More religious stuff than anything. A little dip into an ancestry account. But nothing that connects him to Stella.

"He fell through a couple of weak boards on the deck. Likely termite damage, years of weathering. There was a bash on his head, likely caused in the fall. The entire shower head and the rest of the apparatus fell apart and landed with him."

She set her mug down with finality. "Both cases closed."

Avery pressed her lips together, a retort on the tip of her tongue. It felt like Jets was giving up.

Janis now stared at Avery.

"Look, Harriet 2.0. None of that. I see your look of skepticism. Don't start seconding-guessing the professionals. You should be glad you're off my person-of-interest list. That's what matters. It's time to get on with your life. Pack your duds and catch up with the rest of your hiking pals."

She rose, brushing imaginary crumbs from her uniform. "Gotta go. Tater Tot expects me for lunch." Her gaze flicked to the mayor, who had curled himself on top of Avery's feet. "Want me to drive Maguire back into town?"

"Bork," Maguire answered, rising to all fours.

Avery's hand drifted to pat his head. "I'll walk him in later. I have a few errands and he can keep me company."

Maguire lay back down.

"Fine," Jets answered. "You have anything to say?" She looked over at Olivia, who'd remained oddly silent over the news.

"Nope." Olivia smiled.

With a quick glance and a shrug, Jets headed toward the door.

Avery wondered if Olivia would talk to her about what they'd learned once the cop had left. When she didn't speak, Avery broke the silence.

"I have more errands in town..." she said, her voice trailing away.

Olivia spoke over her shoulder. "More errands? I thought you'd be done by now."

There was something in her detached tone that made Avery wonder. *She isn't interested in the investigation anymore. She doesn't think I am either.* Or maybe it was just that Michael was coming home by the end of the week. The two of them probably wanted time alone. Was Olivia hoping Avery would take Janis's advice and get back to the PCT?

"I am, as a matter of fact, going to pick up my gear," Avery said. "One more night, then I'll hit the trail. That okay with you?"

"You're welcome to stay as long as you want." Olivia smiled.

*Sure, she'd say that. But does she mean it?*

Mayor Maguire padded alongside as she headed to the door. Avery bent to scratch under his chin. "At least I have you, Maguire. Oh, and Sparkles. And Tater Tot. He's pretty cool too." She remembered how the Frenchie had curled up in her lap. He'd taken care of her in the truck that evening, after she found Stella.

On the walk into town, Maguire stuck to her side, matching her stride for stride. His head lifted high, his gait almost regal. Cars that passed by waved at them both.

"You're quite the politician," Avery said. "Everybody loves you."

He glanced up, tongue lolling to one side, with a wide-eyed delighted look.

"Who wouldn't?" she muttered, fishing a bone-shaped treat from her pocket. She held it up. "Look at this. I raided Olivia's stash. Does this make us bonded for life?"

She tossed the dog cookie in an arc. Maguire grabbed it with one bite.

Once they reached town, Avery held up another dog treat for his inspection. He sat on his haunches, eyes locked on the prize. She tossed it right as a voice called from the other side of the street.

Fran Wells-Duran waved a shopping bag dangling from her arm. Her grin warm, her eyes darting between Avery and Mayor Maguire. She crossed the street. "I got the morning off from babysitting," Fran explained. "Want to have an early lunch? I was heading to Thyme Out."

Avery bit the inside of her lip. Fran was being extra friendly. She looked at Maguire with a raised eyebrow, as if asking his opinion.

"Bork," he replied.

"He reads my mind," she explained to Fran, not mentioning her doubts.

"Not surprising," Fran said. "You know everyone thinks he's psychic, at least everyone in Lily Rock, that is. But I've got to say, the mayor rarely stops by my place. Maybe because I'm a cat person."

Avery knew that animals had always liked her. She liked them too. Not just dogs but all kinds. She had an instinct for what animals were feeling. They spoke her language. But the connection with Maguire, it was next level.

"Come on," Fran said. "There will be dog bones and lots of schmoozing at the bakery. The mayor can work the room while we chat."

"Sure. Why not." Avery nodded to Maguire. He led the way to Thyme Out.

Fran kept chatting. "I have a couple of hair products for you to try. Salesman brought me samples this week and I thought, Avery would be a good candidate. They're small enough to slip into your backpack to keep your hair moisturized for the trail." Fran fluffed her own curls to make her point.

*Fascinating*, Avery thought, hearing it said just like in the old Star Trek series she had watched with her dad. Fran was the third person that morning who wanted her to leave.

When they stopped in front of the bakery, Fran reached over to run her fingers through Avery's loose hair. "The cut took off the dry ends, but now you have to apply a mask and massage your scalp."

Slightly embarrassed, Avery looked away. She wasn't used to having her hair journey assessed in public.

"Sorry." Fran dropped her arm. "I forget not everyone wants to talk hair all the time. Professional problem. Let's go in, shall we?"

The two women sat at an empty table on the back patio. Maguire left them to go back inside. "He's looking for more treats," Avery explained.

The server arrived with a menu. They ordered iced tea and salads. When the server returned with their order, Fran leaned closer and lowered her voice.

"I like it here in Lily Rock." She paused to spear a cherry tomato in her salad. "But since Nancy, things have changed. For one, Naomi isn't the same person she used to be. At first, she loved the small-town atmosphere. She thought it suited her and that Lily Rock was the perfect place to bring up a child.

"But I heard about that scene at the library. Naomi has..." She paused to look up. "Developed strong opinions about everything. It's like she's fighting for her own fantasy life, not what's real and in front of her. She wants the world to be a safe place, especially for Nancy. I mean, there's a shadow side no matter where you live. Not just the big cities.

"I've noticed her opinions come out most strongly when

it comes to books. But especially about what books belong in the hands of children."

Fran had mentioned her wife during the haircut, but this confession had a different tone; it merged on anger, sounding dry and opinionated.

"I saw Naomi at the library. She practically got into a knock-down with Meadow, at least by library standards. Has she always been ready for a fight?"

Fran gave a humorless laugh. "Not always. Naomi used to be passionate, sure, but it was the kind of passion that inspired people. Lately..." She shook her head. "It's turned sharp. It feels like she's out to win, no matter the cost."

Avery sipped her tea. "I can be passionate about causes," she admitted, "given the right inspiration and push-back."

Fran leaned in a little more. "But are you dangerous? I've seen Naomi go after teachers and parents like they were enemies instead of neighbors. If someone crosses her the wrong way..." She let the words trail off, but the implication hung between them.

Fran's warning left her with a chill. But Avery kept her expression neutral.

The truth was, she didn't like being dragged into a couple's quarrel. Her parents had put her in the middle growing up. One of the string of therapists had told her that was inappropriate, so she learned to walk away whenever it seemed to be happening again.

She forced herself back into the conversation with a safer topic. "I heard they're no longer investigating Stella's or Theo's deaths. According to Officer Jets."

Fran blinked, her lips tightening before she forced a smile. "Is that so?" She got a faraway look in her eyes. "Honestly, I miss Theo. We'd talk when he came in for a trim.

Which wasn't often. He liked that shaggy I-don't-give-a-damn look. He was...interesting."

"I met Theo on the trail," Avery said. "Didn't even know he lived in town. He showed me the dead drop library. Pretty creative idea, hikers swapping books."

Fran gave a small laugh. "I heard about that."

Avery felt a prickle. "I saw the same book at his place. *The Giving Tree*. Odd, don't you think? That's a children's book."

Fran's fingers tightened around her glass. "Not really. He told me once that he was adopted. He spent time trying to find his parents, but the records were sealed. The topic came up when I mentioned how we conceived Nancy using Naomi's egg, a sperm donor, and a surrogate.

"Theo had a lot of feelings about being adopted and never fitting in. Wanting to know who his biological parents were, their particular circumstances. He liked books about mothers and unconditional love. That other favorite one of his, *Are You My Mother?* He collected used copies and put them in all the little free libraries around town."

"So that explains his interest," Avery said. "But a grown man obsessing over children's books... I just don't know. Makes me feel uneasy."

Fran shifted in her seat. "Those books mattered to him." She looked aside, making Avery wonder, *Why won't she meet my gaze?*

Avery pushed harder with the next question. "Did children's books matter because he was adopted?"

"And because he'd searched, but never found his biological parents. I got the impression that he felt he couldn't grow up until he finally got his answers and connected with one of his bio parents." Fran's jaw set.

"Maybe that's why he kept to himself," Avery said. "Kind of a loner."

Fran let out a too-bright laugh. "The tree house was a cool place. I went up there a couple of times. And that shower..." Her eyes lit up. "Stripping down under the stars, water pouring over you. Tell me that's not the dream."

Avery's eyebrows lifted. She wondered if Fran and Theo might have had a romantic connection. Had they shared that shower?

# CHAPTER THIRTY-TWO

"Time for me to get a few of my errands done," Avery said as the server cleared their table.

Fran glanced over both shoulders before lowering her voice. "So I was wondering... Now that the cops aren't so interested in Stella's death, do you suppose they've taken down the crime tape?"

Avery felt a catch in her throat. Why would she care about Stella's place?

"I guess they could have," Avery said thoughtfully. She softened her tone, doing her best to imitate Olivia's easy way with people. "Other than being an eyesore, why would that matter?"

Fran hesitated but then explained, "I want to have a look inside Stella's house. She has a book I lent her, and I'd like it back."

"Oh, I see." But Avery didn't really. Despite their easy lunch, she still felt suspicious. Getting caught at Stella's house would be an unnecessary risk, mostly for her. She kept her expression mild. "Must be a valuable book," she said, dangling the comment like bait.

"Not valuable but sentimental," Fran admitted. "A copy of *Little Women* by Louisa May Alcott. My mother gave it to me when I was little, and she wrote in the front. You can understand why I'd want it back."

Avery managed a smile. "I read that one high school. Jo March, what a character. Feisty, independent."

"I've always identified more with Meg," Fran said with a small blush.

Tilting her head, Avery studied her.

Meg, the more compliant older sister, easily dazzled by wealth? That didn't quite fit. From what she'd seen, Fran had more bite than blush, more steel than sweetness. The mismatch felt off, like a person trying to be someone she wasn't.

"Does your wife have money?" she asked before she could stop herself.

Fran's cheeks flamed. "She does, actually. She ran a marketing business when we met. Sold it for millions before we moved to Lily Rock. When we got married, I had to sign a prenup."

"Excuse me, ladies." The server held out one hand, her other holding a tablet. "If you're finished, I'll take the check. We've got folks waiting."

"I'll take care of it." Fran reached for her purse.

Avery smiled. "I'll pay next time. I've got to go. I hope you get your book back."

Fran waved goodbye as the server took her credit card and ran it through the card reader.

Avery slipped past the back gate into the alley. She only got a few steps before she heard Fran's voice call after her. "Why don't we go together—swing by Stella's place, see if the cops are gone?"

She stopped in her tracks. "But we don't have a key." She turned to find Fran behind her.

Avery knew full well she did have one, but she wondered what Fran would say.

"Don't worry. I've got my own. Stella handed out keys like candy. I could use the moral support..." Her expression changed to hopeful.

"What about the cops?" Avery asked.

"That Jets is a pain." Fran grimaced.

"Rough-edged," Avery admitted with a laugh. "If you don't mind driving me, I'm in. Let's go see Stella's."

They headed down the alley together, the conversation drifting back to books. Avery mostly listened, unable to shake the feeling that Fran had another reason, besides *Little Women*, for visiting Stella's house.

A short drive up the hill and they saw for themselves—the crime scene tape had been removed. But to Avery's surprise, the little free library had already been repaired.

The wood siding had been sanded, ready for a fresh coat of paint. The door hung evenly, the toggle securing it closed. The post was new, made of redwood.

Inside, a few paperbacks had been stacked neatly, almost too neatly, their spines lined up like soldiers awaiting inspection.

Fran gave a low whistle. "Well that was fast. Already fixed and stocked."

Avery's stomach tightened. She suspected that Marshall Reed had done the work. It had his look. Neat. Tidy. At-the-ready.

Fran's key to the front door turned with a soft click. She walked inside first, followed by Avery. The cottage, light and airy, smelled like a fresh breeze, a hint of freesia in the air.

Avery stood in the center of the living room, feeling as if something were off. *I know*, she thought. *Has Stella's place been staged?*

Fran brushed past, flicking on a lamp.

The couch pillows were plumped. A coffee table held magazines strewn in a decorative array across the glass. Avery's neck tingled. Right in the center of the table was a copy of *Are You My Mother?*, open as if someone had just been reading to a child.

Fran frowned. "That's odd. Stella wasn't one to leave books lying around."

Avery slid her hand across the open pages. She closed it carefully. That book had something to do with Stella's death, she felt quite certain.

They moved into the kitchen, where mugs lined the shelf in perfect order. The counter gleamed, recently wiped clean. Only one thing was out of place: a chipped coffee mug in the sink.

Even before the investigation, Avery often paid attention to what was posted on anyone's refrigerator. Sure enough, she tugged out a paper pinned beneath a magnet. A receipt from the library to return *Julián Is a Mermaid.*

This affirmed Avery's impression of Stella, that she was more like Meadow in her choice of books. She slipped the receipt back under the magnet with a sigh.

*Time to look at the room*, she thought. She wandered down the hall, turning in to Stella's study. She found Fran looking out the window, a sad expression on her face. "You okay?" Avery asked.

Fran turned. "Sure. Fine. I liked Stella, that's all. I miss her."

"Look at this." Avery glanced toward the desk, where a

pen lay on top of a pad of lined paper. She glanced around the room. Unlike the rest of the house, this space felt lived in. Papers on the desk. Books leaning on the shelves in no particular order. The curtain over the window hung in uneven folds.

"The living room and kitchen feel staged. Maybe they haven't gotten to the rest. Looks like Stella was writing a letter." She pointed to the paper. "My last will and testament," Avery read aloud.

Fran came to look over her shoulder. "Maybe she got interrupted," Fran suggested quietly.

"Did Stella know she was going to die?" Avery frowned. "That would put a whole new spin on things. Or maybe she had a premonition." Tears wet her lashes. *Poor Stella.*

Fran rubbed her eyes with the back of her hand. "Don't you start," she said, trying to sound playful.

Avery pulled open one drawer, then another. She flipped through old bills and greeting cards. But it wasn't until the last drawer that she saw the leaflets. At least a dozen. She grabbed them to have a closer look. The one on top had a message.

*We have to stop this now. He's gone too far.*

She didn't recognize the writing, but she felt a shudder. The strong black lines of a pencil. Whoever wrote it had intense feelings. Were they warning Stella or asking for her help?

Fran hovered in the doorway. "We'd better go," she said. "I have my book."

"You said she handed out keys like candy," Avery muttered, easing the drawer closed. She glanced toward the bed, where the quilt lay folded.

Underneath on the nightstand, there was another copy

of *Are You My Mother?* She reached for the book. *Two copies of the same book in Stella's house...*

She stretched to the back of the nightstand drawer and pulled out an old photo of a baby swaddled in a knitted blanket, lying in the middle of a bed. The quilt was the same as the one on Stella's.

Avery read aloud from the looped script, "Summer, 1990."

"A baby?" Fran's voice caught.

She put the photo back, feeling guilty for invading the dead woman's privacy.

"I'm going to have a quick look in the guest room," she told Fran. "Then we can go."

They found a trash bag on the bed, marked by masking tape with "Donations" written across it in black ink. Avery untied the bag to look inside.

There were multiple used copies of *Are You My Mother?* and *The Giving Tree.*

Fran blinked. "Why would anyone collect so many copies of the same books?"

Avery's skin prickled. The books were evidence. Stella may not have collected them; maybe someone dropped them off, hoping she'd pay attention. Stella was kind to a fault.

"Let's go," she said, retying the bag. "I feel like I'm stepping on someone's grave."

Fran needed no coaxing. She was the first to reach for the door.

"Actually, give me another minute." Avery kneeled to look at the other books in the basket she'd seen the last time she came. Two paperback popular mysteries, two Sudoku books, and a familiar title at the bottom. *All American Boys.* She held it in her hand. *Should I take this?*

It didn't feel right to take anything from Stella's house. So she returned it to the basket as Fran opened the door. They walked in silence to the van.

# CHAPTER THIRTY-THREE

By the time Fran dropped her back in town, Avery had formulated her next move. Find more clues to connect Theo with Stella. The photo of the baby on the same quilt as Stella's and his search for his birth parents couldn't be a coincidence. That meant she needed to visit the tree house for more clues.

If Theo had left behind anything—a scrap of paperwork, an email on his laptop, even a stray note—it might clarify what they meant to each other. She couldn't shake the image of the children's books scattered throughout Stella's house, and the thought that someone had been trying to start a conversation with those handwritten messages.

Since the tree house was a favorite stopover for hikers, Avery suspected the owner wouldn't let it sit empty for long. Once it was scrubbed and reoccupied, any trace of Theo, any hint of what he'd been chasing, would be gone.

*If I'm going to find answers, I'd better move fast.*

. . .

She tipped her head back, holding her hand over her eyes to block the sun. The crime tape had been removed. That was a relief.

Without the police and paramedics swarming around, she had a better opportunity to look more closely at the construction. The sealed joints, the tight planking, the way the rope ladder hung, sturdy and strong. *Good bones*, she chuckled. *That's what they say on all the home restoration shows.*

She tested the first rung of the ladder with her foot. Just because she'd gone up one time before, that didn't mean it hadn't been sabotaged. That was the lesson of the shower, and Avery wasn't one to forget.

Once she'd tested the ladder again and found it safe, she began her climb. By the time she hoisted herself onto the landing, her palms were red from gripping the rope.

She looked under the doormat. Sure enough, a key. *I'm sneaking into the house of the second dead person*, she thought. *Nosy or a nuisance—that's what Jets would say.*

Her first impression was that the place had been cleaned. Like Stella's.

The kitchenette gleamed. The floorboards shined with polish. Two shelves were empty. Avery sniffed. Pine disinfectant. Not her favorite, but strong enough to fill the next renter with confidence that the place was germ-free.

Boxes were stacked to one side. *Theo's stuff*, she concluded. *Of course I'll have to tear them open to look for clues.* She felt her conscience prick. *What am I coming to, picking over the belongings of the dead?*

She wasn't ready to start digging in, so she turned to find that the large window offered a spectacular view of the mountain range and Lily Rock. Avery stepped closer.

Outside was the shower, reinstalled, the boards underneath repaired.

She walked out, intrigued by the repairs, and closed the door behind her.

*Good carpentry*, she concluded. *Edges cleanly cut to fit; each board screwed in, not nailed. Yep, a pro did this. Most likely a local carpenter hired by the rental company.*

She looked over the rail to the ground below. *That has to be a ten-foot drop*, she thought. *Theo must have been very frightened going down.* She felt a wave of sadness, thinking of him.

She looked toward Lily Rock in the distance. The sudden steady thump of footsteps on the deck made her spin around.

Avery's throat went dry. *How did she manage that...*

A pair of sharp eyes beneath arched brows glared in her direction.

"Cordelia," Avery whispered.

Wearing jeans and a Romance Writers of America sweatshirt, she held a book under her arm and a surprised expression.

*I bet that's* The Red Ribbon Room. *Her bestseller. Her legacy*, Avery concluded.

Cordelia blinked. "Oh, I didn't expect anyone else here. I was just dropping off my book." Her voice was calm, but Avery heard the tiny falter underneath.

"I like to leave one of my bestsellers for each new renter. Nothing like a cozy romance to get the fires burning." She beamed.

Avery's jaw clenched. She couldn't call Cordelia out now; neither one of them belonged in Theo's tree house.

The older woman's gaze slid past her toward the shower, the repaired boards. Then she tapped the book against her hip, casual and chilling all at once. "Funny thing about a tree house, Avery. They look solid. Until someone postpones a repair and one thing leads to another."

Avery gave her a long look. *She remembered my name. What happened to Miss Forgetful?*

Cordelia looked away and then back. She blinked vapidly, as if even she had lost her train of thought.

"Tsk, tsk," Cordelia murmured. "I suspect they've already boxed up his belongings. I'll leave my book on that empty shelf." She reached into her pocket and used a key to open the door.

"Wait a minute," Avery said sharply. Her pulse thudded. "I know I'm intruding, but aren't you even a little self-conscious? Theo's gone, and here you are, pushing your book like nothing ever happened."

Avery snatched the novel from her hand. "What's so special about this anyway? A nanosecond on the bestseller list before I was even born and what, it's a classic?"

She flipped the cover open; a leaflet slipped free. Avery bent, grabbed it in the air, and read aloud, "How To Be Saved and Know It."

Looking up, she asked, "Are you the one leaving these leaflets all over town? What kind of weirdo are you?" Avery had lost any interest in placating the older woman.

The corner of Cordelia's mouth curved. Whether in amusement or warning, Avery couldn't tell.

"I've seen them around," she admitted. "But I'm not responsible for the distribution."

"Would I find one of these in your little free library if I stopped by?" Avery felt her temper flare, her fists clench.

Cordelia shifted to a little girl voice. "Mommy used to take me to church. I'd wear white gloves and carry a little purse. She told me all good girls go to heaven."

Unsure what to do, Avery shrugged. The rational conversation had folded into a bizarre recollection of Cordelia's childhood. Somewhere she didn't choose to follow. Folding the leaflet, Avery shoved it in her pocket. "Okay then. I have to get going."

"But you never said..." Cordelia took hold of her arm. "The book is my excuse, so why are you here?" There it was. *The real Cordelia.*

"Theo and I were friends...of a sort," Avery said. "I was just curious about the tree house, if it was back on the market to rent."

"Not grieving his loss, then," Cordelia said in a flat, ominous tone. "We're not so different, are we?"

Like an animal caught in a snare, Cordelia trapped Avery with her own judgment. They both had an agenda other than grieving Theo's death.

*How does she do that?* Avery wondered, glancing away. *Go from little girl to sentimental old woman to caught-ya-young-lady. She makes my head spin. Is she losing her marbles or just saving them to pitch at people who get in her way? I just don't know.*

"See ya," she said. "You're right. I'm not being respectful. Gotta go."

# CHAPTER THIRTY-FOUR

Olivia sat on the patio, phone to her ear. The second she spotted Avery, she said, "Gotta go. Avery's here."

She waved. "Good to see you. No backpack? Not ready yet?"

Avery's cheeks burned. She'd forgotten to pick it up.

"I never got there." She flopped into the nearest chair. "I had...another errand. A surprise for you, actually. A goodbye and thanks for having me gift."

Olivia's brows lifted. "You're still leaving, then?"

"The gift won't be ready for a couple more days, and I've got a few loose ends." Avery hesitated, then asked bluntly, "Be honest. Are you just acting polite by asking me to stay?"

"Oh no." Olivia chuckled. "This isn't about manners. It's about rattling around this enormous house, which is big enough for a family of ten."

Some of Avery's tension released. Olivia was so open, she never doubted her sincerity.

"Plus, I have a feeling we're connected somehow," Olivia added, "like I used to be with Cayenne." Her voice dropped to a whisper.

Avery's lips tightened. "How very woo-woo of you."

"It is woo-woo," Olivia admitted with a nod. Then she stood. "Hold on a sec."

When she returned, she carried a slim leather notebook and a pencil with a silver cap. She placed them in Avery's lap. "For you to take notes, *Harriet-the-Spy* style. The eraser is a really good one, in case you make mistakes."

"Thank you." Avery turned the notebook over, doubtful. "Why go to the trouble?"

"Because Janis swears you're a twenty-first century Harriet. And I suspect you weren't off on errands today. You were investigating. Best to write things down right away. At least, I did in the beginning."

Avery stiffened. "You do read minds. Janis is right."

"Not exactly." Olivia's smile softened. "I get impressions, sure, but this time I had lots of affirmation. Meadow saw you walking with Fran. Cookie's staff overheard you talking about Theo over lunch. And a realtor phoned about the tree house listing. He's a friend of Michael's. They work together on flipping local projects."

She took a quick breath before continuing. "The realtor mentioned that he saw you and Cordelia at the tree house, so he called me, since you're staying here. I'm supposed to tell you to call him and he'll set you up for an official viewing."

This detailed report of her whereabouts came as a shock. Back in Beverly Hills, nobody noticed her comings and goings. Nannies had, but not the neighbors, least of all her parents. And nannies could be bribed to keep their mouths shut. But here, people seemed to genuinely care. And that unnerved her more than Olivia's so-called woo-woo.

"Why don't you tell me"—Olivia leaned back, studying

her—"why you keep digging even after Janis closed both cases. It's a rogue move, don't you think?"

The word stuck in Avery's head. *Rogue*. She'd never thought of herself that way—as a rogue. She kind of liked the idea. The thought made her smile.

"I guess it is," she admitted slowly. "Has my pushing back against Janis caused problems for you? Since...well, you work with her."

Olivia's eyes widened as if impressed. "That's a sharp question, Avery. You do cut to the heart of things, don't you." She hesitated. "May I confide in you? Tell you the position I've been in since your arrival?"

Olivia wanted to confide in her? Sweat prickled her palms. She'd expected her to play the mentor, like every other adult who wanted to fix her problems. She never considered that Olivia, the constabulary consultant, might see her as someone worthy of a confidence.

"When I first came to Lily Rock," Olivia began, "I was the thorn in Janis's side. She even suspected me of killing my friend Marla." She gave a wry smile "Honestly, I hadn't planned on staying here at all. Sage and I connected with the band. That was enough of Lily Rock for me. Until Janis nosed her way into my life, forcing me to stay put."

Her expression softened. "And Michael too, once he forgave me for leaving the first time without a goodbye. I had to come back up to settle another matter, and Michael persuaded me to stay longer. But it took some convincing."

Avery sensed there was more, so she remained quiet.

"One thing led to another, and I kept helping Janis out. Before long, it became second nature for her to ask my advice on a case. And then, just a few months ago, she got funding to hire me as a consultant."

Olivia sighed, glancing toward the bridge. "But here's

the thing. That changed everything. Now that I'm paid, I feel obligated to back her up, even when I think she's too quick to call a case closed." Olivia met Avery's eyes squarely. "That's why your persistence matters. You're asking the questions I no longer can."

The briefest brush of insight came over her. That Olivia wasn't convinced that the deaths of Theo and Stella were accidents either. And that meant she wasn't alone in her doubts.

Olivia continued, "Face it, Avery. You're not just curious. You're a rogue trouble magnet. And now you have an official notebook. Which, in Lily Rock, makes you a detective whether you like it or not."

The words caught her off guard. Detective? For half a second, she saw herself from Olivia's perspective. Odd how she could step outside her own body and look back with the eyes of someone else. That hadn't happened before.

Avery smirked. "Perfect. Just what every girl wants on her résumé: professional trouble magnet. I'll need business cards."

Olivia's bright gaze remained steady. "Print as many as you like. You can run away, I know I tried, but the work will keep finding you."

Avery hugged the notebook close to her chest, another joke fading on her lips. Olivia wasn't the town's beloved amateur sleuth anymore. But for her, Olivia was something more important, someone who saw through her public persona to the part of her that wanted to make a difference. To matter somehow.

She might not be ready to admit it out loud, but Olivia was right. She often went rogue and cut to the truth, disregarding the consequences. And Olivia was also right about that other thing. Trouble had already found her. And for the first time, Avery considered her situation from a fresh perspective. *I can't leave without the satisfaction of solving both murders.*

Later that evening, Avery sat propped against the headboard of her bed, notebook balanced on her knees. Words spilled onto the page, a jumble of hunches, overheard conversations, and questions she had not been able to answer. When her hand finally cramped, she dropped the pencil and closed her eyes.

A message pinged on her cell.

> We're meeting tomorrow after dark. Bring All American Boys.

Her heart lurched. No name, no place, no time. Just the demand. Still, she knew this wasn't random. This was her next lead. How did the person know she wanted to bring *All American Boys*? Creepy.

She clutched her phone, pulse racing. Janis wouldn't approve. Olivia either. But so far, that hadn't stopped her. Why change now?

What did matter, what chilled her more than the midnight summons, was the way the sender knew the title of the book she'd been turning over in her mind, the one she'd chosen to defend, if push came to shove.

She shivered. Whoever was out there wasn't just watching her moves. They were inside her head.

Avery dropped the phone onto the nightstand and stared at the ceiling. She could hear Olivia's voice urging caution, Janis barking that the case was closed.

But she knew she had no choice. She needed to prove,

maybe for the first time, that she could see something through on her own and make a difference.

Avery picked up the notebook, flipped to a clean page, and scrawled across the top in big block letters: *Suspects*. Whoever had sent that text message, whatever they wanted, she'd be ready.

# CHAPTER THIRTY-FIVE

Avery poked at her scrambled eggs, the toast cold on the plate. Olivia had left a cheery note propped against the coffeepot. *Help yourself. Key's on the hook by the door.* It was a small thing, but the gesture felt like something a roommate would leave, or a good friend. It felt like trust.

She took a bite of toast, her thoughts circling back to the text from the night before to bring *All American Boys. There must be a local bookstore.* A quick search on her phone answered the question.

The closest bookstore was down the hill in Palm Springs. Of course, Lily Rock had collections of used books at the self-help center. Then there was a used furniture store with a room of books. But she didn't have time to sort through the odd piles to look for what she wanted.

She needed her own copy. And she knew exactly where to find one. Stella's house, in that basket of books by the door. She chided herself for leaving it before.

The problem this morning was transportation. She wasn't in the mood for another long hike. If she still lived in

LA, she'd call an Uber. But in Lily Rock, there wasn't a chance; it would probably have to come from too far away.

Her mind ticked through the possibilities. Marshall, Naomi, Cordelia, even Fran were all tangled up in the Syndicate. Any one of them could be behind the messages, and the thought of being trapped in a car with one of them at this point made her uneasy.

Which left...Brad.

She set down her fork. Brad was Janis's guy. If she asked, she'd be forced to tell him at least some of the truth of why she wanted to go to Stella's. He might raise an eyebrow, maybe even report back. But at least she'd have a ride.

By the time Avery rinsed her plate, her decision was made. Hiking out to Stella's was out of the question; she needed wheels. And for that, she needed Brad.

Notebook in hand, she stepped into the cool mountain air. Pine and woodsmoke curled in the breeze, sharp enough to sting her nose. It should have calmed her nerves. Instead, every step toward the center of town made her more jittery.

She paused at the door to the constabulary to gather her courage. One deep breath and Avery pulled the door open to step inside.

The familiar smell of cool air, old coffee, and dog biscuits brought a smile to her lips. She caught sight of a slobbery squeaky toy, which lay abandoned near the desk. Evidence that Tater Tot had already claimed the office as his morning kingdom.

Brad was hunched over, phone tucked against his ear. He scribbled on a spiral pad. Once he spotted her, he held up a finger, mouthing, "One second."

She hovered near the waiting area, feeling self-conscious, questioning her judgment yet again. *Was she making it obvious? That she enjoyed being around him?*

Brad hung up, flipping his pen between his fingers. He seemed a bit nervous. "Avery. Thought you'd be halfway to the next trailhead by now."

"Yeah, well..." She tried for casual, her hands clasped together. "Plans change. I need a favor."

His brows went up. "Big favor or small favor?"

"Depends on how you feel about taking matters into your own hands." She lowered her voice. "I need a ride out to Stella's place. Quick in, quick out. She gave me a key. So not exactly illegal."

Brad tilted his head. "What for?"

She had no intention of telling him about the anonymous texts. "There's a book I need. For research." She shrugged as though that explained everything.

Brad studied her, the corner of his mouth twitching like he wasn't sure whether to take her seriously. "You want me to be your getaway driver for a book run?"

"Basically." She forced a grin. "I'll even buy you coffee for your effort. Helping an old friend in need."

Brad leaned back in his chair, his eyes suspiciously narrowed, as if she'd just asked him to rob a bank. Then his grin spread.

"Sure. I've always wanted to be an accomplice. But just so we're clear, if this ends with flashing lights and the boss chewing me out, I'm telling her you held me at pencil-point." He pointed to the fancy pencil with the silver cap.

Avery rolled her eyes. "Fine. I'll even sign a confession in your special spiral notebook."

"Deal." Brad grabbed his keys from the desk. "Let's go commit some light literary larceny."

If only she could tell him everything, but this wasn't the time.

"Seat belt," Brad reminded, buckling his own with a

snap. She glanced to the back, to the dog harness and a dry leftover dog treat.

"All set up for Tater Tot," he explained. "Fortunately I get a morning off. The professional trainer picked him up early for a session. I failed miserably at getting Tater to do anything. The only person in town with any control over that dog is Meadow, and she doesn't want him growling at all the library patrons."

"A professional?"

"Yeah. The guy costs a fortune. He calls himself the Frenchie specialist." He turned to her. "So we're going to Stella's. Which book, and why is that one so important?"

She shrugged. "'Cause..." She smiled seductively.

"Janis closed the case. She won't be pleased when she finds out," Brad said dryly.

"I know. Olivia already warned me." She looked outside to avoid his glare.

"So me taking you to Stella's makes me an accomplice to a break-in," Brad confirmed. "Just to make things clear."

"More like my Uber driver," she corrected. "Plus I have Stella's key that she gave me so that I could come and go when she wasn't around. Being dead qualifies as not around. At least, that's my argument, should it come to that." Avery saw the twinkle in his eye. "You don't have to come inside," she added.

"If you think I'm going to just drop you off and drive away, you've got another thought coming." He took the next curve in the road with a grim expression.

She stared out the window again as the truck sped into the next turn. "You sound way too proud of this for a guy who's training to be a cop."

"I am," Brad admitted, eyes flicking in her direction before returning to the road. "Not like I get asked for shady errands every day. My life as the Lily Rock weed dealer has ended. I don't even smoke anymore. Just another upstanding citizen. Usually the edgiest thing I do all day is fetch coffee for the boss or take Tater Tot for a spin around the park, ending with a belly scratch. He's big on that."

Despite herself, Avery chuckled.

This time when he glanced at her, the look lingered a second longer. Her stomach did a quick, traitorous flip.

She cleared her throat. "Just don't ask questions, okay?"

Brad's voice softened, losing some of its teasing edge. "Hey, I trust you. If you say it matters, it matters."

The sincerity caught her off guard. She held her notebook tighter, pulse quickening. His look, his voice—it made her want more.

She forced her gaze back to the window, jaw tight. No. This wasn't the time. Not with secret texts and shadowy Syndicate meetings hanging over her. Whatever this flutter was, she'd deal with it later.

As the truck rounded the bend, Brad spoke. "Relax, Avery. You've got me on your side. And Tater Tot, if you count muscle."

Avery laughed, but then reeled it back in. She didn't want to give him the satisfaction of knowing she found him funny. Whatever this was, whatever she was starting to feel... *Not now*, she told herself.

Brad stopped the truck in front of Stella's. Avery popped out of the passenger side and made her way toward the house. She slipped the key into the lock and eased the door open, giving a quick glance back at Brad.

As the engine idled, he stared over the steering wheel, his expression serious.

The basket by the front door was right where she remembered. *All American Boys* sat on top. The sight tugged her back to that first terrible day. Stella lying on the ground, the basket overturned, books scattered in the dirt. She'd seen the book then.

She drifted toward the living room. Boxes lined the walls, neatly stacked, half-packed. They made their way from the office to the front room. Someone had started clearing away Stella's life.

Like Theo's tree house, soon this place would be polished and staged for rent or sale. *Charming mountain home. Move-in ready*, she thought. It would go fast if priced right.

Maybe Stella left it to someone in her will. *Has anyone thought of that?*

Now Avery realized she'd had a niggling question at the back of her mind, which started when she'd found that baby photo. If Theo truly was Stella's biological son, he might have wanted to stake a claim. A plea for recognition, maybe even for the entire estate. The thought pulled at her heart. *Motive for murder*, she concluded. *Where's my notebook? I need to write it down.*

Maybe Theo did kill Stella.

*But what about this scenario: If Theo stood to inherit from Stella, then maybe there was another beneficiary who'd been cut out. That someone might be angry and willing to silence him permanently.*

"Avery." Brad's voice came sharp from the doorway. "We have to get going!"

She hugged the book to her chest. "Almost done."

Brad stepped inside, closing the door with a soft click. "We shouldn't even be in here." His eyes flicked to the boxes. "If someone sees the truck..."

The sound of a door slamming came from outside.

Both of them froze.

Brad swore under his breath and pulled Avery toward the hall.

She gave a quick backward glance to look through the front window.

Marshall Reed, toolbox in his hand, strode up the walkway. His gait was confident, casual, as if he had a job to do.

Avery's stomach knotted. "What's he doing here?" she whispered. "Making more repairs?"

Brad held up a warning hand. "Doesn't matter. We can either bluff our way out or try to hide."

"Hide it is." Avery took his hand.

# CHAPTER THIRTY-SIX

Marshall's key scratched in the lock as they both ducked behind the kitchen counter. Avery held her breath right as the door swung open. He stepped inside, humming to himself, toolbox bumping against his leg.

She turned to Brad, and he shook his head, holding a finger to his lips.

Marshall rested his toolbox beside the book basket. Holding a screwdriver in one hand, he turned to look closely at the brass plate in the door. Metal scraped against the wood as he began loosening the screws.

Avery looked away. *Who gave him permission to change the lock?* she wondered. The realtor? The estate lawyer? Or was this Marshall helping himself, staking a claim?

Each twist of the screwdriver scraped against Avery's nerves. Brad leaned closer, his whisper hot against her ear. "We need to run. Now."

Marshall's head snapped up, the screwdriver suspended in the air.

Brad yanked her to her feet, making a break toward the door.

*He's going to bully his way past*, she thought, gritting her teeth, what choice did they have?

Quicker than she might have imagined, Marshall dropped the screwdriver to reach for Brad. "You're not goin' anywhere," he growled, large hands gripping Brad's shoulders.

Brad twisted his body to free himself from the grasp.

"Just stop," Avery said. "Explain why we're here. It's my fault." The guilt felt heavy in her chest.

Squaring his shoulders, Brad turned around. He looked at Marshall. "You surprised us coming up the walkway, so we hid because we didn't know who it was. We're relieved to see it's you. Avery just needed a book." He pointed to the copy of *All American Boys* in the basket. "Perfectly innocent."

Avery held the book in front of her as if she was doing a book report. "See? Remember? It's one of my favorites. We talked about it."

Marshall looked from one to the other. "Breaking and entering for a book. I'm pretty sure your boss wouldn't approve."

"We're not breaking in," Brad shot back. "Avery has a key, given to her by Stella. So maybe you're the one who's trespassing."

"That so?" Marshall sounded very calm. He tapped the doorframe with his knuckle, casual as could be, though the muscle in his jaw tightened. He lifted the screwdriver and continued to work with a slow deliberate twist.

"The realtor called me," Marshall explained. He crouched to look at the hole in the door. "People have been seen coming and going. Rather than collect keys from Stella's friends, the realtor asked me to change the locks to secure the place so that it can go on the market."

He paused, glancing over his shoulder, eyes glinting. "This will make a good story at the pub, how Jets's administrative assistant was caught with his girlfriend pilfering the belongings of a dead woman."

Avery's cheeks flamed. "That's not what we're doing." She waved her book in front of his nose. "See!"

"Okay, I get it. Put the book away. Are you sure that's the reason you dropped in?" He sounded skeptical. The way he lifted his eyebrows convinced Avery he didn't believe a word.

Brad took a step forward, voice tight. "It's just like Avery said."

Marshall turned the screw until the plate came loose. "If you say so."

Avery was tired of the sparring. She wanted answers, not another round of Marshall's smug remarks. "So did Stella own this place or was she renting?" she asked, feigning naiveté.

Marshall's hand froze mid-turn. Slowly, he straightened and leveled a glare at her. "Stella owned the house. She left it to her sister, who lives in the desert." He jabbed the screwdriver toward the door for emphasis. "I do work for a few of the local realtors. Just to keep snoopy people out of places where they don't belong."

Brad offered his hand to Avery. "We're done here," he muttered.

But Avery wasn't sure. She clutched the book tighter. She'd gotten an answer, but was it the whole story? Before she could ask another question, Marshall spoke.

"Get outta here, you two. I've got a busy schedule and want to be done. Leave your old key on the porch rail." Marshall waved half-heartedly, finished with the conversation.

Back in the truck, Avery sat in the passenger seat, holding the book in her lap.

Brad spoke first. "Close call," he muttered. "I don't think he'll tell the boss. Not like they're pals."

He shot her a sidelong glance. "What's so important about that book anyway? A personal favorite?"

Avery looked down at *All American Boys* resting in her lap. "You could say that," she said.

When he didn't push, she felt relief. But then she had to ask, "So have you ever heard of the Switchback Syndicate?"

"The what?" Brad sounded surprised. "Another conspiracy group. We've got plenty of those in Lily Rock. Up here, folks keep their theories to themselves. But every now and then, one of 'em pokes their head out and starts yelling in the park."

"What do you do when that happens?" Avery leaned in, curious.

Brad grinned crookedly. "Very politely shut them down. The boss pats her back pocket while I do the talking. That's her way of saying, 'I've got a gun, but I won't use it unless you don't stop yelling and move on.'"

Avery chuckled. "I've seen her do that patting thing. But tell me, how do you actually bring people back to their senses? You must be a pretty good fast-talker."

Brad shrugged, a glint of pride in his eyes. "I just listen. Let people feel heard. I found out that most people like to believe they're smart, not crazy."

Avery studied him. *Okay, I'm going to admit it—maybe he'd make a good cop.*

"You calmed Marshall right down," she agreed.

Brad shot her a quick smile, the kind that crinkled the corners of his eyes. "You saying I could charm a confession out of you?"

Her pulse jumped. "Depends on the question."

He shrugged, eyes on the road. "I learned a lot from watching Olivia interview suspects. She made it look easy, getting people to relax, then slipping in the tough questions when they weren't expecting it. I guess some of that rubbed off."

The truck rolled toward the constabulary, the sun casting a reflection off the bakery window. Finally Brad cleared his throat, drumming his fingers lightly against the steering wheel. "Well, if I ever make it to the police academy, I'll need someone to practice my interrogation technique on. You game?"

She laughed. "Careful. The next thing you know, you'll be bringing out the handcuffs."

He chuckled right as Avery had the oddest thought.

Maybe she wouldn't mind being questioned, at least not by him.

Brad May wasn't just an assistant or a sidekick. He had his eye on something bigger and better. She wasn't sure whether that thought unsettled or drew her closer. But the one thing she did know was that she hated being left behind.

# CHAPTER THIRTY-SEVEN

Later that afternoon, Avery poured herself a cup of tea right as her cell phone pinged.

> See you at midnight. Marshall's place.
> Bring the book.

She shuddered, nearly dropping the honey-covered spoon. Up until now it hadn't felt real. The texts were spooky, and she'd done what they'd suggested, but it had still felt like just a game.

Like playing Clue with real-life human beings.

She'd enjoyed the excitement of figuring out things, getting to know people, poking around little free libraries, hiding in the kitchen with Brad.

But now she felt genuine fear, her head a little dizzy at the thought of the Switchback Syndicate.

Marshall's face, as they'd hustled out of Stella's house, hadn't helped. Gone was the kindly carpenter who'd shown her his three-ring binder of little library designs. Underneath, he boiled with impatience and irritation.

*Add it up,* she scolded herself. *That must be who he really is, an angry guy, looking for a reason to be mad.*

Marshall lived somewhat off-grid, worshiped old sci-fi books, and probably used *Lord of the Flies* as a bedtime story. Head of the Switchback Syndicate? Not a stretch. He'd recognized her over-the-top curiosity, somehow or other, as a threat. Or someone who'd be a good fit for the group. Either way, he was luring her in with those texts.

Her imagination spun out of control. Midnight. Isolated. A drink with something extra. His voice droning on about Heinlein, while she blacked out in a bubbling hot tub. *How did I go from Jessica Fletcher to Clarice Starling in one week?* She shuddered at the memory of Anthony Hopkins in *The Silence of the Lambs.*

Maybe she needed her own plan.

She pictured the four heads bobbing above the water that night in the hot tub, steam curling around them as they whispered. Had one of them killed Stella? She closed her eyes to consider the possibility.

Marshall, of course, was her number one suspect. The part-time carpenter, resident library fixer, his anger simmering just beneath the surface. Then Naomi, Fran's wife and Nancy's mother, with her sharp tongue and her crusade against anything she deemed unsuitable for children. Even Fran seemed dissatisfied with her wife's involvement, her intense opinions about children's books.

At first she'd suspected Theo of killing Stella. Then he turned up dead not long after the Syndicate soak. A maybe, she knew. But who killed him?

Finally there was Cordelia. That woman got on Avery's nerves.

Four adults, naked in a hot tub, debating banned books.

Maybe... Or were they talking about Stella? Had they planned her death together?

The image of Cordelia lingered. Most likely Marshall's age, late fifties. Sturdy and in shape. She'd even scrambled up that tree house ladder without breaking a sweat. But the romance writer had a tendency to wander. At least her mind did. Her body too, Avery reminded herself. Sometimes into the middle of the street, dangerous enough that the constabulary had to intervene.

Probably not Naomi, as much as she'd like it to be.

Avery was certain that one of them had a motive to kill Stella. One of them had a motive to kill Theo. Or had one of them killed both? The only way she'd find out was to show up with her book to this Syndicate meeting.

Later the same evening, she rolled onto her side, then her stomach, then back again. She glanced at her phone. *I need to arrive at the perfect time. Not too early, not too late, but just right. Like Goldilocks*, she thought, though the comparison didn't seem that amusing.

She rolled off the bed, stood, and paced. She stopped for a sip of tea; cold, the honey clumped at the bottom of the mug.

In the bathroom she stared at herself in the mirror. *Come on, Avery. You can't back down now. Take* All American Boys *and pretend it's a book group gathering. That you're special and they wanted to invite you as a guest.*

Wide-eyed, pale, hair uneven, she looked like a woman who'd woken up from a nap. She combed and tied her hair into a ponytail, fingers trembling with anxiety.

*Flashlight. Notebook. The fancy pencil. The dog-eared copy of* All American Boys. *I'm ready.*

At twenty minutes to midnight, she slipped on her boots and zipped her jacket. The tote bag slung over her shoulder. It would take fifteen minutes to hike to Marshall's house in the dark.

She made a quiet exit down the hall, to the stairway. A light snore drifted upward from the great room. She hurried down the stairs. Mayor Maguire, curled up nose to tail, opened his eyes. He'd been waiting by the front door.

"Wanna go for a midnight walk?" she coaxed him in a quiet voice.

He rose to all fours, shaking from head to tail.

"Shush," she cautioned. "Your tags are jingling. Don't want to wake up Olivia." He came closer, walked around, and sat on her right side, nose pointing toward the door.

"Let's go," she whispered, turning the doorknob.

The night air felt welcome. Crickets pulsed in the nearby bushes. Her nervous energy finally put to good use. She headed toward the footbridge, Maguire trotting by her side.

A ribbon of mist drifted upward from the creek below. The cicada chorus drowned out her footsteps. She swung into an even stride, beginning her walk to Marshall's.

On the opposite side of the bridge, she stopped. It wouldn't do to take the road. They might be seen. Instead she veered toward the footpath. Branches arched overhead, darkness settled over the path. An owl called, low and haunting. Maguire's ears raised, but he didn't stop.

The farther she went, the quieter it grew. She lengthened her strides.

Ahead, through a break in the trees, she saw the faint outline of Marshall's cabin. A light inside glowed from the front window.

Maguire gave a sharp bark. Avery whispered, "Yeah, I know." Then, with a quick breath, she approached.

Her boots crunched against gravel, announcing her arrival. The cabin looming larger with each step. Maguire pressed close to her leg, his body taut, right ear flicking. The porch sagged under her weight as she climbed the steps.

For a heartbeat, she stood frozen, staring at the door. She raised her fist and knocked. Three sharp raps that sounded far too loud.

Nothing.

Her breath caught. She took a step backward. Finally the door jerked open.

Marshall filled the frame, his face shadowed, eyes glinting. He didn't say hello. He didn't smile. He just looked at her, then at the bag slung over her shoulder.

"You brought it," he said, voice flat.

Maguire let out a low growl, and she forced herself not to flinch.

"I have the book. And the mayor." She gave a side nod to Maguire. "Can he come in too?"

The dog wasn't interested. He made his own decision and walked away, standing watch at the corner of the deck.

Marshall stepped back from the door, leaving room for her to pass.

His tone shifted, sounding more cordial. "Well," he said. "You're the first one here. Want something to drink?" He pointed to an uncorked wine bottle next to a cooler. "I do have water."

The cabin smelled of woodsmoke and pine sap, the air dense and a little sweet. In the corner, the fire snapped and hissed, throwing restless light across the walls. For a moment, his voice and the glow softened her mood, almost made the place feel safe. Almost.

"How many people do you expect?" she asked, crossing to the cooler. She fished out a bottle of water, twisting the cap with deliberate calm.

"Just the usual. We're much smaller now, without Theo and Stella." Marshall's voice carried a note of sadness, though Avery couldn't tell if it was grief or performance.

She chose the chair nearest the door. A battered rocker that looked older than she was, but it kept the exit close. She was lowering herself into the seat when a light tap sounded, followed immediately by the door swinging open.

"Nancy's asleep," came a hushed voice. "Shush."

Fran and Naomi tiptoed in, closing the door quietly behind them. The baby's head lolled in the carrier, her fists clenched, lips moving in some dream. Avery's throat tightened. What kind of mothers dragged a child to a midnight meeting?

Fran set the carrier on the floor and draped a receiving blanket loosely over the top. Naomi sat beside her on the sofa, their thighs brushing. Fran leaned against her wife's shoulder with a sigh.

The door creaked again, opening wide. Cordelia's voice rose in greeting, but the young mothers silenced her with a sharp shush. The romance writer blinked. She looked at Avery with a sideways glance that held no warmth, but no surprise either.

Cordelia eased into an empty chair closest to the kitchen, while Marshall remained standing by the fireplace, the firelight casting shadows on his face. Then, holding out his palm, he looked at the group with an expectant stare.

As if choreographed, all the women dug into their bags and produced battered old flip phones. Clunky relics from another decade. He stood in front of each with his hand held out. One by one, they dropped a phone into his palm.

Marshall placed them in a small wooden box on the hearth. Then he pulled four other phones out of a similar wooden box. He made the circle again, handing each woman another equally old phone.

Finally arriving at Avery's chair, he tapped his palm with a forefinger for her to hold out her hand. When she did, he put a phone in her palm and walked away.

She turned it over, noting the scratched plastic. Compared to her sleek smartphone, it felt flimsy, outdated, like a toy masquerading as something useful. She set it beside her water bottle, freeing her hands. A quick glance to the closed door reassured her that the escape was there if she needed to run.

At least one question had been answered. They all carried burners. And if the one she'd been given was the same, then any of them could have been behind those anonymous texts.

The thought made her skin crawl. Now she felt certain that every face in the room was a murder suspect.

From the floor, the baby gave a soft, restless sigh. The sound was small, vulnerable, a reminder that she had more in common with Nancy than she might have thought.

# CHAPTER THIRTY-EIGHT

The baby's whimper sharpened into a thin cry. Naomi lunged first, scooping the child from the carrier into her arms.

"Shhh, Mama's here," she whispered, cuddling the bundle against her chest.

Fran was already digging in the tote, producing a bottle with practiced hands. "She needs to eat," she said, her tone clipped, as if Naomi might not know. She offered the bottle, but Naomi shook her head, continuing to pat Nancy's back, her own lips pursed in concentration.

"She just wants comfort," Naomi murmured. "You don't have to offer food every time."

Fran's nostrils flared. "She's hungry. Give her the bottle."

The baby's wail climbed higher. A sharp bark came from outside; Maguire was known to have a soft spot for distressed children.

Naomi finally accepted the bottle, but not without a look of annoyance. Fran leaned in, guiding the blanket around the baby's shoulders with a possessive tug.

Avery sat motionless in the rocker, her throat dry. The

cabin should have felt warmer with the fire snapping in the hearth, but a chill prickled along her arms. These women, so tightly wound around a sleeping child, played tug-of-war. Each looked determined to be the one who knew best.

The baby finally latched with a greedy suck, the cries cutting off in an instant. Relief seeped into the room, but not into Avery.

She leaned back, clutching the arms of the rocker, her pulse quickening. The tenderness between the mothers that she'd expected wasn't there. Instead, she'd glimpsed something sharper, territorial, and fierce.

And it struck her: If this was how they fought over a baby, what else might they fight over?

Marshall lowered himself into a chair, the fire popping behind him. He cleared his throat, slow and deliberate, then lifted his chin.

"This is your phone to communicate within the group," he said. "I've erased all previous messages for the sake of security. Any questions?"

His eyes swept the circle, lingering on each face just long enough to make Avery's skin crawl. She shifted in her rocker, hands tightening around the armrests.

"I've got a question," she blurted. "Why did I get a phone?"

Marshall huffed, a sound somewhere between amusement and irritation. "This is your acceptance into the Syndicate. Didn't you realize we were inviting you when you got our texts?"

*Invitation? Finally a confirmation.*

"That's how we bring in new people," he went on, sharper now. "Watch them a couple of days. Send the first text, then see if they run to the cops or just sit quiet." He observed her expression carefully. "Plus, your boyfriend may be a good connection for us, so long as you can keep your mouth shut."

*Boyfriend... Does he mean Brad? Better not tell him now that he was just a ride to where I needed to go.*

Marshall leaned forward, elbows braced on his knees. He fixed his eyes on her. "I knew I pegged you right for us. Especially when I caught you at Stella's with that book."

Avery's mouth went dry. She reached into her tote and slid out *All American Boys*. "Got it," she said. "Good read."

"Of course, sweetie, you're entitled to your opinion," chirped Cordelia. She rustled in her bag. "I have my copy of my bestseller, *The Red Ribbon Room*."

A ripple, half sigh, half groan, came from the others.

Avery bristled at the reception. She felt sorry for Cordelia. *You'd think her Syndicate friends would be a little more open.*

"I'd love to hear about your bestseller," Avery said brightly. "Start with where the idea came from. Tell me everything about the characters. Spare no detail."

*Am I trying to be nice or just trying to annoy everyone else?* Avery thought. *Too late to take it back.*

Naomi's mouth tightened. Fran glanced at the baby, then Marshall looked away with a groan.

Cordelia lit up. "Well, if you insist." Words spilled from her lips. Something about a locked room that wasn't a room but a large pantry, a ribbon that stood for shame and also courage.

Avery only half listened, taking the opportunity to observe the others and their reactions. Fran kept retucking the blanket around Nancy. Marshall stared at the ceiling. Naomi rolled her eyes, the most obviously annoyed.

When Cordelia paused for a breath, Avery broke in. "Thanks for telling me about your process. But I'm still a bit confused. If I'm part of the Syndicate, what do I need to do? Read all of your favorites? Do I have to have my own little library up and running?"

She wanted to stop Cordelia in her tracks, but more importantly, she wanted to sound eager, as if truly grateful for their attention. She kept talking before anyone could answer. It was time to release her plan, the one that had been at the back of her mind.

"Actually, I have an idea. How about a book burning demonstration? Right in the middle of Lily Rock, in that redwood park. Public but mostly safe. Don't want to light up one of those giant trees, now do I?" It was her turn to glance at each face, her jaw set with determination.

"You all can join in. Bring the books. I'll set up a mic—I know where to get the equipment." She glanced toward the fire. "And before ol' Lily Rock lights up..." She grinned wickedly. "Not an actual fire. I'd never do that. Since my house burned down."

Everyone focused on her now. She took advantage of their silence.

"This will be full-on theater. The barbecue version of a toned-down towering inferno vibe, just like a movie set, with everything simulated. I call it performance art."

Avery extended her arms in the air for dramatic effect. "I'm all about the optics."

She nodded at Cordelia, whose mouth hung slightly open. "Come on. You know it's a good idea. I bet Theo and Stella would have approved." She dropped the names of the dead Syndicate members, waiting to see each one's response.

"Stella would never have approved," Naomi said. "This kind of thing...would have been distasteful in her eyes."

Avery retorted, "Since Stella's no longer with us..."

Avery pretended to dab at her eyes. Then she grinned. "It's time for a new angle. If the Syndicate is trying to make a point—that little libraries promote classic books—then you need to step up your game.

"My book burning performance art supports your cause. But I'm not hiding undercover, meeting at midnight in an off-the-grid bunker." She cast her eye over the room, stopping on Marshall. She didn't call them a bunch of sissies, but she implied.

Avery lowered her voice. "I'll 'burn' a stack that includes your favorite books and your most hated. Just to provoke. Trust me, no one will forget the Syndicate after I'm done.

"Paper flames, LED candles, crackle sounds from a smartphone app, orange tissue that flutters in the breeze. A roast, not a fire. I'll talk while books burn. When people hear the stories, they'll come to listen. Eventually they'll get the gist and laugh. There will be a celebration and no one will call the fire department."

Thrusting her back into the cushion, she felt satisfied. When no one spoke, she added, "The demonstration is a good way for me to show my worth as the latest Syndicate member."

The longer they were silent, the less confident she felt. *Maybe I've gone too far...*

But finally Marshall spoke. "If you go public, then you take the risk."

Fran whipped around, her face flushing pink. "That's what you said to Theo when he put that little library up at the dead drop. That it was his risk. Then it got out of hand. Look what happened to him!"

Marshall shrugged. "Naw, this plan is way above Theo's grade. He had a bit of gumption, I'll give him that. But Avery here?" Marshall nodded in her direction. "She's the real deal. A rabble-rouser of the first order. Reminds me of someone else, back in the day."

"I could bring more books for a signing," Cordelia offered, eyes bright with a new opportunity. "I know I'm the only author in the group, but it would add legitimacy to the book burning, don't you think?"

*No way my book burning is turning into an author fair.* Avery already regretted encouraging the romance writer earlier. She glanced to the sofa.

Fran sat silent and simmering, Naomi hid her face aside as if embarrassed. Neither said a word.

Finally Fran muttered something sharp at Naomi, who snapped back under her breath. Their quiet squabble was interrupted by Marshall's throat clearing. He glanced at Avery and raised an eyebrow before speaking.

"I think your performance art would work. The idea of a book burning reminds me of one of my favorites, *Brave New World.*" As he launched into his story, Avery wondered if he was providing a distraction or was just tired of listening to her talk.

Up until now s'hed been circling suspects, piecing together impressions. Janis Jets had dismissed both deaths as accidents, and maybe the town was content with that assessment. But Avery felt that this group of book lovers had something to do with the so-called accidents.

Maybe the demonstration would bring some insight—someone might get nervous and show their hand.

She pictured them in her mind's eye: Stella, surprised and falling backward, causing the fatal heart attack. And Theo, plummeting to his death when the boards beneath him gave way. Sooner rather than later, Avery hoped to have an answer as to who had tossed the firecracker and who had sabotaged the wood.

# CHAPTER THIRTY-NINE

Avery beat Olivia to the kitchen the next morning. She made a pot of coffee and half a dozen boiled eggs. Two for breakfast and one for later. Olivia could have the rest.

When she brought out her notebook and pencil, she sketched out a to-do list for her book burning.

"Good morning, is that coffee I smell?" Olivia padded in barefoot, wearing a faded Sweet Four O'Clock t-shirt and snug-fitting jeans. Without makeup, her face was fresh, her eyes bright. She reached for a mug, setting it on the counter. "Michael's coming home tomorrow. I hope you'll stay until then."

"Want toast and a boiled egg?" Avery asked.

"Sure." Olivia nodded. She slid into her easy morning rhythm, movements calm, unhurried.

Olivia's presence gently enveloped Avery, soothing her excited nerves. She wasn't going to tell her the plan, but she appreciated her company.

"I met up with a few friends last night," she said lightly.

"PCT hikers?" Olivia asked, her tone curious but careful.

"No. Lily Rock residents." Avery held out a spoon with a warm boiled egg. Olivia took it between two fingers with a smile.

"You're not going to tell me, are you?" she asked gently.

"Nope." Avery shoved a clean plate in her direction just as the toast popped.

Olivia watched her for a brief second and then turned to crack the shell of her egg against the inside of the kitchen sink.

"Do you know where I could find a big barbecue? One of those dome-lidded ones, charcoal-fired?" Avery asked.

Olivia studied her for a moment. "As a matter of fact, I do. A few months ago, we had the Woofstock Festival in Lily Rock. Half the attendees left in a hurry and abandoned their barbecues. Janis hauled what was left to Paws and Pines for their next rummage sale.

"You can take one. Leave them a few bucks in the donation can at the front desk." She watched Avery over the rim of her coffee mug, leaving her next question unspoken.

"Not gonna tell you," Avery repeated, a sly grin tugging at her lips. "But you'll know soon enough."

"You're trouble, you know that?" she said softly; there was no censure in it.

"Yeah," Avery said, rinsing her plate. "That's kind of the point." She flashed a quick smile. "All right if I take this to my room?" She held up her coffee mug.

"Of course," Olivia said.

She carried her mug toward her room, the day sharp with possibility. First the mothers, then Cordelia.

On the hike up the hill, perspiration beaded along Avery's forehead. Without Mayor Maguire trotting at her side, the climb felt steeper, lonelier. More than once, Avery glanced down, half expecting him to materialize.

Instead, it was just her. And if her suspicions were right, she wasn't trudging up to hopefully share coffee and cake and coo at the baby. She was walking straight into the den of two treacherous women who each wanted their own way. The thought didn't cool her sweat; it spiked it, her breath labored.

When she finally stopped to take a rest, she missed the dog more. Maguire would've had the stamina for this climb. He might have eased the way when she showed up unannounced, maybe even distracted Fran and Naomi long enough for Avery to nonchalantly move inside.

But now she was sweaty, jumpy, and about to knock on the door of the two women who might have planned the killing of one or both of the victims.

Avery checked her smartphone; the burner was in her pocket. *Two phones*, she thought. *Just like an LA businessman. Or somebody keeping a secret.*

She made a right turn. Following a long, winding gravel road toward Fran and Naomi's house. Each step made her breath come faster. At the end, a gingerbread bungalow appeared, tucked against a tree-lined slope.

Its trim was painted a cheery forest green, and lace curtains hung in the windows. The overcrowded porch looked buried under the weight of what Avery would refer to as "domestic life."

There were bright plastic toys scattered across the steps, a baby walker tipped on its side, a pair of adult-sized rubber boots forgotten near the railing.

The smell of frying bacon drifted through the open kitchen window. *Breakfast time at the Wells-Durans'*, she thought.

Birds chattered in the nearby trees, their calls rising above the faint clatter of dishes. The house and deck looked like something out of a postcard—homey, harmless. Maybe... maybe not.

*Here you go,* she told herself. *Time to make some trouble.* Her pulse quickened as she sidestepped a stack of wooden blocks parked squarely in her path. She lifted her hand, hesitated, then rapped lightly on the door.

The door opened, revealing Fran with a disgruntled frown.

"I assume it's been a rough morning?" Avery asked, to the sound of Nancy wailing in the background.

Fran blinked, eyes widening. "What are you doing here so early?"

"I need some help." Avery slipped past her with a breezy nonchalance. She made a quick scan of the room, taking in more clutter. Blankets tossed over the sofa, a scattering of wooden blocks on the rug. "Naomi here?"

"I'm making breakfast," came the sharp reply from the kitchen. Naomi appeared a moment later, Nancy perched on one hip. The baby sucked a pacifier. Her rumpled shirt was dotted with baby spit-up, her eyes sharp and assessing as she looked Avery up and down.

"You seem like the kind of people who'd have a craft room," Avery said in her brightest, most chipper voice. "I need tissue paper to create fake flames for the book burning. Plus a glue gun. Every self-respecting mother has a glue gun, right?"

Nancy let the pacifier drop around her neck to gurgle. One tiny fist batted at her mother's chin.

Fran's brow furrowed.

Naomi's lips pressed tight, her gaze narrowing as if weighing whether Avery was joking.

Fran planted her hands on her hips, shoulders sagging. "Craft room? You think we've got time for crafts?"

Naomi shifted Nancy to her other hip. "We've got a glue gun," she admitted reluctantly. "But it's for fixing things, not..." She paused, lips tightening. "Not theater projects."

"Perfect," Avery said, ignoring the edge to Naomi's voice. "Then it'll be nice and broken in."

"You barge in here at breakfast, ask for tissue paper and a glue gun like we're Hobby Lobby. Why didn't you send a text on your burner?" Fran sounded past distressed. Her voice dipped into all-out annoyance.

Avery forced a bigger smile. "I'm kinda freaked out with the two phones. Sorry about that," she added. "I thought the burner was for meeting details only."

Nancy began to fuss, wiggling out from her mother's grasp. Naomi reached for a set of keys hanging on the wall and handed them to Fran. "You do this. I have to feed the baby."

Naomi explained to Avery, "We keep all of our supplies in the shed behind the cabin. Go ahead and have at it. Just bring everything back when you're done."

Nancy broke into a full-on wail.

Once Avery and Fran were outside, the baby's cries grew quiet. Fran shrugged. "I guess we have our order. Come with me."

Avery followed her to a walk-in shed. Fran twisted the key in the lock to open the door. "I have to go. Nancy is a handful in the mornings. It's my day for kid duty, so just let me know when you're done."

Nodding, Avery stepped inside.

The shed was nothing like the house. Where the cabin had been cluttered with toys and laundry and the chaos of a baby, this space was tidy. Shelves lined three walls, stacked with plastic bins neatly labeled Seasonal Decor, Paints, and Electrical, among others.

A workbench anchored the middle of the room, its surface clean, the tools hanging in careful rows on either side. Hammers, saws, and clamps. Everything in its place. A carpenter's dream.

Avery ran her fingertips along the cool handle of a handsaw, imagining the boards on Theo's deck. That would make it easy. A quick cut, a little paint to cover the fresh edges, and no one the wiser until the boards gave way. She spotted a half-used can on the shelf, the color marked Cedar Glow, the rim sticky with dried drips.

On another shelf, tucked behind a box of streamers and balloons, she found a pack of firecrackers with a couple of paper rolls sliding out. Summer Celebrations was the label. Her pulse kicked up a notch. Stella's death, the firecracker that had started her fall... Exactly what she'd been looking for.

Plus the tools and the paint. She wasn't sure it would match Theo's deck, but it would come darn close.

She bent to pick up the glue gun, neatly rolled beside a box of felt squares. As she slid it into her tote, her gaze drifted back to the shelf. The pack of firecrackers gaped open, two red cylinders hanging halfway out like they were begging to be noticed.

Avery glanced over her shoulder. The baby's cry floated faintly from the house, muffled by distance. She reached out, plucked a single firecracker, and slipped it into her tote.

It only took a few more minutes to locate the tissue paper. She picked a bundle of orange, yellow, and red to put in her bag.

Her pulse thudded. The firecracker was proof. Maybe it

could be matched to the one that had startled Stella. Maybe then Janis Jets would reopen the investigation.

Avery pasted on her brightest smile. She left the shed, feeling proud of her evidence collection. In front of the porch, she spoke loudly through the open window. "Found the glue gun and tissue paper. Thanks a bunch." When no one answered, she broke into a fast walk toward the main road.

Avery stopped to shift her tote farther up on her shoulder. But she also wanted a closer look at the Wells-Duran little free library.

She turned the toggle to remove a new copy of *The Velveteen Rabbit*. The spine cracked when she opened the cover. Inside was an inscription: "For Nancy, with love from Grandma."

# CHAPTER FORTY

Avery slid the book into her tote with a sigh. *The Velveteen Rabbit.* Another children's story that held a memory. Not with anyone reading to her, but she'd read it to a neighbor's child when she was babysitting.

Why would any mother give the personally inscribed book from a grandma away? A classic, a keepsake, practically a rite of childhood, left for free to someone else. Either an act of incredible generosity or one of disdain. Maybe anger directed to the giver. Maybe even their own mother.

Was it Fran or Naomi? That was the question.

Something about the book nagged at Avery. A loving gift turned into a castaway. Deciding which stories a child could keep, and which ones to be whisked away.

What emotion would be underneath that action: fear or control or both? They often went hand in hand.

If the Syndicate thought they could dictate which books lived and died, maybe they were capable of pushing people to their death. An extreme comparison, she admitted. But not out of the question.

Avery slowed her pace, since it was a short journey to Cordelia Pratt's house.

The romance author herself opened the door, wearing the same bright red tunic over black workout leggings. Her expression was cool. "Kind of early to just drop in," Cordelia said, her tone edged with suspicion.

Her brown eyes were sharp and clear, no dreamy drift. There was no rambling on. The ditzy romance author losing her grip had disappeared. This Cordelia looked impatient and busy.

"Good morning," Avery sang out, dialing up her chipper tone. "I'm collecting materials from the Syndicate for the book burning. I remembered all those tea lights on your mantel last time. Would you be willing to share them for my staging? I'll bring them back afterward."

Cordelia's gaze slid over Avery from head to toe. "You haven't heard of Amazon?" Her voice was calculating now, an attempt to peel away Avery's fake optimism. "They'll send you tea lights tomorrow. And while you're at it, you could order some new clothes. Those jeans and that sweatshirt... Well, they're very cheap and worn. You could be presentable with a little effort."

The jab landed sharper than Avery expected. She forced a smile. *So the lady has claws after all.*

"Good to know you moonlight as a personal shopper," she said brightly. "But until Amazon adds a category for fake flames and banned book props, I'm stuck borrowing from friends.

"Besides," Avery went on, leaning forward, "you strike me as someone who buys in bulk. Don't you have a million of those lights stored somewhere?"

Cordelia gave a snort, stepping back from the doorway.

"Come in. I'll get my box of replacements. You're persistent, I'll give you that."

Avery kept her voice light. "Persistence is my middle name. I'll just wait for you in the living room."

When Cordelia disappeared down the hall, Avery took her chance. The place felt different from her last visit. More tidied up, as if someone had put things back where they belonged and then remembered to whisk a feather duster around the edges.

The books had been lined up on the shelf, spines squared to the edge. A faint trace of lemon polish lingered in the air.

Her eyes remained on the mantel. Last time, the tea lights had been scattered, half turned over, some batteries already burned out. Now they'd been replaced with actual wax candles with fresh wicks ready to be lit. Too perfect. Too deliberate. As if Cordelia was expecting an important visitor.

*Maybe a boyfriend,* Avery surmised, glancing at the polished surface of the coffee table, the fresh flowers arranged too carefully in a vase. *Romance authors don't crank out all those sensual scenes from thin air. Maybe she was trying on another suitor, as research.*

Maybe Cordelia wasn't losing her edge at all. She was trying to spice up her own love life, gathering material for a comeback book. Revive her brand with a little hands-on information gathering.

The gleam on the picture frames and the tidiness of the books felt like a stage set. Avery's smile faded. What was Cordelia up to?

"Here you go," Cordelia said, placing a cardboard box on the coffee table. "At least two dozen battery-powered tea lights. I was going to donate them anyway, so you don't have to bring them back."

Avery rested a hand on the box, then let her gaze drift toward the mantel. "I noticed your beeswax votives. Getting tired of the battery kind?"

Cordelia blushed, her voice turning girlish. "My new man thinks the smell of beeswax is alluring. He likes the real burn, not just a fake light." She looked aside as though embarrassed by her admission.

*I was right*, Avery thought. *Cordelia does have a new love interest.*

"Who's the new guy?" she asked, slipping into her best girlfriend tone.

"He's a local carpenter," Cordelia said immediately. "Not like Marshall. My guy's a real craftsman. Thornton is very talented. And a bit lonely. Two single people just trying to survive in a fast-paced world."

*Gag me with a spoon*, Avery thought, swallowing hard. The speech itself made her uncomfortable. Flowery but empty.

Avery recognized the name immediately. He'd been one of Meadow's personal projects. He'd stayed in the guest room. At the time he was considered a suspect in another murder. But Meadow knew he had an alibi. She helped him sober up to prove his innocence to Janis Jets.

Avery wasn't going to admit she knew Thorny because she wanted to hear more from Cordelia.

"So who is this Thornton, exactly? One of those Old Rockers?"

"No, he's not that," Cordelia said, a note of annoyance in her voice. "At least he hasn't mentioned it to me. Apparently there was an issue years back. He's a recovering alcoholic.

His wife was incarcerated for a crime. They're no longer together.

"But he's quite the gem. I'm taking a class from him at the town hall. It's filled with women who want to know more about fixing things—you know, small jobs around the house.

"Light electrical, some carpentry. Not crafters!" She held up both hands. "We're much more sophisticated than that. Real tools, tool belts, hammering and nailing." She smirked, her cheeks turning pink.

The way Cordelia said "real tools" sounded like a sales pitch, an elevated hobby, maybe even an Etsy shop. Avery looked around uncomfortably. She half expected Cordelia to pull out a birdhouse or a magazine rack as proof. And then what? Avery would be forced to make noises that sounded like compliments.

"Do I know this Thornton? He hangs out in town, right?" Avery asked.

"I don't think so," Cordelia said. "He's a friend of Olivia Greer's partner. He's legit. And Meadow is his AA sponsor, though I'm pretty sure I'm not supposed to tell anyone that." The corner of her mouth tugged upward, a sly smile. "Thorny and I have become quite close."

"The other ladies must be jealous," Avery said sweetly. "You getting all that special attention from the teacher. Good for you."

She reached for the box of lights, nodding her thanks. "I'll use these, then drop them at a donation site afterward. You'll be there tonight, of course, to show solidarity."

"I wouldn't miss it," Cordelia said. Her smile lingered, but her voice dipped into something firmer, colder. "But next time, use the burner phone to text. I usually don't open my door to strangers."

Avery swallowed back a retort, covering it up with her brightest grin.

# CHAPTER FORTY-ONE

Avery's stomach growled. *Must be lunchtime.* The box of tea lights wasn't heavy, but the awkwardness of hiking on foot made her impatient.

A honk from the road broke into her thoughts. Brad May leaned out the driver's window of his truck, his grin lopsided with boyish charm. Behind him, the window was cracked for Tater Tot, the Frenchie's squashed nose pressed against the glass.

"Need a lift?" Brad called.

"Yes," Avery said with relief. "You came at just the right time. I'll buy you lunch at Thyme Out as a thank-you."

She slid into the passenger seat, dropping her tote and the box from Cordelia next to her feet.

Brad pulled away from the curb. "Whatcha got there?"

Avery felt her ambivalence keenly. It had taken more effort than she'd realized to keep him out of the loop. She wanted a partner to bounce her ideas off of, and she wanted him.

Every time she thought of Brad, her throat tightened. She liked him more than she wanted to admit. His steady voice, the easy way he filled the silence. Unlike her, he was heading somewhere. All of that made lying close to impossible.

Avery forced a casual shrug. "Props," she said, nudging the box with the toe of her boot. "Couple of ladies roped me into helping with a...let's call it a community demonstration."

Brad raised one eyebrow. "Demonstration? Sounds like trouble."

"Not trouble. Theater," she corrected, brightening her tone. "Think cardboard flames, fake candles, and me making a fool of myself in public. Totally harmless."

From the back seat, Tater Tot gave a muffled bark. Avery turned to look him in the eyes. *You don't have to warn me. It's under control. Go back to staring out the window.* She didn't say those words, but it was as if he heard every nuance.

Tater spun around and planted his nose on the glass, his big bat ears alert.

Brad's mouth twitched into a grin. "Harmless. I'll believe that when I see it."

"Then you'll have to come watch," Avery said.

He slowed the truck to approach the town. There was one parking space in front of Thyme Out. Brad slipped the truck into the space, switched off the engine, and jumped outside. He held the back door open.

Avery watched from the curb as Tater Tot waited for Brad to clip his lead onto his harness.

"After you, rabble-rouser." Brad grinned at Avery.

"Me or the Frenchie?" She brushed past.

The bakery was buzzing with the usual lunch crowd. A combination of local men and a table of retirees arguing about the crossword. Cookie Kravitz stood behind the counter, pointing to his new seasonal bake.

No PCHers with their cumbersome backpacks today.

Brad tipped his head toward the specials board. "What sounds good?"

Tater Tot barked a quick greeting to Cookie, who leaned over the counter to offer a homemade dog bone biscuit. "Where's your mom, buddy?"

"She's on the phone with Riverside," Brad explained. "Do you want to take Tater? Avery's paying for my lunch."

"Sure. Send him around the counter." He winked at Brad and then took the leash from his hand, disappearing into the kitchen with Tater Tot trotting behind.

"I'll have a ham on rye," Avery told the young woman behind the counter. "And two of those giant chocolate chip cookies."

"Make mine ham too, except on sourdough," Brad said. "Add extra cheddar, more mayo, double the lettuce and tomato—the works."

Avery found a small table near the window. "No dessert?"

Brad slid into the chair opposite. "I get plenty of his sweets at the constabulary. Cookie sends them over every morning for Janis."

A sharp whine caught Avery's ear. Tater Tot had escaped his leash. He scrambled straight toward them, paws scraping against the plank flooring. With one leap he landed on Avery's lap. Then a quick turn, he faced her to plant a lick on her lips.

Avery wiped her mouth with the back of her hand. "What's the meaning of all this?"

Brad laughed. "He has his preferences. He's kinda like me."

"I have a way with animals," she commented. "You may remember."

"I remember Sparkles taking to you that Christmas. She still won't let anyone as close except Sage. The volunteers who feed her drop her oats and run. She nips at them otherwise."

Tater Tot, still in her lap, glared at Brad. Avery buried her nose in his fur. *You don't have to be so possessive*, she thought. *Brad's okay*.

The dog looked at her face for confirmation and then jumped to the floor as if relieved from duty.

"I miss Sparkles," Avery admitted out loud. "We bonded. She made me feel welcome."

"You miss her." Brad quirked an eyebrow.

"She's like a comfort animal to me," Avery explained. "Not a lapdog like Tater, but I can wrap my arms around Sparkles's neck and breathe in her horsey smell. Makes me feel peaceful."

Brad's gaze softened. There was something there, but before she could put words to it, her phone buzzed in her pocket.

Not her smartphone, but the burner. She didn't want to answer in front of him. He'd ask too many questions.

"Your phone?" he asked, reaching under the table to pet Tater Tot.

Avery glanced to the front of the bakery. Cookie chatted with a pair of tourists near the counter. The retirees were still fussing over their crosswords.

"I need to take this. Excuse me," she said quickly.

"No problem." Brad's eyes were on his screen.

Avery walked past the counter heading toward the restroom. Her heart hammered as she flipped open the phone. The text was from Marshall.

I want to help with the book burning. Put me to work.

He was the one person she least wanted around. But wasn't there a saying about keeping enemies closer? Did that also apply to suspects? She blew out a breath, thumb hovering over the keys. Then she texted back.

I need a kettle-drum barbecue. There are a few stored at Paws and Pines. Any chance you could pick up the biggest one and meet me at the park this evening before the sun goes down? Leave a donation for it too.

The reply came instantly.

On it!

Avery snapped the phone shut. She'd just invited her prime suspect to meet with her at the park in the dark. Brilliant. Or suicidal.

She paid at the counter, got their lunches to go, and then headed back to the table. Brad looked up expectantly.

"I left money at the register. I need to leave." She deliberately used a hasty tone.

"Is that so?" A flicker of amusement crossed his eyes.

When she didn't sit down, he rose to his feet. "Thanks," he said, sounding gruff as she handed him his to-go bag. "Next time it's on me."

# CHAPTER FORTY-TWO

Once Brad dropped her at the house, Avery grabbed her box of tea lights from under her feet. "Thanks so much," she mumbled, slipping her tote over her arm and slamming the door before he could reply.

Inside the kitchen she found Olivia.

"Whatcha got there?" Olivia nodded to the box.

"I'm doing a project. Tell you more later. Feeling a bit tired right now. Think I'll catch a nap." She hurried away.

The tea lights rattled in the box as she took the stairs two at a time. With the door closed softly behind her, she stared at the bed, pulse pounding.

She spread the contents of her tote bag on the quilt and took a deep breath. The rumpled tissue paper reminded her of autumn leaves. She checked the metal tip of the glue gun. Her fingernail dislodged the bead of old glue.

Her eyes fell on the book from Fran and Naomi's little library, *The Velveteen Rabbit.* She ran her hand over the cover. A classic story about being loved and then discarded, thrown on the trash heap. Until the end, when the child sees a lifelike rabbit scurry along the grass. This gives the child hope that his toy bunny is alive and well in the real world.

She wasn't sure what to make of the book. How it had been left in the library. But she knew she'd felt the same. Just like the rabbit. *That's why it's a classic*, she realized. *Because there are many people who know what it's like to be tossed aside.*

This only made her more curious. What kind of mother chucked a classic book gifted by a grandmother?

*A very determined one*, she answered her own question. Maybe an alienated relationship.

The thought sat heavy in her mind, refusing to let go.

## CHAPTER FORTY-THREE

She stood in the center of town, watching the sun's last rays disappear behind the mountain range. The giant sequoias cast long shadows that stretched across the park. The air smelled damp, cool enough to raise goosebumps on her arms.

She spotted him first.

Marshall leaned against the kettle-drum barbecue. His face was tilted up, looking toward the last slant of sun through the branches.

When he turned, the grin was quick, practiced. Too wide, Avery thought.

"Evening, Avery." He nodded.

Her pulse gave a jump. *Evening. Nearly dark. Look out,* she reminded herself.

"Nice of you to haul this thing." She nodded to the barbecue. "I couldn't manage it without a vehicle."

"That would've been quite the sight." His eyes twinkled. "You rolling it down the road, blocking traffic. The Paws and Pines kid unlocked the shed so I could pick the biggest one.

Janis Jets will be glad to see it gone. Took a bit of muscle, but I'm stronger than I look." His gaze slid to hers.

She turned away, not sure what she felt about Marshall's attitude. He seemed less defensive this evening. More cooperative was the vibe she picked up.

A crow called overhead as he flew to another branch, darkness pressing down. Avery shuddered. An omen. Crows were like that. She never knew if they were friend or foe.

"Time to get set up." She aimed for lightness in her tone, hoping Marshall wouldn't notice how nervous he made her.

"I have another idea," Marshall said, reaching into his pocket.

Avery stiffened.

He pulled out his cell. Not one of the burners, but the latest iPhone, its screen dotted with apps. "Look," he said, tapping one. "It projects a fire. Put the phone behind the barbecue, and it'll look like flames are pushing up from the coals."

He gestured to the base of a sequoia toward three gear bags. "I brought some other props I thought you could use. A microphone and a speaker. You'll be heard loud enough to carry across town at this hour. Sure to draw lots of attention."

Avery's memory flashed back to her last visit to Lily Rock, when everyone had just about enough of that giant nutcracker that blared "All Aboard!" from its raucous, tinny speaker. Would she be that kind of loud?

Betty King, the toy store owner, had insisted it was good advertising, though for weeks the whole town groaned every time it went off.

Until someone put a stop to it. By putting a stop to Betty.

*That could be me*, Avery thought grimly, *if I'm annoying enough. Maybe Marshall has his own plan for dealing with nuisances.*

A shiver crawled up her spine. Props, sound system, special effects. He was either her best ally or laying the groundwork for another murder.

"Okay then," Avery said, injecting a lilt to her tone that she didn't remotely feel. "Let's see what you've got."

Marshall rolled the barbecue over and then angled his phone so that it projected jittery orange and red flames in the darkness. Against the steel drum, it looked like fire clawing up from the ground.

"Convincing, isn't it?" His grin flashed, proud—a little too pleased.

Avery folded her arms, willing herself to nod. "Sure," she commented slowly. "Creepy. Theatrical. Perfect for a fake burning."

He moved to the gear bags, unzipping one with the flourish of a magician. Out came a compact microphone and a squat black speaker.

"Bluetooth," he said simply. "I'll set it up to the side, with the flames as the backdrop. You can toss each book one at a time. But only after you've said your piece. That's the rhythm, right?"

"Yeah, Marshall. That's exactly the plan." Avery forced a smile. "You're pretty good at this. Like you've done it before."

He handed her the microphone, his grin widening. "As a matter of fact, before I moved up the hill, I worked in Hollywood. Staging. A key grip."

Avery stepped back. Cold prickled her skin. She'd underestimated him. Judged him by his flannel shirts, his quiet demeanor, his off-the-grid life in the woods. She hadn't thought about his past or what kind of man he used to be.

And now she wasn't sure if she'd invited a stagehand…or a murderer.

# CHAPTER FORTY-FOUR

"Testing, one, two, three." Avery's voice wavered as it crackled through the speaker.

A few curious people had already stopped on the edge of the park, their shapes half-shadowed beneath the redwoods. She didn't recognize any of them. One man cupped his hands around his mouth. "What are you doing with the grill and the flames?"

She forced a bright edge to her voice. "Stick around and find out," she called back.

"Testing, one, two, three," she whispered into the mic. Her whisper sounded loud and clear.

She took a quick look upward at the massive sequoia, aware that Marshall stood partially hidden behind the trunk, arms folded, watching. When he caught her looking, he nodded once.

He'd set up his own hotspot, and the projection app was still running. Everything seemed to be working.

For now.

Avery bent and fished *The Giving Tree* from her tote.

*Lights, camera, action,* she thought, careful not to speak right into the open mic.

She held the book high so the small crowd could see the cover. The fake flames, tissue, and the tea lights Cordelia had given her flickered orange and red at her feet. She inhaled, preparing to speak.

"Okay, everyone," she began, loud enough to carry. "Welcome to Lily Rock's most polite revolution." She gave a little theatrical bow.

"This is a book burning. Sort of. Think fewer torches, more theater. We're here to provoke discussion, maybe give people something to think about. We're here to engage and wonder why anyone would want to ban a book in the first place."

She tapped the cover. "*The Giving Tree.* A classic. A tear-jerker. A bestseller. And let's be honest, a masterclass in codependence." Her eyebrows lifted. "The boy takes and takes, the tree gives and gives, until there's nothing left but a stump. Talk about doubling down on the victim. Sounds less like childhood reading and more like a bad breakup memoir, doesn't it?"

A ripple of laughter rolled through the crowd.

More people crossed the park, curious.

Avery fixed her eyes over their heads, feigning seriousness. "If you love my opinion, clap. If you don't, politely mind your own business. If you're confused, congratulations. You're halfway to being an engaged citizen."

She turned toward the glowing flames, tossing the book into the drum.

The crowd gasped.

Avery faced them. "Tonight, we'll let the stories go up in symbolic smoke. Paper, LEDs, and a speech or two. So that we can all decide which books actually deserve a place on our shelves." She pointed the handheld mic toward the crowd. “So tell me. Who here is ready to stand and share a thought?"

From the back of the gathering, a sharp female voice rang out. "What about adult books?"

Heads turned. Cordelia pushed her way forward, her eyes shining brightly. "Romance. Stories about couples who love each other. What ever happened to those?"

Cordelia yanked the mic from Avery’s hand.

Gasps rippled through the crowd.

Cordelia raised her chin. "People don't want your gloomy allegories and codependent trees. They want passion. They want love. They want..." She hesitated for effect, then threw out her arms. "Happy endings!" She dug into her purse for her copy of *The Red Ribbon Room* to wave in the air.

Laughter broke from the onlookers, though some muttered uneasily.

Now Naomi appeared from the crowd. She stepped forward with Nancy against her body in a carrier. She grasped the book and the mic from Cordelia's hand. Her voice was sharp. "Happy endings? Filling the heads of children with garbage from little free libraries. Half of those books at the dead drop on the trail make their way down into town, ending up in my front yard. Trash. Just plain filth." Naomi tossed the book into the fire with no apology to its author. She turned to glare at the crowd, as if daring one person to disagree.

The laughter sputtered out.

Avery's heart raced. *Could she be my killer? Definitely has some strong feelings, just like Fran warned.*

Right then, Fran shouldered her way through the

crowd. She took the mic. She reached for *The Velveteen Rabbit*.

"Some children's books are toxic," Fran said, her voice steady. "When grandparents give a child one of these so-called classics, like *The Velveteen Rabbit*, for instance, they ought to think about how that story will frighten a little one. A rabbit, tossed aside, worn down, uncared for? That's not comforting. That's cruelty disguised as bedtime reading."

Fran tossed the book into the kettle drum.

A murmur swept the listeners.

Avery felt her stomach clench. The grandmother who'd inscribed the book—had she meant to upset her grandchild? Avery doubted that was her intention. For a moment she felt sorry for a woman she didn't know.

Both of the mothers had strong feelings. But did they have the guts to kill Theo or Stella over a book?

Avery had planned a finale to her demonstration ahead of time. There was one move, hoping to bring the book burning to a grand conclusion. As voices from the crowd grew quiet, she plunged her hand into her tote and pulled out the folded leaflet. The one turning up at all the little free libraries.

She raised it high for all to see. "And what about this?" Her voice rang sharper than before. "This isn't a story about love or loss. Nor a children's classic. This is religious propaganda. Hidden inside a child's book.

"Someone leaves these scary leaflets in all of the little free libraries. Proselytizing to adults—that's one thing. But what about children? Spreading fear is the goal, I can feel it. One of these might turn an early reader away from books entirely, should they find one tucked inside. A lifetime spent in fear of punishment."

Gasps rippled through the grove.

Naomi's face went crimson, her hands clenched tight against the baby carrier at her chest. *Is she speechless? That would be a first*, thought Avery.

Fran stiffened, her eyes flicking to her wife, then back to the leaflet. She reached to snatch it from Avery's grasp, but Cordelia got there first.

She grabbed the paper and crumpled it in her fist. "This is nonsense," she announced, her voice ringing through the night air. "Garbage like this doesn't deserve the dignity of a stage. It deserves the trash bin."

With a sharp flick of her wrist, Cordelia tossed the crumpled leaflet straight into the barbecue drum. She pivoted toward the crowd, hands planted on her hips, chin lifted high. Her wide-eyed glare in the dark gave her an eerie magical look, as if she dared anyone to contradict her.

When Nancy began to whimper, Fran unzipped her from the carrier. She rocked from one foot to the other to soothe the baby's cries.

The crowd chuckled uneasily, their laughter thin around the edges.

Avery stared at the romance writer, wondering why she stood there as if frozen. She looked like an actress having a memory lapse, not knowing her next line.

Avery took the mic and smiled reassuringly. "Stand over there," she whispered to Cordelia, then nodded at Marshall under the giant sequoia. She turned to the crowd.

"Okay then. A little overacting never hurt anyone," she joked, sweeping her gaze across the faces of the crowd. "But we're not finished yet. Anyone else have a book they'd like to burn?"

This time Marshall stepped out from the sequoia. “My turn," he said, taking the mic and reaching to her pile of books for the one on top. *All American Boys*.

His voice carried easily, masculine and with authority. "This one"—he held up the book—"is the kind that tears communities apart. Some schools include it in their curriculum. The message tells kids to hate authority before they even know what authority means."

Avery felt her head spin. What was Marshall doing? Of all people, he resented authority the most. Why wouldn't he like *All American Boys*? His lifestyle was based on staying off the grid, avoiding those in charge. She felt puzzled, followed by skeptical. *Maybe he hasn't even read the book...*

Marshall held it high over his head, the cover catching the reflection of the flames. His expression was calm, almost too calm. "I moved back to Lily Rock to avoid this kind of controversy. I don't appreciate any of you who keep dropping copies of this book in my little free library. What we need more of is order, not division. Not government laws either. That's why this book belongs in the fire."

The crowd murmured, a few nodding, others with blank expressions.

Marshall slid his other hand into his back pocket. He came up with another book, worn around the edges, dog-eared with use. *Animal Farm*.

"Now this one... It's a keeper." Marshall pressed *Animal Farm* against his chest. "Because sometimes you need allegory to remind people how power works. How control has a dark side." His gaze swept the gathering, then settled on Avery. "A true classic."

Her throat tightened. She didn't disagree. *Animal Farm* was one of her favorites too. Her father had read it to her long before she was old enough to understand the meaning. But every time she read it again, she learned something new. It was that kind of book.

But wasn't that the point? That good books stood the

test of time, whispering their meaning from one generation to the next?

A murmur rolled through the crowd, heavier than before. A few people nodded at Marshall's words, their faces solemn, as if he'd spoken some undeniable truth. Others shifted on their feet, uncomfortable.

A woman near the back of the crowd spoke sharply, loud enough for everyone to hear. "What's your name?" She pointed at Avery. "You don't belong in Lily Rock. We're a peaceful town. Go home."

The man next to her muttered under his breath.

Gone was the uneasy laughter that had carried Avery's demonstration earlier. Now the air felt full, taut, stretched thin between approval and pushback.

Marshall's face remained calm, almost triumphant, as if daring anyone to challenge him. "Don't you yell at her," he said firmly. "I'm the one talking."

Avery wondered, *Is he trying to protect me?* The demonstration was supposed to be a parody, a lighthearted subversion. Her hope was that one of the Syndicate would slip, reveal something about Stella or Theo.

Now it was turning dark, into territory she couldn't quite name.

But then, from behind the sequoia, there came a familiar voice. Calm and controlled. "All right, that's enough."

Heads turned. Janis Jets strode forward, face set like granite. Her dramatic entrance was followed by the comic relief. Tater Tot trotted at her heels. Jets plucked the mic out of Marshall's hand.

"So I'm taking my fur baby for a little stroll," Janis drawled, "and what do I find? A bunch of ne'er-do-wells cluttering up my park, arguing about books."

She pointed a finger to Nancy, still huddled on her mother's chest. "That child ought to be home in bed, not dragged to a circus act."

Glaring at the crowd, she continued, sounding slightly bored. "As for the rest of you... Clear out. Books get written faster than you can burn them. And if you really want to read *Animal Farm*?" Her mouth twisted. "Try the old-fashioned way: a library card. I remember one line, the best part, which will save you the trouble of actually reading the book: 'All animals are equal, but some are more equal than others.'"

She barked a short laugh. "I'll show you equal." She clamped a hand around Avery's elbow. "You're coming with me, rabble-rouser. I'm arresting you for creating a public nuisance and disturbing the peace."

Then she turned her glare on Marshall. "And you. I'm charging you with..." She hesitated slightly and then continued, "With unlawful use of props in a public park."

Avery yanked her arm free. "That's not even a thing. I'll go, but you can't arrest him. He's just the key grip."

Jets paid no attention. She seized her wrist with one strong hand and ushered her past the barbecue toward the edge of the park facing the constabulary. Tater Tot followed, issuing a series of short barks as if to urge Janis on.

Before Jets could shove her through the doorway, Avery glanced back toward the park. The crowd had thinned, revealing Marshall Reed.

He stood by the kettle drum, shadows of darkness easing closer, his barely visible in the dark. He wasn't scowling or sulking. His expression looked neutral. Then with a little flourish, he gave her a mock salute.

Avery wanted to laugh. Even if he was the culprit,

trouble recognized trouble, she thought. And Marshall, for all his gruffness, had shared a moment of respect.

# CHAPTER FORTY-FIVE

Brad May walked into the constabulary break room, his hair tousled and his eyes still heavy with sleep. "I was already in bed when the boss called," he explained.

Avery sat at the round table. She gave him a nod but kept her mouth shut.

"When's your interview going to start?" Brad asked, pulling out the chair beside her. "Want anything? Water, food?"

"So you're also the constabulary snack guy?" she said, dismissing his charm. And his good looks. And the way he seemed genuinely concerned.

"Whatever's needed," he said quietly. "What happened anyway? I dropped you off safely at Olivia's; the next thing I know, I get a call you've been arrested. For a book burning, no less."

Avery lifted her chin, a glint of mischief in her eyes. "Do you really think she's going to book me, lock me up in a cell?"

Brad leaned back, his expression softening. "I can't predict that. Never could. She's a difficult personality.

Wouldn't surprise me. She might even charge you with excessive use of tissue and construction paper."

That earned a genuine smile from Avery. She used her hand to hide it, but the truth was, Brad's arrival had snapped her out of a case of extreme nerves.

Until then she'd been replaying the arrest scene with a combination of pride and fear. The burning had landed, wildly successful, but even she hadn't anticipated the crowd pleaser of her getting arrested and hauled off by Lily Rock's finest.

Avery looked up as Jets entered the room. Eyes on her phone screen, the cop thumbed to the next message.

"There's been a new development. Something I want to talk about," Jets said. "Bring her to my office." She nodded at Brad.

The warmth of his hand on her elbow made her customary flinch impossible. She forced herself to go blank so as not to feel too grateful.

They walked into Janis's office. Brad pulled out a chair for her to sit, then he stepped back.

Olivia Greer arrived next, calm and collected as always. She gave Avery's shoulder a light squeeze before sitting beside her. A small gesture, but Avery felt her meaning keenly.

Jets was the last to enter the room. She closed the door and sat behind her desk. "You have a good friend, Avery," Janis began. "He's ready to anti up with your bail."

Avery felt confused. She couldn't imagine what Jets meant.

"Marshall Reed posted it ten minutes ago." The officer swiveled her chair to pin Avery with her eyes. "So, now is the time for you to do some explaining, Harriet."

The nickname again. *Jets wouldn't call me Harriet if she meant to haul me off in cuffs for real*, Avery thought.

Olivia spoke in a gentle voice. "So let's begin with what we all know: that you kept investigating, even after Officer Jets closed the case."

"Yep." Avery flicked an imaginary speck from her sleeve, trying to act as if she wasn't one bit nervous. "Just didn't buy it. That two people would die by accident, both of them tied to the Switchback Syndicate. Both with a little free library."

"Are you usually this nosy about police business?" Jets growled. "I don't remember inviting you to take over a case that I've already closed."

Avery gave a small shrug. "Wasn't yours anymore, was it? You dropped it."

Jets narrowed her eyes. "So who do you suspect?"

"I've got Marshall," Avery began, counting on one finger. "The two moms, Fran and Naomi." She ticked off two more fingers. "And of course the batty romance writer, Cordelia." She dropped her hand into her lap, satisfied.

Jets's gaze sharpened. "That night when we drove up, the one when you were supposed to be minding your own business in the back seat—you were listening in."

"I was," Avery admitted. "Marshall, Cordelia, Theo, and Naomi were all in the hot tub. That's the Syndicate's core. That's what I found out. Only later did Fran admit she was a member but doesn't go to many meetings. Oh, and Stella was also a member. But of course, she had an excuse. She was dead."

Jets didn't smile. "So you say Fran..."

"Fran doesn't attend every meeting. Someone has to take care of Nancy," Avery explained.

Jets leaned her elbows on the desk, eyes locked on

Avery. "What else?" Her tone had shifted to less growl, more interest.

Avery wanted to explain, tired of keeping everything to herself. So the words came in a rush. "Here's what I've come up with."

By the time she'd finished, Jets leaned back in her chair, making a steeple with her fingers. "That's a lot, Harriet. I'm not sure I haven't underestimated you. But what I don't hear is who's risen to the top of your list. Which of that bunch of book lovers had the gumption to bump off one of their own, let alone two."

"I think it might be the same person," Avery said. "Because both deaths appeared to be accidents, but I don't think they were. The tree house boards had been tampered with, deliberately weakened so that as soon as Theo stepped on them, he'd fall through. And that firecracker at Stella's. Her routine of checking her little library was well-known. Somebody was waiting. Not accidents. Not in my book."

"And your number one suspect?" Jets pressed, looking expectant.

"It was Marshall. He has a hard streak in him and he's not afraid to buck the system. Off-the-grid, and then..." She glanced at Olivia. "I checked him out; visited his workshop. I asked him to build a little library for a 'friend'."

She used air quotes around "friend." "He wanted to know who and pressed pretty hard for her address. But I didn't tell him. I thought that was really suspicious."

"Who was the friend?" Olivia asked.

"Actually, I used you. I mentioned a birthday. Sort of made it up on the spot."

"I love a good birthday celebration. Anytime," Olivia said.

"Okay, so I'll buy you candles and a cake," Jets muttered. "Get on with the Marshall story. What happened next?"

Avery leaned back and took a deep breath. "About that time, after Theo's death, I got an anonymous text." She recalled all the details, ending with the meeting at Marshall's and how she'd been accepted into the Syndicate.

"That's when it hit me, a moment of inspiration," she said, pausing for effect. "I'd stage a fake book burning and get one of them to confess."

"Did it work?" Jets asked.

"Nope." Avery sighed more deeply. "I guess getting confessions isn't my gift." She playfully glared at Olivia, who smiled.

Jets looked up at the ceiling. "How about now? Do you still think Marshall's your guy?"

Avery glanced at her lap. When she raised her gaze, she had to admit, "No, I don't. He was really helpful with my demonstration. And then when you were walking me away, he saluted. It felt more like respect, from one rabble-rouser to another. I don't think he's the kind of guy who'd kill someone, let alone two."

Jets stood abruptly. "Well, that's a good thing. Because I've got some information for you, Miss Harriet. Marshall Reed is on his way over. Says he has evidence that'll prove who killed Stella and Theo. The kind that'll hold up in a court of law. Don't forget, he's the one who offered to pay your bail."

Avery's knees started to shake with relief. "So he knows who did it?" She gulped.

"He says he does. So I'll let him explain." Jets glanced at her phone. "We're all heading back to the break room. You included."

A sharp yip came from under the desk. Tater Tot

scooted out, ran around, and leaped straight into Avery's lap. She let out a surprised laugh as his paws scraped at her sweatshirt.

Jets frowned. "Since when did you become Lily Rock's animal whisperer?"

Olivia smiled, calm as ever. "Don't forget, Avery was the first one to stand up for Sparkles. She invited the pony to Christmas at Meadow's."

Jets muttered something under her breath but didn't argue. Avery stroked Tater Tot on the head, brushing over each ear. If Marshall had real evidence, the game was about to change.

Minutes later, Jets sat at the break room table, her laptop in front of her. Olivia sat at her right hand. Avery clutched Tater Tot on her lap, kneading her fingers across his back.

The door opened. She looked over to see Marshall, shoulders stooped, carried a battered messenger bag slung across his chest.

"Mr. Reed," Jets said, tone clipped. "You said you had evidence."

Marshall nodded, then moved to the table, setting the bag down with a weighty thump. He didn't look at Jets. His gaze landed on Avery, and for a fraction of a second, she felt his...what was it? Admiration.

"Yeah," he said, unzipping the bag. "Evidence. Because I knew something was off. Weeks before Stella's death, the rest of the Syndicate got real feisty. People were very angry about their own book preferences. More angry than usual. It was no longer a discussion, more like a war.

"But more than that, those leaflets. They were just mean. And they didn't stop. I talked to Stella—we were old friends. She agreed we had to stop whoever was leaving them."

"Yeah, yeah, yeah." Jets shrugged. "But I'm waiting for the point."

He pulled a laptop out of his bag. "See, before I moved to Lily Rock, I worked cameras. Set dressing, they call it. Surveillance. So when Stella got jumpy, I had the wherewithal to start placing little cams in every free library. I disguised them really well, if I do say so myself. Not inside, but close by in a tree or bush. I'd angle the lens right at the library door to see who was dropping those leaflets.

"Each Syndicate member had a motion-activated camera, which I monitored on my laptop and my smartphone." He pulled out his phone to set on the table and gave a slight chuckle. "Turns out paranoia pays."

Jets leaned forward, suspicion and interest warring on her face. "You're telling me you've got actual footage?"

Marshall opened the laptop, screen flickering to life. "I've got more than footage. I've got the exact moment someone rigged Theo's shower deck." His fingers flew across the keyboard, pulling up a grainy still shot of someone, their hands in work gloves, prying boards loose.

Avery's stomach clenched. The image wasn't clear enough to name a face. But the stance, the size, the angle of the wrist. It narrowed the field.

Marshall looked up, his voice low. "I didn't want to believe it. But one of us in the Syndicate killed Theo. And Stella too."

The room went still, except for the hum of the nearby refrigerator. Tater Tot had stopped squirming, his big eyes directed at Marshall.

# CHAPTER FORTY-SIX

Marshall showed the footage of Theo's tree house two more times.

"That's enough," Jets said. "I don't see the little library. Did he have one?"

"More on that in a minute." Marshall played with his laptop. "I admit I installed an extra camera at Theo's."

"What about Stella?" Avery asked, too impatient to wait. "Do you have footage of her death?"

"Sure do." He thumbed through his phone, paused, then tapped Play.

The video rolled. Stella appeared on the grainy screen, a basket of books hooked over one arm. She looked very content, smiling to herself. She paused in front of her little library, eyeing the contents.

She raised a veined hand, holding up a familiar book: *All American Boys*. Avery's breath caught. She watched carefully to see what happened next.

Then came the sharp flare of light, the sudden pop, and a lit firecracker. Stella jerked, startled, her basket tumbling from her arm. She fell from view. Only her shoes and legs remained in the corner of the frame, splayed beneath the little library.

Avery detached her stare, feeling a wave of sadness. When she looked back, she saw the next bit of video. In the frame was Cordelia Pratt, plain as day, face glowing in the after-flash. Her red lips curled in a small half smile. Her hand clutching another firecracker.

She ducked back into the brush, disappearing from the frame.

Now all Avery could see on-screen were Stella's legs and feet, the toppled basket, the strewn books, and the charred splinters of the little library.

One person, two crimes. Cordelia had sabotaged Theo's deck, and she'd tossed that firecracker too. Avery looked over at Marshall, whose eyes looked bleary with tears.

The screen went dark. Avery held her hand pressed against her chest.

Olivia drew in a sharp breath, eyes wide. "Oh, Stella..." she whispered, her voice breaking with genuine sorrow. "She didn't see it coming."

Janis sat back hard in her chair. "Well, I'll be," she muttered, her tone more stone than sympathy. "Caught red-handed hiding in a shrub. Was that a backup firecracker I saw in her hand, just in case the first one didn't do the job? Now that's premeditated right there."

She slapped a palm against her knee. "And here I was thinking Cordelia would be the least likely person to kill anyone. What with her romance novels and the way she wasn't all there." Jets tapped her head with a forefinger. Then she glanced at Olivia, her mouth held tightly.

"Do you suppose for one minute all of that ditzy stuff

was just an act to keep me off the scent?" Jets's eyes narrowed. "I thought she was prancing around town quoting her own romance novel because she forgot she wasn't famous anymore."

"Maybe," Olivia answered. "But now you can see how clever Cordelia played it. But my problem is imagining why anyone would want to kill Theo and Stella over a book."

Avery spoke up. She turned to confront Marshall. "Back to my other question: Why did you install a camera on Theo's deck facing his shower?"

Marshall let out a deep sigh, nearly a groan. "I can explain," he said. "Theo's little library was on the trail, the dead drop. But I had another reason for the camera outside his tree house."

Janis held up a hand. "Okay, okay. I sense another long-story-short coming up. Which is never short. An excuse for mansplaining, in my book. I want the whole sad explanation. I really do. But hold on because I have to get that Cordelia dame in a cell." She yanked out her phone.

"Brad? Yeah. Stop whining. Sleep on your own dime. I need you to pick up the romance woman. Cordelia Pratt. She'll be at her house. Pretend you're dying to read her book or something. Bat your baby blues.

"We don't have time for backup. Just get her here. Tell her I want to talk publishing. She's a narcissist, it won't matter if she believes you—she'll eat it up. Call me the second you're on your way."

She hung up and slid the phone onto the table. "Now, Marshall, pull up a chair. Start at the beginning, and don't leave out a single detail."

Avery shifted in her chair. Tater Tot clung to her lap, his warm body a welcome presence. Whatever Marshall was about to say, she felt certain that it would change everything.

Marshall dragged a chair across the floor and lowered himself into it with a tired groan. His eyes settled on a spot between the floor and Avery's shoes. "I didn't set out to be a snoop," he began, voice low. "I formed the Syndicate for personal reasons. I like the concept, books moving through town, people talking about ideas instead of who's sleeping with each other."

Marshall paused, appearing to search for words. "But I also wanted to keep close to Stella and Theo."

Janis's tone was clipped. "You and Stella were what... together?"

"Not the way you're thinking," Marshall said, a flash of irritation in his voice. "We were old friends. We reconnected after I moved back. Turns out we had more in common than I realized, other than books and the outdoors. She told me something I'd never expected. She said she'd given up a baby, my baby, years ago. She didn't want to tell me and she had the records sealed."

"So you were shacking up," Jets insisted. "Isn't having a baby together the very definition of being together?" She tapped her desk with her fingers, looking impatient.

Avery felt her brain whirl. Maybe there was a connection with the dog-eared children's books in the free libraries, mostly about mothers and children.

"But we didn't get back together," Marshall said. "We were thrust together because of Theo. He found Stella and got in touch."

"So he was the long-lost baby," Jets surmised.

Marshall nodded. "He reached out a few months ago on email. He asked Stella questions, wanted to meet his biological parents. Somehow he'd gotten the files unsealed.

"Stella was terrified. She'd lived with her guilt for so long, and she feared that underneath he'd judge her. Once he realized she was just human, not the mother he'd imagined, he might leave her. The second time saying goodbye would be more than she could handle.

"I tried to tell her she'd be missing a chance and that was worth the gamble. We were trying to sort it out and she finally relented." He shut his eyes, shook his head. "I didn't realize how messy it would get. Not until those leaflets started showing up.

"At first I didn't connect them to Theo. I thought they'd go away. People would toss them and that would be that. But then I made the connection. He was the one."

Marshall's voice roughened. "I saw the leaflets in books in the library. Stuck under windshields. Pinned to telephone poles. Whenever one would appear, Theo would be hanging around, as he wanted to see people's expressions when they read the words.

"That was when I knew Theo was unhinged. But it wasn't just the leaflets. He'd buy multiple copies of books like *The Giving Tree* and *Are You My Mother?* He'd leave them in all the little libraries. Apple doesn't fall far from the tree," Marshall muttered. "If anyone, I should know what obsession feels like. And paranoia. After all, he was my kid.

"My final confirmation was the time he kept playing with a chain around his neck. He wore it in the hot tub and I saw a cross. Talk about panic.

"So to keep an eye on him, I started installing the cameras quietly—I didn't announce it. Whenever someone called me to fix a hinge or slap on a coat of paint to their little library, I'd install a cheap camera. Nail it to a nearby bush. Discreet.

"This didn't solve my problem with Theo entirely.

Because his little library was the dead drop on the trail. So I had to take another surveillance step." Marshall ran his hand over his short-cropped hair. "I added two cameras to his tree house. Not inside!" He registered alarm. "I'm no perv. I placed them in tree branches, focused on the stairway, and one on the shower."

"No perv," Jets scoffed. "Yet you had full view of your son's shower, and anyone else who might have wanted to join him."

"Spying on naked people...not my deal," Marshall dismissed her instantly. "I invite naked people in my hot tub all the time. Just nature."

Jets shook her head and made a note in her iPad. "So keep talking, upstanding citizen," she said dryly. "Why don't you make a big fat excuse about why you didn't tell me immediately about Cordelia and the firecracker. Theo might still be alive if you had. I could arrest you for obstructing the course of justice right here and now," she insisted.

Olivia raised an eyebrow in her direction.

Jets sighed, continuing to drum her fingers on the table. "Go on then, Marshall. Tell me the rest."

He leaned forward, elbows on his knees. "After I got the cameras installed, I kept watch. Stored the videos on the cloud. Like I showed you earlier."

His jaw tightened. "Didn't take long for me to confirm Theo was leaving the religious propaganda. I found other similar leaflets online. So I looked into where they came from. I finally put together that Theo had gotten involved with some kind of religious cult when he was younger. I guess I can call it that.

"I knew that Theo wasn't going to stop. Not with the leaflets or the children's books. *Are You My Mother?*, *The*

*Giving Tree*—he had multiple copies. Then he'd stuff those leaflets inside. It felt like an outlet for his frustration, or revenge for being adopted.

"We—Stella and I—felt responsible for his behavior. Maybe he knew I was watching him. He wasn't stupid, just emotionally unstable." Marshall's eyes filled with tears. He used his sleeve to wipe them away.

Then he cleared his throat. "But he died before Stella and I could decide what to do to help our son out."

Avery had most of her questions answered. But she still had one more. "That doesn't explain why you were at Stella's place when Brad and I were there."

Jets's hand came down on the table. "What's that? You and Brad—you did what again?"

"We went to her house, but I had a key," Avery insisted. "Stella gave it to me. Brad was just giving me a lift."

Janis shook her head, her eyes glaring. "He's my assistant, Harriet. Keep your mitts off him. The boy gets into enough of his own trouble without the likes of you."

Olivia turned her head to hide a smile.

Janis's words lifted the somber mood, making Avery more eager to jump in with her side of the story.

"We were just looking for evidence of how Stella might have died. Maybe a clue or two," Avery said quickly. "Brad didn't want to help me. I kinda begged."

"I bet you did," Jets muttered, rolling her eyes.

"I told you the truth then," Marshall interjected. "I was hired to fix things up to get Stella's place ready to stage and rent."

In the pause, Brad's voice floated down the hall. He sounded firm and polite. "Right this way, Miss Cordelia. Watch your step. Do you need a hand?"

Cordelia swept into view, her chin lifted, eyes darting

over the room. She made her entrance like a woman ready to accept the Romance Author of the Year award.

Brad closed the door and the room fell silent.

Avery crossed and uncrossed her legs, followed by a quick look in Marshall's direction. He sat with his hands clasped, staring directly at the floor.

# CHAPTER FORTY-SEVEN

Brad avoided eye contact with Avery. He held handcuffs dangling from one hand. "Boss?" he asked.

"Not yet," she snapped.

Jets folded her arms on the table. "Sit down, Cordelia. This isn't what you think. Unless, of course, you'd like to skip the boring parts and just confess." Her tone was almost hopeful.

Brad blinked hard. Avery waited to see if he'd roll his eyes. Then across the table, Olivia smirked, a flicker of quiet solidarity.

How had her life taken this turn? One week ago she'd been hiking the Pacific Crest Trail, wondering where she'd live after the fire. Now she was practically starring in her own true-crime drama.

Jets gripped her iPad with both hands. "Cordelia Pratt, you're under arrest. Got you on video with a firecracker in one hand and a saw in the other. I *told* Thorny not to teach you ladies to use tools," she muttered.

Cordelia's forehead lined with confusion. "That is

preposterous! A lady of letters does not use pyrotechnics nor saw wood under a shower."

"And that's a real confession right there," Jets drawled. "I've got video and now you admit the shower sabotage. I never said anything about how Theo fell to his death, now did I?"

Cordelia leaned in, squinting at the video Marshall held in front of her face. "Well, that angle is dreadful. Shadows can do terrible things to a woman's jawline. Anyone could mistake me for—"

"Save it," Jets cut in. "You're not being booked for bad lighting." She rose to her feet. "I'm charging you with the deaths of Theo and Stella. I'll let the courts peel back your "poor demented me" act. My bet? They'll call it premeditated murder. Maybe you can workshop your next romance novel from a jail cell."

Marshall broke the silence, turning to Cordelia. "Why? Why did you kill them? I don't get it."

Avery thought she did, but she held back, letting Cordelia answer.

The romance writer lifted her chin, eyes flashing. "Those two kept removing my books from their little libraries. Replacing them with trash. Stella had the gall to return them behind my back. And Theo..."

Her voice cracked with fury. "Theo tossed *The Red Ribbon Room* straight into the garbage. My work! My legacy!"

Her voice, wild and unrepentant, made Avery shiver.

"I was ready to deal with the mothers next," Cordelia continued. "And then you, Marshall. You strutted around like you were in charge of the Syndicate. Inviting them behind our backs." She glowered at Avery. "I had big plans to take it over once you were gone."

Avery's skin crawled, she didn't think that rage could come from this seemingly benign woman.

Jets huffed, unimpressed. "Congratulations, Cordelia. You're quite the piece of work. It's time for me to quote from a book." She straightened, a wicked glint in her eye. When no one asked, she went ahead anyway.

"Ah, what the hell. Here you go: Off with her head!" She turned to Brad. "Get her outta my sight."

# CHAPTER FORTY-EIGHT

Olivia's car crunched up the gravel road. Avery slumped in the passenger seat. She felt every ache and pain in her body. What a night.

A black truck sat parked near the house, its hood gleaming faintly in the dark.

"Michael's home." Olivia sounded breathless.

Avery barely had time to unbuckle before Olivia ran across the footbridge, straight into his arms. Their laughter rose above the sounds of the creek, warm and sure.

She waited for the stab of envy, but the sight of Michael with Olivia only brought a quiet joy. They belonged together.

She sat a bit longer to give them the chance to reunite.

"Bork."

Maguire's paws scrabbled against her window, tongue lolling sideways in a goofy grin.

"Silly boy, move out of the way," she muttered, pushing open her door.

He trotted ahead and then over the bridge. Never in her

life had Avery felt more like a third wheel. Maguire stopped halfway across, looking back expectantly.

"I'm coming," she sighed. She walked slowly over the bridge, looking out toward the shadow of Lily Rock. When she got to the end, Michael kissed Olivia quickly on the lips.

He kept an arm around her with a grin toward Avery. "Well, if it isn't Elf Two. Never thought I'd see you again." He reached to fold her into their embrace.

Her throat tightened. Michael had changed. A little more gray, a few more lines, but the warmth was the same. He seemed a lot less sad. And with Olivia beside him, they felt like more than a couple. Like they were destined by some unstoppable force beyond her understanding.

Michael slung an arm around each woman as he steered them toward the house. "Come on inside. Dinner's nearly ready. And I want to hear everything. You arrested the killer, right?"

Olivia's eyes sparkled as she nodded toward Avery. "She's the new sleuth in town. I just got to watch. Janis calls her Harriet, like the book *Harriet the Spy*. Ever read that one?"

Michael chuckled. "Not me. I was more of an *Encyclopedia Brown* man myself."

Their banter rolled on as Avery listened. How did they do it—make her feel part of them with seemingly no effort?

Michael dropped his arms. He turned to her. "So, I was telling Olivia, let's find you a place up here in Lily Rock. She mentioned the fire. You're presently unhoused, right?"

She couldn't believe her ears. He had a plan for her? She wasn't sure if she was angry or overwhelmed because he cared. When she didn't say anything, he kept talking.

"I can remodel any place you like, now that you're back," he explained. "How does that sound?"

How could she disagree? That face, his big warm eyes. Irresistible.

She shrugged. "Not a terrible idea," she finally admitted.

"Good, that's settled." He glanced toward Olivia, then back at Avery with a grin. "Welcome to Lily Rock, Avery."

"Bork," agreed the mayor, lifting his paw for a shake.

# EPILOGUE

Two Weeks Later

Marshall Reed stood at the microphone, scanning the crowd. Nearly thirty people filled the Lily Rock Town Hall. His gaze stopped on Avery, seated in the far back corner with her notebook balanced on her knee.

"Good evening," Marshall said, his voice carrying easily. "Welcome to the bi-annual meeting of the Friends of Lily Rock Library. This should be short. In the past few weeks we've been sorting out our charter and mission statement. Updating to better suit the needs of the community."

A ripple of polite applause filled the room.

"Please stand, or not, for the Pledge of Allegiance."

Avery hid a small smile. She could tell from his tone that the "or not" was a concession. A few days ago, when they'd discussed this meeting, he'd been resistant to even leading the pledge. Their conversation had been short but wildly fun.

"Turn the Switchback Syndicate into something new, open to everyone?" he'd asked, sounding skeptical.

"That's right," Avery had said. "No burner phones. No secret texts. No midnight hot-tub strategy sessions. Just a town group that supports books and community. Seems radically old-school—a perfect fit for Lily Rock, don't you think?"

He'd laughed and given her a hug. As if a great weight had been lifted from his shoulders.

Now, as the applause faded, Marshall caught her eye and mouthed, "You were right."

When the meeting adjourned, he found her by the cookie table, ladling out punch.

"I think you're something else," he said softly. "This'll be...interesting. Starting over with both of us in charge."

"Not me," Avery said, raising an eyebrow. "I've had my fill of books and opinions for a while. You're the guy. Ask Naomi. She practically lives at the library. She'll be your spokeswomen."

"You're so busy you can't help a guy out?" He pretended to be shocked.

Avery's grin turned sly. "I'll invite you over as soon as my renovation's done. I have a surprise for you. Something Michael's helping with."

He leaned closer, curious. "And what would that be?"

"My new support animal requires a specialized facility," she said lightly. "That's all you get for now."

Marshall laughed under his breath. "You know, we're a lot alike."

"Both radical extremists," she teased.

"That's us," he agreed, lifting his punch cup in a mock toast.

After saying goodbye to Marshall, Avery stepped

outside to the boardwalk where Sparkles waited. Tied to a bike rack the pony dozed, one hoof raised.

Thank you for reading this advance review copy.
If you enjoyed this story, please consider leaving an honest review on Amazon and Goodreads when the book releases
April 9, 2026

# AUTHOR'S NOTE

Dear Readers,

I hope you enjoy book one in the newest branch of the Lily Rock Mystery universe. I'm finding Avery Denning to be the perfect protagonist as she navigates the space between her own special gifts and her longing to belong.

My heartfelt thanks go to **Christie Stratos** of Proof Positive for her editing expertise and steadfast support of all my books. She finds what I miss and brings her keen eye to everything that works (and occasionally misbehaves) in my genre.

To **Ebook Launch, Dane and Alisha**, thank you for another stunning cover. Hand-drawn yet distinctive, it perfectly captures our new amateur sleuth. The finished book looks amazing on my shelf, and for those who read paperbacks, I hope it looks fantastic on yours as well.

To the man known as **Husband** in all my newsletters: Thank you for walking with me every day—literally and figuratively. You ask questions about my characters as if they were family (and for all intents and purposes, they are). You also give each manuscript its final read before I send it out into the world, and I swear, the man doesn't miss a thing. What an eye for detail.

Finally, to our small terrier mix, **Adam Westie**. This summer, we lost his sister Minnie, and the three of us were bereft. Husband and I were worried that Adam might give up when he stopped eating and wandered the house looking for her around every corner. But the little rascal turned his own corner. He started eating again, rediscovered the joy of walks, and has embraced life as a solo dog who now gets to sleep in our bed and go on road trips.

Our Minnie lives on in the character of **Mayor Maguire**—she's like *The Velveteen Rabbit* in reverse: She went from real to imaginary instead.

Thank you, dear readers, for being part of the ever-growing Lily Rock universe. I hope you fall in love with our new sleuth as much as I have. I'm already plotting the next Avery mystery, and yes, Sparkles the irascible pony is making another appearance. Shh...don't tell Janis. Avery has a new plan.

Happy Reading,
**Bonnie Hardy**

# 📚 WELCOME TO LILY ROCK BOOK CLUB DISCUSSION QUESTIONS

Whether you're here with a book group, curled up solo with a cup of tea, or you just flipped to the back because you're curious—welcome. This section includes ten discussion questions to spark reflection, laughter, and (possibly) debate.

Avery Denning is new to sleuthing, but Lily Rock is no stranger to mystery. And in a town where secrets hide behind every pine tree and paperback, we hope you enjoyed this twisty tale.

🔍 **Discussion Questions**

1. A Journey Begins

Avery returns to Lily Rock after time on the Pacific Crest Trail. What personal growth is visible from the start? In what ways does the town still see her as the girl who left?

2. Books with Meaning

The Little Free Libraries are more than just props—they're woven into the plot and the characters' emotional lives. What stood out to you about Stella's connection to books?

3. Hidden Truths

Theo's identity is a major reveal. Did you suspect his connection to Stella? How did this twist change your perspective on earlier chapters?

4. Aging & Memory

Cordelia is battling cognitive decline but remains shrewd and sharp in unexpected ways. How did your perception of her shift throughout the story?

5. Found Family

Avery has no interest in building roots—but slowly forms connections with Olivia, Brad, and others. How does this reflect one of the central themes of the story?

6. Trust Issues

Would you have trusted Brad? Why or why not? How does his dynamic with Avery echo the town's tension between past mistakes and future hope?

7. The Politics of Reading

Books like *All American Boys* and *Julián is a Mermaid* appear on purpose. How did their inclusion deepen your understanding of Stella—and her risk?

8. The Syndicate

The Switchback Syndicate walks the line between mischief and activism. How did your opinion of this group evolve? Would you have joined?

9. Olivia & Avery

As Avery's mentor figure, Olivia Greer plays a quieter role in this book. How does her presence help or hinder Avery's growth? Do you see parallels between them?

10. Tone & Humor

Despite the murder, Lily Rock keeps its cozy charm. What moments made you smile? How do animals, food, or setting help create a sense of comfort?

### Want More Lily Rock?

Find all the books in the Lily Rock Universe—including Olivia's adventures, the Redondo & Rose series, and holiday novellas at: https://bonniehardywrites.com/

# THYME OUT SIERRA SNOWCAP COOKIES

***A Cookie Kravitz July 4th Signature Bake***

## COOKIE INGREDIENTS

**6 cups all-purpose flour**

**3 teaspoons baking powder**

**1 teaspoon baking soda**

**3/4 teaspoon pink salt**

**1 cup whole sour cream**

**2 cups granulated sugar**

**1 cup salted butter, slightly softened**

**4 large eggs, room temperature**

**1 teaspoon almond extract**

## FROSTING INGREDIENTS

**1 cup salted butter, slightly softened**

**3 cups confectioners' sugar**

**1/2 teaspoon almond extract**

**1/2 teaspoon vanilla extract**

**1/8 teaspoon pink salt**

**2 tablespoons whole milk**

## INSTRUCTIONS

**Make the Dough**

**In a large bowl, whisk together flour, baking powder, baking soda, and salt.**

**In a separate bowl beat the sour cream, sugar, butter, eggs, and almond extract until well combined.**

**Fold dry ingredients into the wet mixture until fully incorporated. The dough will be sticky. Cover the bowl and chill the dough for 1 hour or until the dough is firm enough to roll out.**

**Divide the dough into 4 even balls. Roll out one quarter at a time. Keep the remaining dough in**

**the fridge until ready to use. Roll each quarter to 1-inch thickness. Use a cookie cutter 2 inches in diameter to cut out circles.**

**Bake**

**Preheat the oven to 250 F, and set the rack to the lower-middle position.**

**Arrange the cookie circles on parchment or silicone-lined baking sheets, leaving 2 inches between each cookie.**

**Bake 8-10 minutes before transferring the cookies to a wire rack to completely cool.**

**Make the Frosting**

**Whisk butter until light and fluffy.**

**Add sugar and continue to whisk. Add the almond extract, vanilla extract, and salt, and whisk until fully incorporated.**

**Decorate**

**Frost cookies after completely cooled.**

**Top with red, white, and blue sprinkles, and if you're feeling particularly patriotic, a small flag on a toothpick (found online or at a local craft store).**

## A NOTE FROM COOKIE KRAVITZ

***"Frosted cookies can be kept in an air-tight container for a couple of days. You can freeze unfrosted cookies for up to two weeks.***

***Of course, I never freeze cookies for Thyme Out. Unless I make dog bones. You'll have to ask Mayor Maguire if he can tell the difference."***

# ABOUT THE AUTHOR

Bonnie Hardy, a retired professional turned author, is celebrated for her expanding mystery universe set in California's mountain and desert landscapes. Her cozy Lily Rock Mysteries follow amateur sleuth Olivia Greer, known for her uncanny ability to draw out confessions from the most unlikely people, while her Redondo & Rose: Neighbors in Crime series transports readers to Palm Desert, where mentalist Rex Redondo and his grounded next-door neighbor, doula Vivienne Rose, uncover secrets in the sunbaked desert.

Bonnie's three time award winning historical mystery series begins with "An Unsuitable Job," introducing Josie MacFarland, a former Harvey Girl turned private investigator in 1929 New Mexico. Against the backdrop of the elegant Castaneda Hotel, Josie becomes the first-ever "Harvey House Detective," navigating a world that doesn't welcome women in charge. Inspired by Agatha Christie, Bonnie's tales of mystery and community masterfully blend fast-paced whodunits with clever sleuthing, rich emotional undercurrents, and the enduring spirit of women who won't be underestimated.

www.ingramcontent.com/pod-product-compliance
Lightning Source LLC
LaVergne TN
LVHW091957080526
838231LV00033B/379

* 9 7 8 1 9 5 4 9 9 5 5 1 2 *